THE COUNTRY CLUB MURDERS NOVELLAS

ONLY THE GOOD DIE YOUNG, SOMEWHERE IN
THE NIGHT, AND RICH GIRL

JULIE MULHERN

ONLY THE GOOD DIE YOUNG

A COUNTRY CLUB MURDERS NOVELLA

CHAPTER ONE

July 1974
Kansas City, Missouri

My daughter finds bodies. It's a deplorable habit—almost worse than spitting tobacco or picking one's nose in public (or at all).

If I've asked her once, I've asked her a hundred times—*Ellison, please stop.*

Does she listen?

No, she does not.

Then she forces a smile, as if I'm the one who's being difficult.

If it were her daughter finding corpses, I bet she'd sing a different tune.

They're on vacation now—Ellison and my granddaughter—in Europe. Knowing Ellison as I do, I'm sure she's bought out half the boutiques in Paris and ordered enough shoes to keep an Italian cobbler busy till Christmas. She's spoiling Grace rotten.

Not that I blame her. They needed a vacation. They grabbed their passports and jumped on a plane. And I'm glad they're gone because, for all the times I scolded Ellison about finding bodies, I found one, too.

~

THE DAY SEEMED ORDINARY. IT STARTED IN THE USUAL WAY—A Continental breakfast in the sunroom, a peck on my cheek from my husband before he left for work, a few calls, then the club. I breezed into the clubhouse, nodded good morning to the receptionist, and made my way toward the card room.

"Frances."

I recognized the voice, and my spine stiffened. Muriel Jarrett. Our mothers had disliked each other. Muriel and I carried on their tradition. Ellison and Muriel's daughter, Prudence, had taken the antipathy to a new level. They despised each other.

Of course, Prudence (an amoral tramp) did carry on with my son-in-law, so Ellison's feeling were entirely justified.

I forced a chilly smile and turned. "Muriel."

"I hear your daughter is gallivanting across Europe."

Gallivanting? I wouldn't abide censure from the mother of an adulteress. "Ellison and Grace took the summer to travel. A change of scenery can be a balm to the soul. And after Henry's infidelity…What is Prudence up to this summer?" I knew the answer. Nothing.

Prudence lived off the proceeds of a modest trust. She didn't work. She didn't have children. And no man in his right mind would take on that horse-toothed harpy. (Ellison's description, not mine—but Ellison was spot on).

Muriel studied the floorboards and her gnarled hand tightened around her cane. "Prudence is taking it easy."

"How nice. And you? Travel plans?" I asked only to be

polite. Muriel had spent every August in Estes Park since the beginning of time.

"The cottage in Colorado to escape the heat. You?"

"The cottage in Harbor Point." Just like she went to Colorado, we went to Michigan. But our cottage was a six-bedroom house with a wrap-around deck, and the lake was our front yard. Her cottage was an actual cottage.

"Will Marjorie and her family join you?"

Marjorie was my oldest daughter. She'd married a man from Ohio then moved to Akron. "For two weeks in July." Muriel hadn't stopped me to discuss vacations. What did she want? I glanced at my watch.

Muriel adjusted her glasses. "Have you spoken with Caro?" Carolyn Langley was friends with each of us.

"Not this week. Her mother-in-law is giving her fits." John Langley's aging mother wanted to stay in her own home, and John and Caro had bent over backward to make that happen. Well, Caro bent over backward. John made pronouncements. Do this. Do that. Make the problem go away.

"The old bat needs to be in a nursing home."

I agreed. Not that I'd ever admit to agreeing with Muriel. "Caro hired round-the-clock nurses." At least she'd tried. Evelyn Langley was accustomed to a cook and a housekeeper and a laundry maid and a man to see to her garden. An employee who didn't polish silver or run a sweeper over the rug was an anathema. Evelyn fired nurses as soon as Caro could hire them. In desperation, she'd hired a service. Last I heard, it wasn't going well.

Poor Caro. I'd call her when I got home. Perhaps she and John could come over for cocktails.

"Evelyn will run through John's inheritance."

Were things tight? I bit back the question. I didn't discuss my friends' finances. Especially not with Muriel. I lifted my chin and looked down my nose. "I wouldn't know about that."

Especially not with Muriel.

Muriel blushed an unbecoming shade of red, and her lip curled, revealing long teeth (Prudence came by her *horse-toothed harpy* moniker thanks to her mother).

I glanced at my watch a second time. "If you'll excuse me, I'm due at the bridge table." I turned and walked down the hallway laid with Oriental runners. Ancient floorboards creaked beneath my feet, and the creamy walls held Audubon prints and botanical studies. I kept my shoulders straight and my chin high, but I felt Muriel's burning gaze on my spine. She didn't like being dismissed. Not one bit.

The best way to annoy her further was to pretend she wasn't there. So that's what I did.

We'd reserved the small card room. Only two tables fit. An ultra-suede cloth covered our table. The second was left empty. Two card decks were fanned across the table's surface, along with a score pad and a pencil sharpened to a fine point. Side tables held glasses of ice water and bowls of mixed nuts. The view from the windows was lovely—lush, emerald-hued greens, gorgeous flower beds, and a flag decorated with the club's crest fluttering atop a distant pin.

I breathed deep and let the stiffness in my spine relax. I played bridge at least twice a week. I adored the game and was a competitive player, but the cards were secondary to time spent with dear friends.

Lillian Rush was already seated.

I took the seat next to hers. "Darling dress." She wore a navy blue shift with a collar piped in scarlet. "New?"

"This old thing? You've seen it a hundred times. Have you heard from Ellison? How is she?"

Unlike Muriel, Lillian's concern for my daughter was real.

"I spoke with her a few days ago. She was in Paris eating her weight in macarons." I warned her about that. "She bought out

Galeries Lafayette and Printemps. Now she's visiting every art gallery on the Left Bank."

"She is a painter."

I gave a curt nod. Ellison's painting hobby had unexpectedly become a successful career. I was proud of her success, but I'd warned her that her husband wouldn't appreciate a wife who earned more than he did.

Did she listen?

No, she did not. Ellison never listened.

Muriel passed by us in the hallway, and Lillian wrinkled her nose as if she'd caught a whiff of garbage. "Why is she lurking?"

"She wants to talk to me."

Lillian lifted a questioning brow.

"She's worried about Caro. She says Evelyn is being difficult." There was no way I'd repeat her gossip that the Langleys might run out of money. "She wonders why they don't put Evelyn in a home."

Lillian shrugged. "Evelyn doesn't want to go."

"Where's the tipping point?" I mused.

Lillian collapsed the blue deck and shuffled. "What do you mean?"

"At what point is the stress on Caro and John too much?"

"Only they know." Lillian's fingers deftly fountained the cards and her gaze landed on my right hand. "New ring?"

I nodded and admired the piece of coral that had been hand-carved into a shrimp design. It was a lovely shade of red, topped with a circle of diamonds, and set in white gold. "We celebrated an anniversary."

"Harrington has excellent taste." She gave the cards another shuffle, then she tsked. "Back to Caro. You were lucky with your mother and your mother-in-law."

My mother had stayed strong and independent and sharp as ten very pointy tacks until a heart attack took her. She lingered in the hospital for three days—long enough for us to say our goodbyes, long enough for my sister to travel from Singapore—then she'd quietly left us. I adjusted my ring, which still needed to be sized, and agreed. "That's me. Lucky."

Joanna, who wore a tennis ensemble that showed off her deep tan and the wrinkling around her knees, stepped into the card room. "Good morning." She checked her watch. "Am I late?"

"Right on time," I replied. "We were talking about Evelyn Langley."

Joanna pulled a face. "How is she? How's Caro?"

"Not good," Lillian replied. "It's too bad John didn't have sisters. So much falls to poor Caro." John had three brothers, but he was the only Langley man living in Kansas City.

"Caro's a saint," said Joanna. "If Norton asked me to take care of his mother..." She shuddered at the mere suggestion.

Lucky for Joanna, Norton's mother, who was meaner than an asp, was still healthy at ninety-three. Lord only knew how vicious she'd be if (when) her health failed.

Patty burst into the card room. "I'm late. I'm sorry! I couldn't get off the phone." Patty wore a tan skirt embroidered with orange mushrooms and a matching orange t-shirt. She was a good friend, so I refrained from telling her orange made her look sallow, and the scoop of her shirt was too low for a woman whose chest had taken sixty-plus years of sun.

"Who kept you on the line?" asked Joanna.

"My daughter. She's worried about Melissa."

"That's her youngest?" I asked.

Patty nodded. "She's been taking diet pills."

Lillian shook her head. "There's so much pressure on young girls these days. To be slender, to be pretty, to be smart."

In my day, no one cared about smart. I kept that thought to myself. "Shall we play?"

~

THREE HOURS, FOUR RUBBERS OF BRIDGE, AND ONE CLUB sandwich later, I rang Caro's doorbell, and her housekeeper opened the door.

I donned a pleasant smile. "Is Mrs. Langley at home?"

The woman nodded. "Won't you please come in, Mrs. Walford?"

I searched my memory for her name and came up with a blank. A shame. She wore a uniform and had her hair pulled back into a neat bun. Exactly *comme il faut*. Ellison had recently hired a housekeeper who wore muumuus. I did not approve. And don't get me started about the wildly inappropriate earrings the housekeeper, Aggie, wore with those muumuus or her sproingy orange hair.

"Thank you," I murmured as I swept by her into Caro's tasteful front hall, where an antique Georgian table held an arrangement of stargazer lilies. Their sweet scent perfumed the air, and I breathed deep.

"Frances?" Caro appeared in the door to the sun room. "What a nice surprise." She meant, *what are you doing here*?

"We haven't spoken in a few days. I wondered how you're getting on."

"Edith, iced tea and cookies in the living room, please."

The housekeeper nodded. "Yes, ma'am"

Edith. I'd have to remember that for next time, "How's Evelyn?"

Caro sighed as if she were Atlas, and the weight of the world was too much for her. "She's not answering her phone."

"Perhaps she's napping. Isn't there a nurse?"

Twin furrows appeared above Caro's nose. "Evelyn probably told her not to answer the phone just to worry me." She rubbed an open palm across the back of her neck. "Her evil plan is working. I'm worried."

"Would you feel better if you checked on her?"

She gave a reluctant nod. "But I just asked you to sit and drink iced tea."

"I can drink tea any time. If you want company, I'll go with you."

Her expression lightened. "Would you mind?"

"Of course not. We can take my car."

"Thank you. I'll grab my handbag."

We climbed into my Mercedes and drove the four short blocks to Evelyn's house. Caro's expression darkened with each block.

"How can we help?" I asked as I turned right on Evelyn's street.

"We?"

"Your friends. We know caring for Evelyn isn't easy."

"Cocktails. Lots of cocktails."

"I'm serious."

"So am I. Evelyn is not being reasonable." She leaned her head against the neck rest, closed her eyes, and sighed deeply. "It's almost as if she believes John and I owe her. That we should put our lives on hold for her. John can't do that. He can't. He has a company to run. So, when a nurse doesn't show up, or she fires one because they refuse to dust the dreadful figurines she collects, she calls me. If she's missed the weather forecast on the evening news, she calls me. If she needs a ride to the doctor or the hairdresser or the dentist or the Plaza, she calls me."

"Can you hire a driver for her?"

"She fires them. She says they drive too fast or too slow, they brake too hard, or they fail to use their turn signals. I'm at the end of my rope."

I parked at the curb in front of Evelyn's house and turned off the car.

Caro made no move to open her door. "I'm tired, Frances. And I resent the way she treats me. It's causing a problem in my marriage."

"Have you told John?"

She nodded. "He doesn't have the answers."

"What about his brothers?"

"They don't care about my marriage." She barked a bitter laugh. "They're all too happy to armchair quarterback from Connecticut and California and Chicago."

"She's not your responsibility."

"But she is John's. And John and I are a team."

"Let's check on her, then we'll go for a glass of wine."

Caro gave a near imperceptible nod. "Thank you."

"I haven't done anything."

"You're here. I'm usually here by myself."

John didn't sound like much of a teammate. Perhaps I should tell him.

I opened the car door. "Let's get this over with. Then wine."

Together we walked up the front walk, and Caro pulled a set of keys from her purse.

She rang the bell. When no one answered, she unlocked the door, and we stepped inside.

Evelyn's house was dated. Art déco furniture that was popular in the 1920s played a major role in her decorating scheme. The air smelled of moth balls and copper and Shalimar.

"Mother Evelyn?"

No one answered.

"I hope she hasn't fallen. Wait here?" She hurried down a hallway, but returned seconds later, shaking her head. "She's not in the kitchen."

"Her bedroom?"

"Mother Evelyn?" Caro called up the stairs.

Silence was the only response, and a chill ran down my spine.

Together we climbed the steps, our heels sinking deep into the peacock-patterned carpet.

"Mother Evelyn?" Worry tinged Caro's voice. She led me to

a room at the front of the house and cracked the door, then gasped and stumbled backward.

I peeked over her shoulder.

I too gasped.

Caro no longer needed to worry about taking care of her mother-in-law. Evelyn Langley lay on the floor, unmoving, waxy, in a veritable lake of crimson. Her mouth hung open. Her skin was a pale gray. She was obviously dead.

And I'd found my first body.

M y chin tried to quiver. Tried. But I would not falter. Not when my friend needed me. I took a deep breath and steeled my spine.

Caro made a keening noise and wobbled, and I took a firm grasp on her elbow and stopped her from sinking to the floor of her mother-in-law's bedroom.

"What do we do?" The barest whisper escaped her pale lips.

"Breathe." Sensible advice.

She shook her head as if breathing wasn't a viable option.

"Take a breath," I insisted. Perhaps, as she filled her lungs, she'd realize hiring and firing nurses was no longer her problem and she could retire from her job as Evelyn's chauffeur. "Do it, Caro."

She took an open-mouthed breath. "Now what?"

"Call your husband, then I'll call mine."

Her gaze shifted to the phone on the bedside table, and her shoulders shook.

I didn't blame her. Making calls with Evelyn in the room was…wrong. "We'll use the extension downstairs."

She wobbled again, and I tightened my grip on her arm. Together, we descended the steps.

"Thank you, Frances." Her words came out as shaky as her knees.

"For what?" My knees weren't one hundred percent. Not that I'd admit weakness.

"I'm so glad you're with me. What if I'd found her when I was alone?"

I thought of Evelyn and her waxy skin and the blood, and two thoughts popped into my brain. First, did Ellison experience this horror when she swam into or tripped over a body? Had my sweet daughter dealt with the gut-wrenching chill that iced my blood? My hands clenched. Second, and equally disturbing, I, Frances Walford, had found a body.

After all the scolding I'd done, Ellison could never know.

"I'm glad you weren't alone." Too bad it wasn't John with her.

"We can use the phone in the kitchen."

I followed her to the back of the house and watched as she dialed John's number. "It's Carolyn Langley. I need to speak with my husband." She winced. "I don't care. This is an emergency. Interrupt him." She pressed her free fist to her mouth. "I see. If he checks in, have him call me at his mother's. It's an emergency. Thank you." She hung up, and when she looked at me, tears stood in her eyes. "He's not at the office. Emily will try to reach him."

Annoyance tightened my shoulders, but I forced a reassuring smile. "I'll call Harrington." I picked up the receiver and dialed my husband's direct line.

"Walford." His voice calmed my stuttering heart.

"Harrington." Why did I sound so squeaky? I cleared my throat and adjusted my posture. My mother always said posture was a sneak peek at what others were feeling. Slumped shoulders? Sadness or defeat. A straight spine meant a woman ready to take on the world.

"What's wrong, Frannie?" Concern hung from every word.

"I'm at Evelyn Langley's house with Caro. Evelyn died."

"Where's John?"

"Out of the office. Caro and I are here alone."

"How did Evelyn die?"

"She fell?" I frowned. Why had I made that a question?

Long seconds clicked by as my husband decided on a course of action. "I'll call the police."

"The police?"

"I'm on my way, Frannie. Stay strong."

I huffed. I was always strong. "Of course."

"That's my girl. I'll be there as soon as I can."

"I love you."

"Love you, too."

I would have liked a minute more of his voice and its comfort, but he hung up.

I returned the receiver to its cradle. "Harrington is on his way."

"Thank God." Caro sank into a ladder-backed chair at the kitchen table and rested her face in her hands.

"What can I get you?"

She looked up. "Is it awful if I say scotch?"

"Not in the least. Where is it?"

"The bar is set up in the living room."

A moment later, I pushed a glass with three fingers of good scotch into her hand, then took the chair next to hers.

She sipped and shuddered. "Thank you."

"What else can I do?"

"Nothing." She took another sip. "Thank you for this." She held up the drink. "For being here with me. How can I ever repay you?"

"Don't tell anyone I was here."

"What?" She tilted her head.

"I might have scolded Ellison about finding bodies and..."

"And you don't want her to know you found one."

"Exactly."

"My lips are sealed." She mimed zipping her lips. "Mothers of daughters have to stick together. We might judge our daughters, but they judge us right back. And they're much harder on us than we are on them."

The truth of her statement wrapped around me. I'd forgive Ellison or Marjorie most any sin, but I'd been hard on my mother. I couldn't forgive her willingness to always put my father first. Above her own wants or needs. Above her children. If she'd paid more attention to my sister, taken a firmer hand, Sis might have had a family. Instead, my sister was a globe-trotting Bohemian.

"My lasting memories of Evelyn won't be good ones." Caro sipped again. The level of scotch in her glass was dropping at an alarming level.

Did I tell her to slow down?

No, I did not. But I wanted to.

"Truth is, even before her health failed, Evelyn wasn't the easiest mother-in-law. I won't miss her." She stared into what was left of her drink. "But John loved her. This will hurt him." She slumped, as if she were anticipating her husband's pain. "At least he can stop fighting with his brothers."

"He argued with his brothers?"

She answered with a quick nod. "Evelyn was burning through money. They were appalled."

"It was her money."

"You're right. But she sent ten thousand dollars to some Baptist preacher she saw on TV. And she was an Episcopalian. They saw her frittering away her fortune, and they were all intent on there being money left when she died." She glanced at the ceiling and grimaced as if picturing the body upstairs. "We knew she was a fall risk."

"That's why you hired nurses."

Caro glanced around the kitchen as if she expected someone to be with us. "Where's the nurse? She should be here."

"Maybe Evelyn fired her."

"The agency is supposed to call whenever that happens. No one called."

Ding dong

Caro stiffened

"You sit." I rose from the table. "I'll get the door."

I strode into the front hall, wiped the scowl from my face, opened the door, and froze. Only iron control kept my jaw from dropping.

What were the chances that he'd show up here? Drat the luck. "You."

"Mrs. Walford." Brown eyes sparkled and expressive lips quirked. And, for half a second, I understood why Ellison found Detective Jones so attractive.

"What are you doing here?" The unwelcome surprise of his presence sharpened my voice to a fine edge.

"Mr. Walford called me."

"Harrington called you?" The tone I used when I said *you* might have been slightly insulting, but it was better than my first urge—to close the door in his face.

"He said you found a body." The man was silently laughing at me. I could tell.

"We don't need a homicide detective. Evelyn fell."

"Since I'm here, perhaps I should take a look."

I could sense a stubborn streak. He wouldn't back down. Rather than argue, I stood aside and allowed him entry into the house. "Suit yourself."

Why had Harrington phoned Detective Jones? Why? My husband and I would have words about this.

"The body?"

I waved at the steps. "Upstairs in the master bedroom."

"Anyone else here?"

"Her daughter-in-law is in the kitchen."

"Her?"

"Evelyn Langley, the woman whose death you don't need to investigate."

His eyes twinkled. "I'll be the judge of that."

If Detective Jones thought he could waltz into Evelyn's house and involve me in a murder investigation, he had another think coming. "She fell."

His lips quirked a second time. "You already mentioned that. Now, if you'll excuse me?" He didn't wait for my reply. Instead, he climbed the front stairs, leaving me gaping.

That was unacceptable. I snapped my jaw shut and followed him, pausing only when Caro called my name.

"Frances?" She stood at the bottom of the stairway.

I turned. "Harrington rang the police."

Her gaze followed Detective Jones. "He's the police?" Awe colored her tone. Was any woman besides me immune to his charms?

"Can you make some coffee? We may be here a while." I was nowhere near the coffee devotée my daughter was, but I needed a jolt of something, and making coffee would give Caro something to do.

She nodded and headed toward the kitchen.

I hurried toward Evelyn's bedroom where Detective Jones studied the body. His gaze took in the large pool of blood.

"What broke the skin?" he mused.

"When you're older, it's easier to break skin. She hit her head on the floor."

He shook his head as if my excellent point had failed to convince him. "When you found her, did you touch anything?"

"No." My lips pursed. "You can't think she was murdered?"

"I can't rule it out."

I straightened my spine. "You can. You can report that she fell."

"If she was murdered, she deserves justice."

Since I couldn't argue that, I turned and left. Caro needed me. And I needed to escape Detective Jones's suspicions.

I found Caro in the kitchen, clutching her nearly empty glass as if it were a life preserver and she was drowning. "I tried calling again. I still can't reach John."

The coffeemaker gurgled, and we both looked at it as if it might start speaking.

"Detective Jones will take care of everything until John can get here."

"Detective?"

I nodded. "I met him after Ellison found Madeline Harper's body."

"But Madeline was murdered." Her skin paled. "Evelyn wasn't murdered. She fell. It was an accident."

"Exactly what I told him. He insists on being thorough." An attribute I usually appreciated.

Ding dong.

Caro sagged.

"I'll get it," I offered.

"Thank you, Frances."

I hurried to the front door and found my husband on the other side. Despite the relief that eased the tension in my neck and shoulders, my eyes narrowed. "You called Detective Jones?"

Harrington shrugged. "I had his card."

"But he's a homicide detective."

Harrington nodded. "He can rule out homicide, then we'll call the funeral home."

"What if she didn't fall?"

My husband tilted his chin and lifted his eyebrows.

My lips pursed with distaste, but the words had to be said. "There's a lot of blood."

"Oh?"

"I worry someone may have bashed her on the head."

"Murder?" A shadow passed over my husband's usually sunny face.

"Maybe." There was so much blood.

He lifted a brow. "Like daughter, like mother?"

"This is nothing like Ellison finding bodies." I couldn't allow doubt. Well, couldn't acknowledge doubt. "Besides, I'm sure Evelyn fell."

He nodded, but I got the sense he was humoring me.

"Promise me you won't tell Ellison."

"Frannie..."

"Promise." On this, I would not compromise.

"Fine. I won't say a word." Clearly, Harrington expected me to come clean. To admit to Ellison I'd found a body. That conversation would happen when hell froze over.

He glanced over his shoulder at the car parked in the drive and frowned.

"What's wrong?"

"Ellison called."

"Did she find a body in Paris?"

"Glass houses, Frannie." He made a fair point.

"Why did she call?"

"Aggie was called out of town." Aggie was Ellison's muumuu-wearing housekeeper.

"And?"

"I picked up Max. I told her we'd keep him till Aggie gets back."

"You did what?" There was no way my voice could adequately convey my displeasure. I crossed my arms and scowled.

"He's in the car."

I leaned around him and spotted Max. "Harrington." Censure fully saturated my tone. And who could blame me? My daughter's dog was a disaster on four legs. Compared to Max, the apocalypse was a gentle stroll through Loose Park.

My husband tugged at his collar. "I'm worried it's too hot to leave him in the car."

"The windows are down." And Max's silver head was stuck out of the car. His pink tongue lolled, and he wore a doggy smile, as if he were on a grand adventure. Or a search and destroy mission. The very last thing poor Caro needed was Max. "Take him home."

He blinked. "You're serious?"

"Look at him. He'll jump through that window as soon as our backs are turned. Then we'll have to search for him." I closed my eyes and searched for a solution. "He can't stay in the car."

"You don't want him to overheat."

"Don't be ridiculous. I don't want to play chase with a dog who's smarter than half the humans I know."

"Don't let Ellison hear that."

"That I don't want to chase her dog?"

"That you think Max is smart. She'll discover you secretly like him."

I sniffed. "He's not bad looking."

"You like him."

I gave my husband the full force of my most vicious scowl, and he held up his hands. "I won't tell Ellison you have a weakness for her dog. Promise." Then he grinned, and I was reminded how lucky I was. So many of my friends stayed with their husbands for financial reasons or laziness. I still loved mine. He was still as handsome as ever. And, God love him, he tolerated my sometimes prickly demeanor.

I didn't let him see the softening in my attitude. Instead, I scowled harder. "Why did Ellison call you? I'm her mother." And I hadn't heard from her in a week.

"Frannie..."

We all knew Harrington was more likely to say yes. Ellison had wrapped her father around her fingers from the moment she drew breath. He'd pluck the moon from the sky if she asked him. Instead, she'd asked us to take her dog. "It's such an inconvenience."

"You won't even know he's there." That was a big, fat lie. "I'll run him home now. Or you can take him home, and I'll stay."

For a brief second, the day felt almost normal—Harrington with his optimism, me with my scowl—and my lungs fully inflated. But normal was a mirage. Nothing was normal, not while Evelyn Langley grew cold in her bedroom.

"Caro needs me."

"Then I'll take him home." He dug his keys from his pocket.

"Harrington." I rested my hand on his forearm.

"What's wrong, Frannie?" He searched my face as if I'd revealed a rare sign of weakness.

I considered brushing aside his concern, but then I thought about Evelyn's body, and the amount of scotch Caro was drinking, and Detective Jones acting as if Evelyn death wasn't an accident. I stared into my husband's eyes. "It was awful."

He wrapped me in a hug and rubbed small comforting circles on my back.

It was so tempting to stay there in the comfort of Harrington's arms. But Caro needed me. I steeled my spine and drew away. "Thank you. I needed that."

His warm gaze searched my face, and he nodded. "You're sure you're okay?"

"I'm fine." Still a lie.

He gave the briefest of nods at my falsehood, then drove an animal bent on world domination (or, failing that, utter destruction) to our house.

CHAPTER THREE

I nursed the lukewarm contents of a mug and waited with Caro. We sat at Evelyn's kitchen table. The kitchen was in need of an update. Evelyn still had metal cabinets, and there was a pinkish linoleum on the floor. Also, the woman collected kitschy salt and pepper shakers. They were displayed in a specially made shelf on the far wall, and owl with enormous eyes stared at me.

"Why hasn't John called?"

I didn't have an answer, and Caro downed the rest of her second drink.

Detective Jones appeared in the doorway, and his gaze caught on my friend's empty old-fashioned glass, but rather than comment, he asked, "May I please have a cup of coffee?"

"Of course." Caro stood, swayed, grabbed the edge of the counter, and pulled a mug from the cabinet above the coffee maker. "There's milk in the fridge."

"Black is fine." He accepted the mug and took a seat at the table. "I'm Detective Jones."

"Carolyn Langley." Her voice was ghostly faint. "What's happening?"

"The medical examiner will take the body."

"Take the body?" Cora's voice faded to barely audible.

"I'm sorry for your loss."

Deep wrinkles cut across her forehead. "Why are they taking the body?"

"For an autopsy."

"No." She shook her head and crossed her arms over her chest. "That simply won't do."

"It's a suspicious death, Mrs. Langley."

"She fell," I insisted. And my opinion bore repeating as many times as it took until Detective Jones accepted the truth.

"I have my doubts," the detective replied.

Cora's narrow shoulders shuddered. "This is so...sordid. Frances, will you try John's office again? Please?"

I patted her hand. "Of course."

She rattled off the numbers, and I dialed. "Hello, this is Mrs. Harrington Walford calling. I need to speak with John Langley."

"He's out of the office, ma'am."

"It's an emergency." I glanced at Detective Jones. "His mother fell."

"He's not here, Mrs. Walford."

"Where is he?"

"I couldn't say."

Couldn't or wouldn't? I didn't believe a word the receptionist said. She was covering for John, and I sincerely hoped that poor Caro didn't have to deal with a philandering spouse on top of a dead mother-in-law. "Do you have a way to reach him?"

"No, ma'am."

"Do you expect him to return to the office?"

"I don't have his schedule."

"If he returns, please have him call his mother's home."

"Yes, ma'am."

"They haven't found John?" Caro sounded broken.

My distinct impression, that John might be found in a hotel room with another woman, remained unvoiced. "Not yet."

"Does your husband have any siblings?" Anarchy asked.

"Three," Caro replied.

"Perhaps we could call one of them."

"His oldest brother, Douglas, lives in Stamford, Connecticut. His twin, Fitz, lives in Chicago. And his youngest brother, Evan, lives in Denver. They're not nearby."

Detective Jones smiled at her as if she'd showed him the road to Shangri-La. "Will you tell me about them? Please?"

"Douglas is a corporate type in New York. Very important. Always busy. His wife doesn't like him." Caro slapped her hand over her mouth.

She'd drunk way too much scotch. That wasn't the sort of tidbit one dropped to a homicide detective.

Jones's eyes twinkled. "Your secret is safe with me."

"Evan runs his wife's family's company. She's lovely. Three children."

"And Fitz?"

Cora's mouth pursed. "The black sheep." She let that secret go without covering her mouth.

"He lives in Chicago?" Detective Jones prompted.

"That's right. He trades bonds."

"When were they last in Kansas City?"

"Douglas and Evan came for Mother's Day. Fitz was here last week."

"Did they get along with their mother?"

"Cora, you don't have to answer." She needed her husband here. That or a lawyer. I should have called Hunter Tafft the moment Detective Jones arrived. I should have taken the dratted dog home and asked my husband to stay with Caro. Harrington might not be a lawyer, but he was whip smart and he'd protect my friend. Even from herself.

Caro glanced at her lap and ignored my warning. "Evelyn's been difficult of late."

"How so?"

"She insisted on staying in her home. No matter the cost or inconvenience."

"Inconvenience?" Detective Jones sounded suspiciously sympathetic.

"She fired her nurses." Caro looked around the kitchen as if she expected a woman clad in white to jump out of the broom closet. "Someone should have been here. With her. The agency didn't call. They're supposed to call me when a nurse isn't here."

"The agency called you with problems?"

"Yes." Caro eyed her empty glass.

"Not her son?"

"He has other responsibilities."

"Did you like your mother-in-law?"

Caro paused, and I could sense her weighing the cost of a lie. "No."

"Never?"

"Never," she confirmed.

"Why not?"

"She never let go of her sons. She believed their roles as her sons were more important than their roles as husbands or fathers." She jerked her head up. "Is the safe still locked?"

"The safe?"

"Her jewelry. If her death wasn't an accident, this has to be a robbery."

"We'll check the safe." The gentle way he spoke made me realize he'd found the safe, and as far as he could tell, the contents were untouched.

"When did this happen?" I asked. "When did she die?"

"The medical examiner will give us a better idea, but my guess is she died early this afternoon."

Tears filled Caro's eyes. "So awful. I didn't like her, but I didn't want her dead. Not like this."

"Then how?" asked the detective.

"Gently. In her sleep."

I wrapped an arm around Caro's shoulders, and she leaned into me and murmured, "Thank you for staying, Frances."

"Of course."

Brnng, brnng.

Our heads swiveled, and Caro stiffened.

"I should get that." She stood. Slowly. Rising from her chair seemed to require Herculean effort. "Hello." She clutched the receiver as if it kept her upright. "John." Her husband's name came out in a rush. "Where have you been? It doesn't matter. You need to come to your mother's house." Her gaze shifted to Detective Jones. "She fell. She's gone."

The knuckles on her right hand whitened around the receiver. Her left hand smoothed a non-existent wrinkle from her skirt. "I don't know, John." She closed her eyes. "The police are here. A detective." She listened, and her chin lifted. "I'm not the one who disappeared this afternoon. Just get here." She hung up the receiver with more force than was strictly necessary then faced us. "John will be here shortly."

The brightness in her voice didn't fool me. "Do you want another drink?"

She nodded. "Please."

I fetched her a single finger of scotch, and we waited together until John arrived. He burst into the kitchen wearing a brow etched with worry and gathered his wife into an encompassing hug.

She had her husband. She didn't need me. "I'll let myself out."

"Thank you, Frances." She pulled loose from John's embrace, clutched my hand, and gazed at me with watery eyes. "I don't know what I would have done without you."

"You're welcome." I gave her a brief hug then nodded goodbye to John and Detective Jones.

The detective followed me to my car, which earned him an aggrieved sigh.

"What is it?" I demanded. I wanted my husband, my home, and a scotch of my own. Not a conversation with a homicide detective.

He rubbed the back of his neck.

He wanted information about Ellison. I was sure of it. The two of them had taken an unacceptable shine to each other. I readied my non-answer.

"Is there anyone in Evelyn Langley's family who wanted her dead?"

Perhaps he wasn't interested in Ellison. "Caro is a dear friend."

He waited for more.

"I won't gossip about her or her family."

"Someone murdered her mother-in-law. Questions have to be asked."

"But I won't be the one to answer them."

"We'll need a statement."

"She fell." That was my statement. I climbed into the car and left him standing on the curb.

"Harrington?" I called for my husband the moment I passed through the front door.

He appeared in the hallway to the kitchen. "Need a drink?"

"A double."

He nodded. "How's Caro?"

"She was well on her way to three sheets when I left."

"How are you?"

"Fine." Not fine. Evelyn's blood spreading across the floor

filled my vision. Ellison had found three bodies. Three. Three times the horror. And I'd scolded her for it. For a brief instant, I regretted that censure. Then I remembered that my daughter approached danger when any sane person ran the other way. If anything, I hadn't offered enough censure. "Where's the dog?"

"Backyard."

"Unsupervised? He's probably halfway to China."

"I was outside with him till you got home. We can have drinks on the patio."

"But dinner..." Our housekeeper's day off meant dinner at the club.

"There are potatoes baking and a salad in the refrigerator. I'll grill steaks."

"You're a marvelous husband." He was also a far better cook than I ever dreamed of being.

He handed me a cocktail. "I have a marvelous wife. Go. Sit. I'll be out in a minute."

I offered a quick peck on the lips, then headed to the brick patio where a scalloped shade in a bright pink hue covered a glass-topped table. Matching pink geraniums and white petunias rioted in nearby terra-cotta pots.

I sank into a chair, adjusted the pink cushion beneath me, and searched the yard for Max.

Ellison's dog was busy sniffing every scent. He lifted his head, stared at me for a few seconds, then leapt at a squirrel who'd been foolish enough to leave the safety of its oak tree.

The squirrel barely made it to safety.

Max stood and stared at the chittering beast just out of his reach.

"Max!"

He ignored me. It was nothing personal. He often ignored Ellison, and she was his favorite person.

"Max!"

He turned his amber gaze my way.

"Leave the squirrel alone."

He gave me a doggy eye roll.

"Behave."

He turned his back and resumed sniffing.

Harrington put a charcuterie board on the patio table, and I popped a red grape in my mouth.

"Dinner in thirty minutes."

"Can I do anything?"

"Not unless you'd like to eat outside."

"It's a lovely evening."

"Then I'll let you set the table."

Max, who'd sniffed cheese and summer sausage, joined us on the patio and sat, his gaze fixed on the appetizers.

"Do not feed him," I warned.

Harrington scratched behind his ears. "Who's a good boy?"

Max preened.

"Cheese gives him gas."

"Sausage won't hurt him." Harrington offered Max a slice, and the dog snarfed it down.

Disapproval pursed my lips. "You shouldn't feed him from the table."

Harrington smiled. "You're right, Frannie."

"I'll get the silverware and place mats." I wasn't fooled. Harrington would give Max more sausage when I turned my back.

I stood and left them to it, but turned when I reached the door to the house. "No cheese, Harington. I mean it."

"Yes, dear."

Lord, how I hated "yes, dear," and "yes, Mother." It was my family's code for *we've heard you, we don't want to argue, and we'll do what we want.* "If that dog develops gastric issues, you'll be the one getting up with him in the wee hours."

"Yes, dear."

This "yes, dear" called my bluff. Harrington was the breadwinner, which meant sleep lost to children, pets, and worry that the hose was running fell firmly on my side of the bed.

When I returned with everything we needed to set the table, Max was sprawled across the patio bricks, and the cheese on the platter looked untouched.

We ate a lovely dinner. I lifted a perfect bite of medium rare steak to my lips and said, "Evelyn fell, hit her head, and died."

"I hope you're right."

"Of course I'm right." I spoke with more confidence than I felt, but faking an attitude could convince most anyone.

Most everyone except my husband. He swallowed the last sip of wine in his glass then patted my hand. "Shall we clear?"

Max, who'd waited patiently, eyed the few remaining bites of steak on my plate. His stubby tail gave a hopeful wag, and I tossed him a cube.

"Now who's feeding from the table?"

"No one enjoys a nag, Harrington."

Max followed me into the kitchen and easily caught the remaining bites of steak I tossed to him.

Harrison watched from the doorway with his arms crossed and the hint of a smirk on his face. "If I didn't know better, I'd think you're fond of that dog."

"Don't be ridiculous."

Max regarded me with liquid eyes, and I offered him the last bite.

He took it from my fingers with surprising delicacy.

When I rinsed the plate, he gave a disappointed huff.

"You made out like a bandit," I told him.

He lifted a single brow then settled on the floor.

"Just behave yourself, mister."

He didn't listen. He never listened.

Which was why I shouldn't have been surprised when I stumbled into the empty kitchen the next morning and found a disaster. I stared in horrified wonder at the open cabinet doors and the wrappers littering the floor.

Harrington had a junk food addiction that I quietly ignored. I pretended the cabinet filled with Ding Dongs and Pringles and Hostess fruit pies didn't exist. He ate corn chips and moon pies without me.

Max had tasted it all. I bent and picked up a bit of cellophane. "Max!"

He didn't come, which was no surprise.

I stalked through the house, searching for him. "Max!" I was no fool. I knew he'd hide from the outrage in my voice, but I couldn't dull the sharp edges.

I found him under the dining room table. "Get out from there right now."

He didn't budge.

"Frannie, what's wrong?" Harrington still wore his seersucker pajamas.

"Have you seen the kitchen?"

Harrington raised his brows and disappeared. He returned a moment later, covering his mouth with his hand as if I he could hide his amusement from me. "You'll take him to the vet?"

"Me? They were your snacks."

"I have an early meeting."

I wasn't sure I believed him. "Fine. You get him out from under the table, I'll change." I hurried upstairs, called the vet, and changed from my nightgown into a linen coat dress. I add pearls and lipstick, fluffed my hair, then returned to the scene of the crime.

Max, who looked green around these gills, wore a leash.

"How does Ellison put up with you?"

He groaned.

"It's a good thing you're good-looking. Harrington, help me get him in the car."

He led Max outside and boosted him into the passenger seat of my Mercedes. "Let me know how he is."

I pressed my lips into a thin line and drove to the vet's office, where a young woman in scrubs accepted his leash.

"What did he eat?" She eyed his distended belly with concern.

"Two cans of Pringles, a dozen Ding Dongs, and a box of moon pies.

She frowned. She was judging me.

"Also, a box of Bugles."

"Bugles?" She regarded me without an ounce of comprehension.

"They're a snack shaped like horns. Children put them on their fingertips." I curled my knuckles till my fingers were claws. "I'll get you and your little dog, too."

She paled, as if I were an actual wicked witch.

"It's from—never mind. They're corn snacks."

"Anything else?"

"Probably."

She nodded as if she'd done this before. "We know Max. Well. We'll take good care of him." She led Ellison's dog to the back room, and I took a seat in the waiting room where I perused the morning paper. Evelyn's death wasn't included in its pages.

"Frances?" Hortie Beecham stood at the counter holding a cat carrier.

"Hortie." I nodded a hello. What were her parents thinking, naming her (or any child) Hortense? "Good morning."

"How's Ellison?"

"Still in Europe. Her dog is staying with us." Which explained my presence at the vet.

"Grace is with her?"

I nodded.

"Such a tragedy about Henry."

My son-in-law had become something of a disappointment, but I nodded.

"Did you hear about Evelyn Langley?" she asked.

I kept my expression neutral. "I did."

"So fortunate John saw her yesterday."

"John saw her?"

She nodded. "I saw him stop by around lunchtime. Frances, what's wrong?"

"A goose wandered over my grave. What time?"

"Time?"

"What time did you see John?"

"I'd have to think about it." Her forehead puckered. "I was leaving to go to Barbara's for bridge."

"Mrs. Beecham, we're ready for you and Felix."

I scowled at the woman waiting to lead Hortie to an exam room, and she retreated a step.

"The time, Hortie?"

"Lord, I don't know. Noon? One? Why do you ask?"

I swallowed my annoyance. "Just curious."

Hortie, Felix, and the young woman disappeared into an exam room, and I resumed reading the paper. Surely if Evelyn's was truly a suspicious death, there'd be an article. It didn't matter that John had been there the afternoon she died.

"Mrs. Walford?"

I looked up from the obituary page.

"Max is ready. We pumped his stomach."

The dog wore an angry expression.

"His tummy will be delicate. When you feed him, you should serve scrambled eggs or rice."

My housekeeper would *love* that. The corner of my eye twitched with the effort required to keep my mouth shut.

Unaware that I did not employ a short-order cook, the young woman followed me to the car and helped load Max.

I thanked her, then told him, "You're nothing but trouble."

His amber gaze held mine for long seconds, then he vomited on my seat.

CHAPTER FOUR

I pulled a driver from my golf bag and watched Joanna tee off. Her ball flew, hugging the fairway's edge, and finally thudding into the rough.

She grunted her displeasure.

I settled my ball on the tee and swung. My shot didn't fly nearly as far as Joanna's, but it did land in the center of the fairway.

"You heard about Evelyn?" she asked.

I replaced the driver in my bag, and we boarded the golf cart. "I did." I would not share that I'd found Evelyn's body. Not when I'd been so vocal in my displeasure when Ellison found corpses. If my luck held, Caro would never mention my presence, and my daughter would never know.

"Richard was on the golf course with John when Caro found her."

"Really?" That was a relief. At least John wasn't having an affair.

"They met for a late lunch then played eighteen. They were having drinks in the men's grill when someone told John there was an emergency at his mother's."

"I'm sure Caro needed him." Such an understatement.

Joanna's lips pursed.

"What?" I asked.

"Richard said John sighed and finished his martini."

My hackles rose. "Poor Caro."

"Evelyn had regular emergencies," said Joanna, who always looked for the good in people and made excuses for their failings.

"I imagine she did. But Evelyn was John's mother, not Caro's. Seems like he should have been the one asking how high when Evelyn said jump. Not Caro." John should have leapt from his chair, not finished his martini. "Caro needed him."

"He didn't know that. He was told emergency at his mother's. According to what he told Richard, emergencies could include being out of gin, a fuzzy picture on the television set, a light bulb that needed changing, or her newspaper arriving late."

"I assume Caro handled most of those emergencies."

"Undoubtedly. But John still got the calls."

I parked the cart, took a five-wood from my bag, and positioned myself above the ball. I breathed deep, allowing the tension that had gathered in my shoulders to ease. I swung and hit the golf ball onto the green.

When I took my seat behind the wheel, Joanna said, "Nice shot."

"Thank you."

"Do you think an eight iron or a nine iron?"

I eyed her ball. "I'd use a nine."

She nodded, and we drove closer to her ball.

"You're right, Frances." Of course, I was. "I certainly hope John felt guilty when he discovered what Caro had to deal with by herself."

I parked the cart, and Joanna approached her ball. She brought her nine iron back, and I noticed the club face was too open. Not that I'd tell her that. Joanna pouted when I made suggestions about her golf swing. Some people just couldn't take constructive criticism.

The club thwacked the ball, and, as I suspected, her shot sliced, landing in a bunker to the right of the green.

My lips remained sealed as she dropped her club into her bag. "Drat."

"Happens to the best of us," I replied.

She frowned.

"Let it go," I urged. There was no point in pouting over an errant golf shot. "It's a beautiful day." The sky was a perfect azure blue. The grass was lush and shaded a vibrant green. A light breeze rustled the leaves. And, for once, the humidity was bearable.

"You're right." Joanna climbed into the cart. "Richard always says a bad day at golf is better than a good day at work. The weather is glorious." She grinned. "And I'm aces with a sand wedge."

She had to be. Of course, I kept that observation to myself.

"I talked to Caro last night."

My heart hiccupped as I drove the cart near the green and claimed my putter. "Oh?"

"She told me the medical examiner took the body." Joanna tsked. "Why, I don't know. It's ridiculous. Evelyn's death is obviously a tragic accident."

"I'm sure the medical examiner will concur." An accident. A fall. Detective Jones was wrong. Had to be. Otherwise, like my daughter, I'd found a murder victim.

The thought was so unsettling, I missed a makeable putt and scored par instead of making a birdie.

Joanna pitched out of the bunker, made a short putt, and bogeyed.

We recorded our scores on our cards and drove to the next tee box.

"What time did Richard and John have lunch?" I asked.

Joanna looked up from placing her tee. "Why do you ask?"

"I ran into Hortie Beecham at the vet's, and she said she saw John at Evelyn's around lunchtime."

"She would know. She watches everything that happens on that street."

"There's one on every block." The tiresome woman who lived across the street from Ellison felt honor bound to call me whenever anything happened at my daughter's house. Sadly, that meant she called often. "What time was lunch?"

"I'm not sure what time they met." Joanna's brows lifted above the rims of her sunglasses. "Do you think John's a suspect?"

"Evelyn fell." That was my story, and I was sticking to it. Like glue.

"Right." She tapped her lips with a lacquered nail. "But if she didn't—"

"It might be nice for John to have an alibi." I finished Joanna's sentence.

"Good heavens. It's like being in an episode of *The Streets of San Francisco*. Horrible and exciting at the same time. You're probably used to it—what with Ellison and all those bodies."

"It wasn't that many," I snapped. It was.

We played eighteen holes, and both scored in the mid-eighties.

"Do you have time for a bite?" asked Joanna as we walked toward the ladies' locker room.

"I wish I did. I left Max with the housekeeper. I should probably make sure my house is still standing."

"Max?"

"Ellison's dog. He already destroyed my car."

"How?"

"Don't ask." The scent of dog vomit soaking into the seat would linger (at least in memory) forever. "Also, I should stop by Caro's." Hopefully Max hadn't devoured the Bundt cake I asked the housekeeper to bake.

We stored our clubs in our lockers, checked our hair, patted the shine from our foreheads, and headed toward the exit.

"You're here?"

Heavens to Betsy. Where had Muriel Jarrett come from?

She stared at my new golf skirt and the matching shirt with a scalloped collar, drew her shoulders back, and let her upper lip curl away from her horse teeth. "You do know Evelyn Langley is dead?" Her voice held a sneer. "I spent the morning at Caro's."

"I planned on visiting her this afternoon." Why was I explaining myself to Muriel?

"Caro's true friends were there this morning, when she needed us most."

"Yet here you are at the club," I observed.

"I'm picking up dinner." Muriel sounded affronted. "The family is arriving this afternoon, and no one has brought food yet."

Joanna smiled gently. "That's kind of you, Muriel."

Muriel sneered as if she doubted Joanna's sincerity.

Shame on Muriel.

Joanna was truly nice.

I didn't have that problem. "Whatever would Caro do without you?" Sarcasm dripped heavy in my voice.

"At least I'm there when she needs me."

It was tempting to bite back, to tell her I was with Caro when she found Evelyn. Tempting, but foolish. I held my tongue, and Muriel swanned away as if she'd won a point.

She could have her point. I was playing the long game.

I walked to the car I'd borrowed from the dealership after I'd taken my sedan for a deep cleaning and thought again about Evelyn's death. Detective Jones might have his suspicions, but the simplest answer was undoubtedly correct. Evelyn had fallen, hit her head, and died.

When I got home, I found a chocolate Bundt on the cooling rack.

"That looks divine," I told my housekeeper.

Penelope, who wore a light blue uniform and kept her hair in a neat bun, smiled. "As soon as it cools, I'll drizzle it with dark chocolate."

"Wonderful. Thank you." I looked around the kitchen and frowned as a shiver of unease took hold of my spine. "Where's Max?"

Penelope winced. "He was underfoot."

"Is he in the backyard? Unsupervised?" The dog was fully capable of destroying every flower in the yard.

"No, ma'am. You told me not to do that."

"Where is he?"

"The back bathroom. I just needed a few minutes to clean up the kitchen."

"It looks clean now."

She gave a reluctant nod.

"I'll let him out." I walked toward the back half-bath. It was located next to the laundry room and hadn't been updated since 1952. As far as I knew, Penelope was the only person who ever used it.

"Penelope," I called. "Why is there water on the floor?"

"Water, Mrs. Walford?"

I rounded the corner and found a flood. "Merciful heavens!"

The water seemed to be coming from the half bath, and I yanked open the door.

A tidal wave soaked my shoes, and a very wet Max dashed past me.

"Max!"

He kept running.

"Penelope!" I didn't call, I yelled. "Catch Max." I waded into the bathroom, turned off the cold water tap, and surveyed the damage. Water was everywhere. It was probably leaking into the basement.

Rather than chase Max, Penelope joined me in the bathroom. Her eyes were wide, her skin was pale, and her hands shook.

"How?" I demanded.

"I promise you, I didn't put the stopper in the sink or turn on the water."

I believed her. "He's an evil genius. Where is he?"

"I can't catch him," she huffed. "I'm too old to chase that beast. I'll fetch a mop."

It didn't matter how old she was (younger than me), I was the one who wrote the checks. "Please. Catch the dog."

She turned away in a huff.

Why had Harrington agreed to keep the hound from hell? Why not send him to a kennel? There was a facility near Paola where the dogs who boarded did nothing but run and play and swim in a pond. Max would love it.

An hour later, the water was cleaned up, the cake was iced, and Max was loaded into the kennel owner's van. I'd paid a premium for the immediate pick up, but Harrington wouldn't mind. Not when the alternative was the utter ruin of our home.

I sighed as I looked into the vanity mirror. Most days, I didn't feel old enough to have so many lines on my face. Today, I felt every year that trailed behind me. I fastened a pearl neck-lace at my throat then searched my jewelry box for my new ring.

It wasn't there.

My heart fluttered. Had I taken it off last night? I couldn't remember. Rather than panic, I removed each piece from the box. Gold beads, gold chains, a diamond pendant, more pearls, a sapphire cocktail ring, a cameo brooch that belonged to my grandmother. No coral ring.

I hurried to the phone and called the club. "This is Frances Walford on the line."

"Good afternoon, Mrs. Walford."

"Has anyone turned in a coral ring?"

"No, ma'am."

"You're certain?"

"Yes, ma'am."

If I'd lost the ring at the club, someone would have turned it in.

Where else could I have lost it? The only other place I'd been was Evelyn's. Was her house a crime scene? If so, would the police let me search for my ring?

My choices were clear. I could call the detective and ask for his help or tell Harrington I'd lost my anniversary gift within days of receiving it.

I swallowed a sigh and reached for the phone.

CHAPTER FIVE

T he Bundt cake in my hands was perfect. Of course. I'd never bring anything less than perfection to a grieving friend.

Cora's front door swung open, and John stared at me as if were a stranger.

"I brought a Bundt." I held out the cake. "I'm so very sorry for your loss." I should have led with the sentiment, not the cake. But the cake was real, the sentiment less so.

"Thank you." He widened the door. "Please, come in. Caro will be glad you're here."

Caro would be glad. I offered him a chilly smile.

"I should thank you." He rubbed the back of his neck. "For yesterday. Caro needed a friend."

"Don't mention it." I meant that. None of the friends and neighbors crowding Caro and John's house could ever know I'd been with Caro when she found her mother-in-law's body.

One of them would tell Ellison. They'd line up for the chance. And I'd prefer she never learned the truth.

"Where should I put this?" I tilted my chin toward the cake.

"Dining room table. Cora's in the living room."

I deposited the Bundt on a lace-covered table, then found my friend.

Caro wore a navy suit and clutched the pearls at her neck. She looked pale beneath her tan and she squinted as if she were fighting a headache. Perhaps she was—she had put a sizeable dent in a bottle of Johnnie Walker. She saw me and smiled, beckoning me to her side.

I'd caught her between conversations, and she stood alone. Her gaze scanned the crowd, making sure her guests had plenty to drink. Someone had set up a card table and covered it with a linen cloth. The small table groaned beneath the weight of pitchers of iced tea, bottles of wine, vodka, gin, scotch, and bourbon, and an array of mixers. The profusion of bottles looked out of place in Cora's elegant living room.

I gave my friend a brief hug, and she squeezed, as if she needed me.

Then, she stiffened. "Frances, you know Doug, and his wife, Patricia."

I released her from my hug and extended my hand to Doug. "I'm so sorry for your loss."

I hadn't seen Doug in eons, and the years had not been kind. The part in his gray hair started just above his ear, and long strands clung to his naked pate. His face looked puffy and red, and his hand, when he took mine, was limp and clammy. "Nice to see you, Frances."

Patricia yawned, barely covering her mouth or her boredom. She wore a black dress with a neckline better-suited to a cocktail party. My dress was perfect for the occasion—a dove-gray linen coat dress. Like Cora, I wore pearls, but I didn't clutch mine.

"Frances's daughter is an artist," Caro told Patricia.

"Really?" Patricia could not have been less interested.

"She paints," Caro explained.

That earned a snide smile. "Pretty little landscapes?"

My spine stiffened. How dare she denigrate Ellison's paintings?

"Patricia is terribly chic and modern," said Cora. "She collects abstract art."

Patricia gave a tiny, superior nod. She was one of those easterners who was surprised that Kansas City had an airport, not a hitching post. I loathed people like Patricia. When they thought of the cities that dotted the Midwest and South, they assumed the inhabitants were hicks. They never, ever considered how provincial their world was.

But this was Cora's sister-in-law. And Caro had enough problems without me putting Patricia in her place. I swallowed my dislike. "Caro and John are friends with the Kellers. They have a world class collection of modern art. Perhaps they can arrange a tour while you're here.

Patricia lifted a brow, clearly doubting the possibility that any good art existed in a state without Atlantic coastline. "Which artists?"

"Pollack, Stella, Mapplethorpe—" I suppressed a disapproving wince "—Lee Krasner, Roy Lichtenstein, Jasper Johns, and Andy Warhol."

"Really?" A tinge of interest colored her voice. "Here? In Kansas City?"

Her husband's arm draped around her shoulders. "Patricia is convinced this is the wild west. She expects six guns and saloons, not fine art."

"Sorry to disappoint," I replied.

Her answering smile was colder than an ice storm, and she shrugged off her husband's embrace. "I've visited Kansas City with Douglas before. I know there aren't any saloons."

There were plenty of saloons, but I kept that to myself. This was the woman who, according to Caro, didn't like her husband. He probably didn't like her either. With good reason.

Cora's gaze bounced between us, and an awkward silence fell.

"If you'll excuse us, I believe I need another drink." Patricia walked away. "Douglas, are you coming?"

"I'm sorry," said Cora.

"Not your fault." I patted her arm.

"She's—"

"Frances?"

I turned, then smiled at Lucy Langley. Unlike her New York sister-in-law, Lucy was actually pleasant. When she and Evan first married, they'd lived in Kansas City and she'd absorbed seamlessly into the community. It was only at her father's behest that she and Evan moved to Denver. I hadn't seen her in years, but she still carried an air of youth, and her eyes sparkled behind her glasses.

We kissed the air next to each other's cheeks. "Lucy, I'm so sorry for your loss."

"It's terrible for Evan and the kids."

"Remind me. How old are they now?"

"EJ is thirty-five. He and his wife have two children. They're around here somewhere. Blaire is thirty, and her daughter just turned four. How are Ellison and Marjorie?"

"Ellison lost her husband earlier this summer." Lost her husband. That sounded as if she'd misplaced him, like a library card or a set of keys or a ring. Speaking of, I crossed my fingers that I'd find my ring at Evelyn's. "Ellison and Grace are in Europe for the summer. Marjorie and her family are still in Ohio. They'll join us in Michigan later this summer."

"Evan," Lucy called to her husband, who stood near the fireplace, "Come say hello to Frances."

Evan excused himself from his conversation, strode across the room, dropped a quick kiss on my cheek, and said, "Thank you, Frances."

I stiffened. Did he know I'd been with Caro when she found Evelyn?

I caught Caro's eye, and she gave a quick shake of her head. She'd kept my secret.

I sent her silent gratitude.

"For being here, I mean." Evan's eyelids drooped as if he actually grieved. It was nice that someone mourned Evelyn.

I made a mental note not to torture my children in my old age. When I died, I wanted real tears. Real grief. I wanted them to miss me when I was gone. "I'm so sorry for your loss."

"Mother had a good run. I think she'd prefer eternal rest to a nursing home." He cast his gaze at Caro and frowned as if she'd threatened Evelyn with a fate worse than death.

"It's still a terrible loss."

"We appreciate your sympathy. Having friends and family nearby is a comfort."

Lucy rested her hand on her husband's arm. "Speaking of family, where's Fritz?"

"He's not here yet." Caro's voice was mild, but I heard the censure lurking behind her simple reply.

Lucy nodded once, as if she understood everything Caro wasn't saying.

"It's a shame we couldn't do this at Mother's house," said Evan. "That friend of your daughter's declared it a crime scene."

My spine stiffened. How did Evan know about Ellison and Detective Jones?

"Ellison knows the detective?" asked Lucy.

"She found a body in the pool at the club earlier this summer, and he investigated. I'd hardly call them friends."

"It was awful for poor Ellison." Caro offered me a small grimace. "For Frances and Harrington, too."

"Perhaps Ellison could call the detective?" Evan suggested. "We'd like to get in the house."

"Ellison is in Europe."

"Too bad," he replied.

"Is Detective Jones certain there was foul play? It's possible your mother fell."

Lucy adjusted her glasses. "That's what I said."

"There was a wound facing up," said Evan.

"Surely she could have turned her head."

"True," he ceded. "But how to explain the other wound? It's impossible to fall on the floor and impact both sides of your head."

Lucy gasped as if she hadn't considered murder. Caro turned white as milk.

"Why would anyone kill Evelyn?"

"A burglary gone wrong," Evan suggested.

"There was nothing missing," said Cora. "Nothing out of place. I can't help but hope the police made a mistake."

Evans's face pinched. "This is hardly the place for this discussion." His gaze landed on me. "I'd appreciate it if you didn't share the detective's suspicions. You know how people talk."

Each of the Langleys would be a suspect.

"My lips are sealed."

Lucy offered me an apologetic frown and tugged on her husband's arm. "Kaye and Mark Pierson are here. We should thank them for coming."

He let himself be led away.

Caro sagged. "The family has decided to be beastly."

"My mother always said to judge people by the company they keep. Those are the people we choose. Family is an accident of blood."

She huffed. "Doug chose Patricia."

"Which says nothing about you."

"Maybe she's less abrasive in New York."

"Undoubtedly." I bet she was worse. "Did you find out what happened to the missing nurse?"

"They left a message. I just hadn't picked it up yet."

"Ah." I glanced around the room. No one was nearby. "I hate to bother you with this, today of all days, but I lost a ring yesterday."

"Oh?" Caro nodded at Lillian Rush, who'd entered the living room and was heading our way.

"No one turned it in at the club."

Caro fixed a tight, polite smile on her face.

"Did you see a coral ring at Evelyn's?"

The smile slipped. "No. But I wasn't looking. Perhaps, after the funeral, we can look for it."

That simply wouldn't do. I couldn't wait days to find the ring. I had no choice but to meet Detective Jones at Evelyn's.

CHAPTER SIX

My fingers tightened around the steering wheel as I drove to Evelyn's house. Was Detective Jones right? Had someone murdered her?

A vision of Evelyn swimming in a pool of her own blood flashed through my mind, and my stomach tightened. For a brief second, I completely understood Detective Jones's need for justice. Evelyn hadn't deserved to die, and catching her killer was paramount. In the next instant, I remembered Evelyn was beyond caring about justice. Would she even want justice if it meant destroying her family?

Because, if someone killed her, it was probably a relative. Patricia was my favorite possibility, but if that woman were to kill someone, it would be with a knife to their back.

The car behind me honked, and I realized I'd been at the stop sign for more than a minute. I offered an apologetic wave and turned right.

If Evelyn had been murdered, and a family member sent her to her grave, the motive was clear.

Money.

She'd been running through money as if hundred-dollar bills

grew on trees. Frittering generational wealth went against every tenet my parents drilled into me. But it was *her* money. Evelyn had the right to spend it as she liked. I believed that, and I'd laugh if Ellison or Marjorie presumed to tell me how to manage my finances. On the other hand, Evelyn sending ten thousand dollars to a preacher she watched on television didn't wow me with her good judgment.

There wasn't an easy, black-and-white answer. I sighed my frustration, turned onto Evelyn's street, and shifted my focus to a more immediate problem. Hortie Beecham. I got lucky the last time I was here. Hortie had been away from home, unable to mark my presence or track my movements, unable to report that I'd found a body. I couldn't count on luck a second time. I pulled into Evelyn's driveway and parked behind the house (not that Hortie would recognize the loaner car, but I couldn't risk her seeing me).

The back door hung open, which seemed odd. Especially since Detective Jones's car was parked in front of the house.

I stuck my head into the kitchen and looked around. "Detective Jones?"

Empty. Where was he?

A trickle of unease chilled my spine, and I swallowed the urge to call his name a second time. Instead, I pushed through the door and tiptoed into the front hall.

Not a soul in sight. Fine. I didn't need a homicide detective to greet me at the door. I'd find my ring and leave.

The late afternoon sunlight that filtered into Evelyn's living room was no match for the teal and gold geometric fountain wallpaper. The room was so dark, it reminded me of a tomb. The joyless art didn't help. And the gray velvet crescent couches reminded me of coffins. I caught my reflection in the starburst mirror above the fireplace and frowned. I looked tentative. Almost scared. I didn't do tentative or scared. I did strong. That's what I'd taught my girls.

I straightened my shoulders, crossed to the bar cart, and spotted my missing ring nestled between two bottles of gin.

A relieved sigh rose from my toes as I slipped Harrington's gift back onto my finger.

I could leave, escape this house and its art déco shadows, avoid the memory of Evelyn in a pool of blood, and make it home in time to make a few calls about an upcoming gala I was chairing.

I stepped into the hallway and paused. I couldn't just leave. Detective Jones had made a special trip to let me in. It would be rude to leave without alerting him.

So where was he?

I approached the foot of the stairs and my gaze fixed on a side table covered with a basket for mail, a Lalique lamp, and an Erté bronze of a woman in a leopard print evening gown.

She was slender and elegant and held out her hand as if she expected a dashing man to claim her fingers.

"Det…" His name died on my lips, and I shivered. Something was not right.

I claimed the Erté statue. The woman's heft comforted me as I tiptoed up the stairs.

My feet led me to Evelyn's bedroom door.

The door was shut, and my free hand circled the handle, but I paused.

I heard voices. Two men. I strained to hear what they were saying. The blood rushing to my ears made eavesdropping difficult.

If Detective Jones was with another cop, I'd look like a fool for toting Evelyn's expensive bronze statue like a weapon.

But the feeling from behind the closed door was dark and dangerous, and I tightened my grip on the statue.

One of the men on the other side of the door grunted. Then came a crash, loud enough to wake the dead.

I swallowed a surprised squeak.

The bedroom door flew open, and I gasped. "John?" No. That couldn't be right. John was with his wife, their family, and fifty of their closest friends. I knew that. He'd seen me to the door not twenty minutes ago.

Also, John would never snarl at me or lift his arm as if he intended to hit me.

It was Fritz.

But not the Fritz I knew. Not the affable ne'er-do-well. This man's features were twisted in anger. His eyes were tight, his mouth thin, and his cheeks ruddy. He stared at me, and his lips drew away from his teeth.

There could be only one reason he was here, only one reason Detective Jones lay behind him in a growing pool of blood.

I took a giant step back.

Fitz took a giant step forward. "What are you doing here, Frances?"

"I lost my ring. I came to find it." I didn't show him the carved coral on my right ring finger because that hand was tucked behind my back, clutching his mother's bronze statue.

"You shouldn't have come."

Was Detective Jones unconscious? Dead? Why didn't he get up? Was my heart going to beat out of my chest?

I retreated another step. "Your mother?" A pointless question. I knew the horrific answer. "You killed her."

"She'd lost her mind. She was giving my inheritance to worthless charities, and Caro and John refused to stop her."

"But—"

"Her death was an accident." His expression softened, and he held out a hand, as if he might convince me Evelyn's death was a huge misunderstanding. "I didn't mean to kill her, but she refused to sign the power of attorney."

"You clubbed her over the head and let her bleed to death." My mother always told me my tongue would get me into trouble. I sealed my lips before I said anything else to anger him.

"I didn't mean to do it. She wouldn't listen to reason." It was almost as if Fritz believed his mother's death was an unfortunate mishap. Maybe he hadn't meant to kill her, but she was still dead.

"You could have called for help and saved her life." Mother was right. My tongue was going to get me killed, but I couldn't stop the words from coming.

Fritz shrugged. I'd seen plenty of shrugs in my life. None as cold as his. The man had let his mother bleed to death, and his only emotion was the lift and fall of his shoulders.

He advanced a step.

My grip tightened around the statue.

"I'm sorry about this, Evelyn, but I can't leave any witnesses." His hands closed around my neck, and he squeezed.

My body froze. My heart raced. My mouth dried. I couldn't die like this. I simply refused. I thought about begging or reasoning or scratching at his face. In the end, I swung.

The statue's heavy base hit Fritz in the temple, and the blow's impact traveled up my arm.

Fritz fell. Hard.

And he didn't move.

I waited to feel. Remorse. Anger. Anything. My only emotion was a fear that he might rise.

I rushed past him, stepped over Detective Jones's body, yanked the receiver from its cradle, and dialed. When the operator answered, I said, "Hello. We need help." My voice was thin and reedy, as if my lungs weren't getting enough air.

"What's the nature of your emergency?" How could the blasted woman sound so cool? I had an emergency.

I glanced at the two men on the floor. Neither moved. What if Fritz woke up? My stomach flipped, and I beat back the need to run screaming from the house. "A killer attacked a police officer. He's not moving."

"Which one? The officer or the killer?"

"Either."

"I'll connect you with the police."

I waited, my gaze fixed on Fritz's unmoving body.

After an eternity, a woman said, "Hello."

"There's a police officer who's been injured."

"And you are?"

"Panicked." Any reasonable person would be.

"Where are you, ma'am?"

"Evelyn Langley's house."

"The address?" Couldn't she trace that?

"I don't know. Fifty-fourth street between Ward Parkway and Belleview."

"The police are on their way."

I glanced at Detective Jones. He hadn't moved a muscle. "And an ambulance?"

"Yes ma'am. What's your name?"

Nope. She wasn't getting my name. "I'm a friend of the family."

"Who's family?"

"Evelyn Langley's."

One of the men moaned.

"I need to check something."

"Ma'am?"

Ignored her, dropped the receiver onto Evelyn's bed, and crouched next to the detective. "Was that you who moaned? How badly are you hurt?"

He didn't answer.

Blood soaked his plaid jacket (no loss there), and his skin was pale. His eyes remained firmly closed.

How had Fritz incapacitated a trained police officer?

I scanned the room. A fireplace poker lay abandoned on the floor. That explained the crash and the pool of blood around the detective's head.

I leaned forward till my cheek brushed against the detective's chest. I strained to hear a heartbeat.

The light shifted, and I looked up from my spot above the detective's chest.

Fritz was on his feet. He clutched the doorframe and glared at me as if I were solely responsible for all his problems.

"Wake up." I poked Detective Jones.

He didn't move.

Fritz did. He lurched forward, and my heart skipped a few beats.

"Wake up!"

The detective was unresponsive.

Fritz took another step.

My shaking fingers slid inside the detective's ugly plaid sports coat and closed around his gun. I pulled the .38 from its holster, cocked the hammer, and pointed the muzzle at Fritz. "Not another step!"

His face twisted into a fearsome sneer. "You wouldn't shoot me."

"I would." Shame on him for doubting me.

"It takes courage to take a life." He took another step.

Was he suggesting I was a coward? "Courage? Killing an old woman wasn't courageous."

His sneer deepened. "What would you know about needing money? You've never wanted for anything in the whole of your over-privileged life."

That was rich coming from a Langley. He'd grown up with more money than Midas. "If I did, I wouldn't kill for it."

He took another step.

"If you get any closer, I'll shoot."

He stepped.

Bang!

Fritz fell, and I stood, keeping the gun aimed at him, despite my shaking hands.

He clutched his thigh, and blood welled between his fingers. "You shot me!"

I tried to calm the tremors in my hands. "I warned you. If you're lucky, the ambulance will arrive before you bleed out."

At my feet, Detective Jones stirred, then his eyes fluttered open. They were brown and blurry, but as I watched, his gaze sharpened. "Mrs. Walford?"

I nodded.

"What happened?"

"You caught a killer."

He winced.

"He gave a full confession. He killed his mother for his inheritance."

The detective sat up and rubbed his head. Only then did his gaze shift to Fritz, who lay in his own pool of blood.

"Police!" The cry came from the first floor.

"Upstairs," I called. Relief flooded my veins and my knees wavered.

Seconds later, uniformed officers poured into Evelyn's bedroom.

I crouched and put the detective's gun on the floor. Then, I held up my hands.

"I'm reaching for my identification." Detective Jones slipped his hand inside his jacket and produced a shiny badge.

The uniformed officers relaxed, and I lowered my hands.

"What happened?" demanded a middle-aged man whose gut said he needed to lay off the donuts.

Detective Jones and I exchanged a long look.

I wanted no part of this investigation.

"Homicide division," said Detective Jones.

The officer frowned at the gun I'd left on the floor. "How did a civilian get your service revolver?"

Detective Jones grinned. "Why don't you tell him how that happened, Mrs. Walford?"

"When you and Fritz struggled for the gun, it fell to the floor and went off, shooting Fritz in the leg. I simply picked up the gun and kept it aimed at Fritz till you arrived."

I waited for Fritz to contradict me, but all the fight had leeched out of him. He seemed as flat as a fallen soufflé.

"What about the statue in the hallway that's covered with blood?"

"No idea." I lifted my chin and looked down my nose. "This incident has been most trying. I should like to go home."

The officer's mouth opened and closed. Like a fish.

"We'll need a statement," said Detective Jones.

"You know where to find me." I swanned out of the room before anyone could stop me. Then, I descended the stairs, climbed into the loaner car, and drove away.

That I pulled over because my body shook too hard to drive was nobody's business but my own.

CHAPTER SEVEN

Strictly speaking, it was too early for gin.

I didn't care.

I clutched that gin and tonic as if it were a life preserver and I was adrift in the ocean. I clinked the ice in the glass as if the cubes were heavenly harps offering me salvation. And the lime? It was a small wedge of happiness.

I needed to pull myself together. Quickly. I knew that. Harrington would be home soon, and I did not wish to recount my afternoon. He didn't need to hear the story that began with my losing my ring and ended with me shooting a killer.

I swallowed more gin, took a deep breath, and held the air in my lungs.

Ding dong.

I didn't move. Not a muscle. Well, except for my arm. My arm lifted my glass to my lips for another sip of gin.

A moment later, Penelope appeared at the cased entry to the living room. "There's a detective here to see you, Mrs. Walford. He says his last name is Jones."

I sighed.

Her gaze brushed against the glass in my hand. "Should I tell him you're not available?"

Tempting, but he'd come back. Maybe when Harrington was at home. "No. I'll see him."

Penelope gave a brief nod, then led Detective Jones into the living room.

"Mrs. Walford." He inclined his head.

"Detective." I offered him a regal nod. "Please, sit."

He chose a wingback chair and surveyed my tasteful living room—the velvet loveseats, the English antiques, my collection of Halcyon Days boxes, and one of Ellison's paintings above the fireplace. He stared at the painting for long seconds, as if he could memorize each brushstroke.

"May I offer you a drink?"

"No, thank you." He glanced at my right hand. "You found your ring."

"I did. How is your head? How are you feeling?"

"I'll live."

"There was a lot of blood." He'd obviously showered since I last saw him. His hair was no longer crimson, and he wore a different (though equally ugly) plaid jacket.

"Head wounds bleed." He shrugged as if that sea of blood (his blood) was of little concern. His gaze bored into me. "You shot a killer with my gun."

Oh, dear. I pursed my lips.

"You lied to the police."

Lied seemed too strong a word. I'd created an alternate truth. I refused to fidget. Instead, I forced myself to look into his eyes. "I do not wish to be associated with a murder investigation."

He rubbed the back of his head. "You could have run."

I tilted my head. "Pardon me?"

"After you clubbed Langley with the statue, you could have run. Instead, you stayed with me and called for help."

I took another sip of gin. The level in the glass was getting dangerously low.

"He'll be charged with second-degree murder."

"Second degree?"

"Langley swears he didn't plan to kill his mother."

"So he confessed to you?"

"He did."

"He tried to kill me." My hands rose to my throat. I'd slathered the bruises with arnica, then hidden them with the Hermès scarf Ellison sent me from Paris.

"Do you wish to press charges?"

"You'd call me as a witness?"

The detective's lips quirked. "That would be unavoidable."

"No. I won't press charges." I tightened my fingers around the glass. "I did shoot him."

"A clear case of self-defense."

I leaned back in my chair and felt the tension in my neck and shoulders ease. Perhaps I could pass on that third gin and tonic. "Why was he at Evelyn's house?"

"He's in debt to some dangerous people. He planned on stealing his mother's jewelry."

"Why didn't he take the jewelry when he killed her?"

"He wanted her death to look like an accident. He claims he went to her house to discuss her spending. They argued. He hit her, and she fell to the floor."

"With what?"

"Pardon?"

"With what did he hit her?"

"Ah." A smile twisted his lips. "The same statue you used on him. Apparently, Mrs. Langley kept the statue by her bed. After Fritz hit her with it, he carried it downstairs, washed it off, and left it in the front hall."

"Was she dead when he left her?"

"He says he doesn't know. I suspect she was.

"Poor Evelyn." I finished the last of the gin. "So, it's over."

"Yes, ma'am. Although I feel as if I owe you."

My mind latched onto a solution to the mess I found myself in. "Make me a promise, and we'll call it even."

"A promise?"

"You will never, ever tell my daughter about what happened."

He gaped at me.

"She will never know about my finding Evelyn's body, Fritz's attempt on my life, my whacking him over the head with a statue, or my shooting him. Promise me you won't tell her."

"Why don't you want her to know?"

"That's my business." I would not cede the moral high ground. If Ellison ever found another body, I needed the ability to scold.

His brow creased. "Why would I tell her?"

Because I'd seen the way he looked at her. Worse, I'd seen the way she looked at him.

Also, I had a terrible feeling Ellison wasn't done finding bodies or involving herself in murder investigations. "Humor me. Please, give me your promise."

"As you wish. I promise."

Dare I press my luck? "Do you think that silence could extend to my husband?"

He chuckled. "So, this stays between you and me?"

"That would be ideal." I'd be kept out of the papers, the trial, everything.

He paused, and I worried he might say no. "You're sure?" he asked. "You are the heroine in this story."

As if I'd ever willingly be associated with murder. "I'm positive."

Again, he paused, and my nerves demanded more gin.

Too bad the glass was empty.

"Please, detective." I hated to beg, but needs must.

Finally, he nodded. "You have my word."

The relief in my veins was more intoxicating than a whole bottle of Gordon's. "Thank you."

He stood. "I'll see myself out. And, to be clear, I should be the one thanking you."

"For?"

"For staying. For calling for help."

"You're most welcome."

"I'll be seeing you, Mrs. Walford." He offered me an infectious grin and his brown eyes sparkled. For an instant, I understood why Ellison found him so appealing. Not that I would ever, ever admit that. He would find no chinks in my armor. Nor would she.

I straightened my shoulders and directed my fiercest scowl his way. "Not if I see you first."

He chuckled as if he found both the sentiment and my expression droll.

And I couldn't help but worry that he was right to be amused. I would see him again. Sooner and more often than I'd like.

SOMEWHERE IN THE NIGHT

A COUNTRY CLUB MURDERS NOVELLA

CHAPTER ONE

November 1975
Kansas City, Missouri

The holiday season might bring people together, but family dinners also drove them round the bend.

Or was that just me?

One of Mother's cherished customs was rushing through our Thanksgiving meal so we could see the Plaza lights come on. Each year, more than 100,000 colored lights decorated the Plaza's Spanish-inspired buildings. Towers looked like delicate lace. The buildings looked fit for fairies. Even the parking garages were transformed.

Simply put, the Plaza during the holidays was magical.

Less magical was the stress of arriving in time to see the lights come on. It wasn't as if we didn't have other opportunities to see the lights. They shined brightly until after New Year's.

But Mother insisted. Which is how I found myself packed in

a limousine with Mother, Daddy, Anarchy, Grace, Beau, and Karma.

As I thought about the mess we'd left with Aggie, my house-keeper, I clenched my hands until my nails dug into the heels of my palms.

"Ellison," said Mother, who'd never once concerned herself with the amount of work she'd left for her help. "That's a sour look you're wearing."

"Is it?" We could be at home right now, drying the last of the dishes, getting ready to curl up in front of the fire in the family room with mulled wine or hot chocolate. Instead, we were racing around like chickens with our heads cut off.

"There are people who'd give their eye teeth for your Aunt Matilda's view. She's kind to invite us." Mother gave a put-upon sigh. "Even if she did give her guest parking spaces to Jane's family. She knows your father refuses to park anywhere else."

Hearing the clear censure in Mother's voice, Daddy, who'd undoubtedly rather be home watching the Cowboys play the Lions, patted her knee. "Parking down here is a zoo. Besides, the limousine is nice." He took a sip of his very stiff scotch and leaned back into his seat.

Mother pursed her lips and shifted her gaze to my half-sister, who'd relocated from San Francisco to Kansas City over the summer. "The holiday lights are spectacular. You'll love them."

"I'm sure I will." Karma and Mother were always scrupulously polite.

"Have you ever seen the lights come on, Beau?" asked Karma.

"Yes." He sounded nowhere near as enthusiastic as Mother.

"It's very exciting," Mother insisted.

As exciting as flipping a light switch.

I batted down that uncharitable thought. It was Thanksgiving. I refused to be negative. Not even in the privacy of my head. Where was my holiday spirit? The Plaza lighting ceremony was the official start of the Christmas season. I needed good will toward men, or at least good will toward Mother. "Who else will be at Aunt Tilly's?"

Mother scrunched her nose as if she'd smelled particularly pungent trash. "Jane and her brood. They were invited for dinner." It ate at Mother's craw when Jane's family was asked for dinner, and we weren't.

"Mother, if you dislike them so, why go?" It was a reasonable question. Another reasonable question? Why drag us with her?

She shook a finger at me. "Ellison Russell—"

"Jones," I corrected.

"Jones," she ceded. "Don't take that tone with me. Your aunt looks forward to this every year, and I can hardly decline an invitation just because we don't care for her in-laws."

Mother called Aunt Tilly's in-laws outlaws. She was convinced Aunt Tilly counted her silver when they left.

"Who's Jane?" asked Karma.

"Aunt Matilda is my father's sister," Mother explained. "She married George Webster. Jane is George's niece."

"And Aunt Tilly's," I added.

"Only by marriage." Mother dismissed my excellent point.

"Jane married a man named Kowalski," I added. The mere mention of the name annoyed Mother.

"Like Stanley?" asked Karma. I didn't miss the amusement dancing in her eyes.

Mother scowled. Deeply. To her waspy ear, Kowalski sounded so very ethnic.

"Yes," I replied. "Exactly like Stanley. Except Jane's husband's name was Mike."

"Was?" asked Anarchy.

"He had a heart attack a few years back." Probably from the stress of getting to Aunt Tilly's apartment in time for the lighting ceremony. "Mike and Jane had two children, Clover and Mike junior. They're both married."

Mother sighed as if Clover and Mike were heavy weights to bear. "Clover's husband's name is Wyatt. Mike's wife's name is Karli."

Anarchy chuckled. "Karli Kowalski? That's very alliterative."

Mother's lips curled in distaste. "The fool woman did it to herself. As for her first name, it's spelled with a 'k' and an 'i.'"

"We see them once or twice a year," I told Karma.

"Which is more than enough." Mother might have said more, but the limousine pulled to a stop next to the glass front door, and we all piled out of the car and headed to the elevator.

As we waited for the elevator to arrive, Daddy asked, "Anarchy, what are your family's holiday traditions?"

Anarchy reached for my hand and gave it a quick squeeze. "An annual argument about serving turkey instead of tofu." My husband had a Bohemian upbringing. He'd rebelled by becoming a meat-and-potatoes-eating, straight-arrow police detective.

"And you, Beau?" Dad shifted his gaze to the latest addition to our family. "Do you have a favorite holiday tradition?"

I held my breath. Beau's whole life had recently been upended, and the last thing I wanted was to upset him.

"Pie," he replied. "We ate pumpkin pie for breakfast on the day after Thanksgiving."

Mother jabbed at the elevator call button as if hitting it a second time would make it arrive faster.

"That's a great tradition," said Anarchy. "I say we continue that one."

Beau grinned.

"It's not healthy." Mother was in a mood, and we hadn't yet interacted with Jane. It promised to be a long evening.

"It's one day out of the year." I kept my tone mild.

She eyed me critically. "You do realize most people gain ten pounds over the holidays?"

First off, I was fairly certain she'd made that up. Secondly, I was not the one who planned on eating pie in the morning. I offered her a tight smile. "I wonder how many calories are in a scotch and soda."

"One-hundred-and-forty," said Karma. "Although the way this family pours, the number is probably higher."

Unlike Mother's ten-pound-holiday-weight-gain number, Karma's sounded legitimate.

"How do you know that?" asked Mother.

Karma smiled brightly at Mother. "I had a diet coach back in California."

Mother pursed her lips and closed her eyes, and I could see the wheels turning. Three times one-hundred-forty. She paled as she added four-hundred-twenty calories to her daily tally.

"A slice of pumpkin pie has around three-hundred-and-twenty calories." Karma flashed me a quick grin, so quickly Mother couldn't see.

I adored my sister. Truly, I did.

The elevator doors slid open, and we pressed inside.

A moment later, we knocked on Aunt Tilly's door, and her houseman, Hudson, welcomed us inside. He'd added a sprig of holly to his white coat and wore a silk bow tie decorated with tiny turkeys. He looked quite festive.

When Hudson had our coats draped over his arm, he asked, "A scotch and soda for you, Mrs. Walford?"

Mother offered him a grateful smile. "Yes, please." It might cost her one-hundred-plus calories, but there was no way she could deal with Jane and her family without scotch.

Hudson gave a brief unsurprised nod. "A scotch for you, Mr. Walford?"

"Please."

"Mrs. Jones?"

"Sparkling water with lime." Anyone else's house, I'd ask for wine, but Aunt Tilly poured Lancer's.

"Mr. Jones?"

"The same."

"And you, miss?" Hudson smiled at Karma.

"Scotch and soda."

"Miss Grace?"

"Scotch and soda."

"Grace!" Mother sounded scandalized.

My daughter, who wore a Laura Ashley dress she loathed to please her grandmother, grinned. "Just kidding. May I please have a Tab with two limes?"

Aunt Tilly's houseman nodded, then turned to Beau.

"Hudson, this is Beau. The newest member of our family."

"Pleased to meet you, Beau. What may I get you to drink?"

"A soda, please, if it's not too much trouble."

"No trouble at all." Hudson nodded toward the living room with its wall of windows. "They're just finishing dinner. They'll join you in a moment."

"Thank you, Hudson." Mother swanned into the living room and perched on a brocade covered fauteuil. Aunt Tilly's apartment was furnished in dainty French antiques and shaded in soft blue, pink, and gilt. The paintings were Dutch still lifes in ornate frames. It was the most feminine room imaginable, and it made Daddy itch.

No surprise, he stepped outside onto the balcony. He wouldn't last long. Not without his coat. The temperature had reached forty this afternoon, but with the sun long since set, it was cold outside.

"Frances, you're here!" Tilly had mastered the art of sounding thrilled to see everyone she met. Her tone suggested Mother's arrival was the best thing to happen since sliced bread. Which was lovely until you heard her use the exact same tone with the plumber or the woman who came every Monday and did her laundry. "And Ellison. How pretty you look." She held out her manicured fingers to Anarchy. "We met at the wedding. Call me Aunt Tilly."

"A pleasure to see you, again." Anarchy gave her the grin that made my knees turn weak.

Aunt Tilly swayed and fluttered her eyelashes at my husband before switching her focus to Karma. "You look so much like Marjorie. The two of you could be sisters."

They were sisters. Well, half-sisters.

Karma managed a polite smile. "Dad's genes."

"I suppose that must be it." Tilly turned to Beau and caught his chin in a vise-like grip. "And you're Beau. Frances told me about you. What a handsome boy you are."

Beau, who wore a navy blazer and rep tie, did look handsome. "Nice to meet you." He cast me a desperate glance.

"You may call her Aunt Tilly."

"Nice to meet you, Aunt Tilly."

"Aunt Matilda," Mother corrected.

My great-aunt was tall and thin and chic and looked twenty years younger than her actual age. She was feminine and fun and, because she spent most of her time in Palm Springs, we didn't see her often enough. "Aunt Tilly is just fine," she told Beau as she released his chin. "Now that you're all here, the party can start. You all know Jane." She nodded to her niece, who wore a rust-colored pants suit with a turquoise blouse. Jane had once been a pretty woman, but decades of cigarette smoking had cut deep lines into the skin around her mouth. Tonight, her lipstick had bled into those lines. Not a good look. Nor was her frosted blue eyeshadow.

Aunt Tilly shifted her gaze to a stranger. "And this is her husband, Earl."

Husband? When had that happened?

Earl wore a handlebar mustache, long sideburns, and an

open-collared shirt. No tie. No jacket. Also, he was at least ten years younger than Jane. Maybe fifteen.

Mother's disapproval rose like mist from a morning meadow. She stared with singular focus.

Uncomfortable in the silence, I cleared my throat.

Anarchy held out his hand. "I'm Anarchy Jones, Ellison's husband."

The two men shook.

"How long have you been married?" Mother's eyes were narrowed to mere slits.

Jane giggled. "Two weeks. It was a whirlwind romance."

"We got hitched in Vegas." Earl possessed a country twang.

"You got hitched." Mother's voice was dry as dust. She and Jane didn't like each other. Mother believed Jane maintained a relationship with Aunt Tilly in hopes of inheriting money that belonged, at least in Mother's mind, to our family. "How romantic."

Jane blinked in the face of Mother's sarcasm.

Not that I'd argue the point with her. Getting "hitched" in Vegas sounded about as romantic as a colonoscopy.

"It was beautiful." Jane was starry-eyed. "The chapel was filled with flowers, and the minister's wife sang *We've Only Just Begun*. She sounded just like Karen Carpenter."

I forced a smile. "Best wishes to you both."

"I see you've met Earl." Clover, who'd entered the living room a moment after her mother, sounded less than enthused about Jane's new husband. She took after her mother. Pretty. Blonde. And Clover's face wasn't ravaged by cigarettes. Although…her mouth was tightly pursed.

"Just now," I replied.

Clover leaned forward and ghosted a kiss near my cheek. "Sorry about this," she whispered. Then, she held out her hand to Anarchy. "Clover Bowman. Nice to meet you." She glanced over her shoulder. "And this is my husband, Wyatt."

The two men shook.

Wyatt Bowman was a bean counter. A straight arrow. He and Anarchy had that in common. They also had to put up with family craziness. There, the similarities ended. Wyatt was slight, with thinning hair and a tremulous smile. Meanwhile, Anarchy was tall and strong and had eyes the color of perfectly brewed coffee.

Hudson appeared with a tray of drinks.

As I accepted my club soda, I wished I'd requested something stronger. "What time is it?" The real question? How long until we could politely leave?

"We have fifteen minutes until the lighting ceremony." Aunt Tilly waved at the wall of windows. "Grace, why don't you show Beau the TV room? The other children are already there. We'll call you when the lights are about to go on."

Grace didn't need telling twice. She grabbed Beau's hand and disappeared.

As they left, Karli and Mike arrived. Her cheeks were flushed, and her eyes were shiny. Either they'd been kissing or arguing. Given the unhappy tilt of her lips, I guessed the latter.

Except for Jane and Earl and Aunt Tilly no one looked happy. I glanced toward the door to the balcony. Daddy was still out there. Probably freezing. Lucky, lucky man.

"Everyone has a drink?" Aunt Tilly held up a glass of scotch and water. "Wonderful. Let's sit."

Mother resumed her perch on the fauteuil and offered Jane a tight smile. "How did you two meet?"

"My car broke down. The mechanic said it would cost five-hundred dollars to fix it. Which is more than it was worth. So, I decided to buy a new car." She giggled again. "Well, a new-to-me car. Earl was the salesman."

Mike, who sat next to me on the couch, made a funny noise, like pieces of gravel rubbing against each other.

I added two and two and got four. A new-to-her car. A salesman. Jane had married a used car salesman. No wonder Clover and her brother wore bemused, angry expressions.

"Did you attend the wedding?" I asked Clover.

"Mother surprised us," she replied coolly. "She didn't tell us she was dating."

What was that strange noise Mike was making?

I glanced his way.

His jaw worked. The man was grinding his teeth. Hard enough for me to hear. Mike was a big man. Tall. Beefy. And starting to go soft around the middle. We'd never had much use for each other. But I didn't need to know him well to sense the barely contained fury radiating from his person.

Earl, who had his arm draped around Jane's shoulders, gave Mother a slick grin. "When you know, you know. Right, babe?"

Jane snuggled closer to her new husband. "It was love at first sight."

Mike ground his teeth harder. If he kept it up, he'd break a molar.

"What a charming story." Mother sounded anything but charmed.

"Did you buy a car?" asked Karma.

Jane nodded. "Earl got me a good deal on a Pinto."

Oh, dear Lord.

The door from the balcony opened, and Daddy stepped inside.

"Harrington," said Mother. "Meet Jane's new husband, Earl. I'm sorry, I don't believe I caught your last name."

"Hicks."

Mother closed her eyes as if the name pained her. "Meet Earl Hicks."

Daddy stepped forward and extended his hand. "Pleasure to meet you, Earl. I'm Harrington Walford."

The two men couldn't look more different. In his charcoal-gray suit paired with a crisp white shirt and festive red tie,

Daddy could have modeled for Brooks Brothers. Earl looked like…well, a used car salesman. But they shook.

"Harrington--" Mother pointed "--Hudson left your drink on the console."

Daddy claimed his scotch with alacrity, then he bent and brushed a kiss against Aunt Tilly's rouged cheek. "You get prettier every time I see you."

She swatted at his arm as her face flushed with pleasure at the compliment. "I do declare, you say the nicest things."

"Nothing but the truth."

Silence fell. Uncomfortable silence. And I fidgeted in my seat. "Did you all have a nice dinner?"

Earl rubbed his belly and tipped a glass of what looked to be straight scotch at Aunt Tilly. "Good eats. A first-class spread."

Oh my. What came next? Loosening his belt or a belch?

I didn't want to know the answer. "Do you have family in town, Earl?" There was an outside chance the newly married couple would split holidays. If we were lucky, they'd go someplace else for Thanksgiving next year.

"Just me. I was an only child, and my folks are gone."

Hope died a quick death, but I forced a smile. "So, where are you living, Jane?"

"Earl's apartment was too small for us. He moved into my house." Her hand traveled from his knee to high up on his thigh, and she fluttered her eyelashes. "Our house."

Next to me, Mike snorted, loud enough to draw all eyes.

"Mom." Grace hovered near the entrance to the living room. "Can you come?"

I stood. Grateful for the interruption. "Of course. Is everything all right?"

She nodded, but her gaze was shifty.

Something was wrong. Beau? Were the other kids being mean to him?

"Excuse me." After I sorted whatever was happening with

the kids, I'd find Hudson and ask for a real drink. The evening definitely called for scotch. I followed my daughter into the hallway. "What's wrong?"

"Mikey locked himself in the bathroom."

Mikey was sixteen. And not my child. How had he become my problem?

Then, I smelled it. Pot. "Are you kidding me?"

"I knocked, and he didn't answer. I'm worried."

Not my problem. Not my problem. But Grace was looking at me as if I had the power to solve this problem. I rapped my knuckles against the bathroom door. "Mikey?"

Mikey remained stubbornly silent.

I twisted the locked handle. "Mikey?" I rapped once more. Harder.

There was no answer, and the silence seemed ominous.

Grace clasped her hands. "What if he smoked pot laced with LSD?"

I winced. I hated that my daughter knew to worry about things like that. I prayed she was wrong as I said, "Go get Anarchy."

She didn't move. "But..."

I understood her reluctance. Anarchy was a police detective. If he found Mikey doing drugs, there might be criminal charges. But if Mikey was dying, Anarchy was the best person to help him. "Tell Anarchy there's a problem, Grace. Mikey may need his help."

She nodded, then disappeared down the corridor, and again I rapped on the door.

Again, there was no response.

Anarchy arrived with Mike, who shouldered past me and hammered on the door. "Mikey, open the door, son. Now."

The other children gathered around—Beau, Mikey's younger sister Gina, and Clover's daughters, Heather and Ivy.

I offered them a weak smile. "Why don't you go back to the television room?" It wasn't a question, more like a suggestion.

Gina, who'd paled to the color of fresh fallen snow, shook her head. "I'm staying here."

I planted my hands on my hips, channeled Mother, and gave them a fearsome scowl. "Grace, take everyone to the TV room. Now."

The children took giant steps backward, and Grace gave a short, unhappy nod, before herding the kids, including a reluctant Gina, back down the hall.

"We need to take the door off the hinges," said Anarchy. "Does your aunt have a screwdriver?"

"I'll ask Hudson."

I raced to the kitchen, where Hudson was handwashing Aunt Tilly's Haviland china.

If he was surprised to see me barging into the kitchen, he didn't show it. "What may I do for you, Miss Ellison?" he asked.

"We need a screwdriver."

Hudson wiped his hands on a dishtowel then reached for the vodka.

"No, no. An actual screwdriver."

Ever unflappable, Hudson opened a drawer, revealing both a flathead and Phillips.

I took them both. "Thank you, Hudson. When you get a moment, may I please have a scotch and soda with a twist?"

He nodded as if my sudden request for alcohol came as no surprise. "Yes, ma'am."

I hurried back to the bathroom and held my breath as Anarchy and Mike removed the door. Then, I peered inside.

Mikey lay on the tile floor, not moving.

"Call an ambulance." Anarchy used his cop voice, the one that demanded immediate action.

Mike stumbled backward, away from the entry to the bathroom, then took off down the hallway, presumably to call for help.

Anarchy and I stepped into the tiny room, and he fell to his knees and checked for a pulse. "He's alive."

"Thank heavens." I took my first full breath since he and Mike had gone to work on the hinges. "What can I do?" Mikey's skin was the color of dirty Silly Putty, and his eyes remained firmly closed.

"He's breathing on his own." Anarchy sat back on his heels. "Any idea what he might have taken?"

"My son does not do drugs." Karli spoke from the doorway to the bathroom. A crowd of concerned adults surrounded her.

"Someone was smoking pot in here." The smell hung heavy in the air. I pointed to the roach on Aunt Tilly's tiled floor. "Who else?"

Her mouth puckered as if she'd been sucking lemons, and she planted her hands on her hips. "Not Mikey."

Denial wasn't just a river in Egypt.

"Grace thinks the pot was laced with something."

I heard a gasp and knew it was Mother's. "How does my granddaughter know what a marijuana cigarette smells like?"

Because she was a teenager in the 1970s. Recognizing something and using it were two different things. I said as much.

Mother pressed a palm to her forehead. "Harrington, I need another drink."

Karli joined me next to her son's body. "Mikey, honey, wake up."

Mikey didn't move. Maybe she should lean closer? The overwhelming smell of her Charlie perfume mixing with gin on her breath was as good as smelling salts.

I blinked my watering eyes.

Karli tapped her son's cheek. "Mikey, it's time to wake up now."

No one said a word. Especially not Mikey.

"The ambulance is on its way." Mike pushed his way into the bathroom and joined his wife at his son's side. "What can we do for him?"

"We wait," Anarchy replied. "His breath is shallow, but he is breathing."

"But his color," said Clover from her spot just outside the door. "He looks like a corpse."

True, but not helpful.

Karli sobbed, and Mike patted her shoulder as if he didn't know what to do to comfort his wife.

"Don't fall apart when your son may need you." Jane sounded judgmental—as if she couldn't abide Charlie perfume, copious gin, or her daughter-in-law's narcissism.

Karli turned and gave her mother-in-law a vicious glare. "Don't talk to me about being there for your children."

Jane's face flushed an ugly red, and her fingers stretched as if she longed to slap Karli across the face.

"Someone should go to the lobby and wait for the ambulance," I suggested. It would help clear the crowd spilling into the bathroom. And clear some of the tension, too.

"I'll go." Wyatt went so far as to raise his hand when he volunteered.

Everyone shuffled around, and he disappeared down the hallway.

A long—endless—moment passed, then Mother said, "Well, we've missed it."

"Missed what?" asked Jane.

"The lights."

I stared at Mother. A boy was unconscious on the floor, maybe dying, and she was worried about missing the lights come on?

"How can you say such a thing?" Jane demanded. "That's my grandson."

"A delinquent who—"

"Come on, Frannie." Daddy tugged on Mother's elbow. "Let's get you a drink."

Mother allowed him to remove her from what promised to be a nasty argument.

"How long will it take the ambulance to get here?" Karli wrung her hands.

"St. Mark's is only a few blocks away." I didn't add that the driver would have to get through the craziness and traffic on the Plaza.

"He's still breathing?" she asked.

"He is," Anarchy confirmed.

Mike wrapped an arm around his wife. "He'll be okay, honey."

She pushed him away. "You don't know that. How could this happen?"

"Mom?" Grace stood in the hallway near the doorway. "How's Mikey?"

"Breathing. An ambulance is coming. Do the girls know what he was smoking?"

"Pot. He offered to share. We all said 'no.'"

"Thank God," Clover whispered.

Karli gave her sister-in-law a scowl that could peel paint, then she turned her glare on Grace. "You didn't try and stop him? You didn't come and find an adult?"

I would not allow her to blame my daughter for her son's choices. "This is not Grace's fault, Karli."

"She let my son take drugs."

"Your son chose to take drugs. He needs more parental supervision, not a mother who blames everyone else."

Karli's fingers curled into claws. "How dare you?"

"Let's all calm down." Anarchy's voice was even. Authoritative. It demanded calm.

"Make way." An EMT pushed through the bottleneck at the bathroom door.

Anarchy and I stood, allowing room for someone with actual medical training.

"If you folks would step back?" said the EMT. "Give us some room."

Everyone but Mike and Karli retired to the living room, where Aunt Tilly had the lights turned low. Outside, the Plaza blazed with color. Everyone took a cursory glance then perched on delicate chairs. Everyone except Mother. She took her fresh drink onto the balcony and stared at the lights.

Daddy offered Jane an apologetic smile. "Frances was worried that Ellison had found another body. She's a bit sensitive about that." He took in Jane's horrified expression, and added, "I'll keep Frannie company." He escaped onto the balcony, leaving Anarchy and me with Jane, Clover, Wyatt, and Aunt Tilly.

We watched a second EMT push a gurney down the hallway to the bathroom, and Jane pressed her palm to her mouth.

I frowned. "Where's Earl?"

Jane tilted her head as if she was puzzled by his absence. "He must be with the children."

That hardly seemed likely.

"I don't know about you, but I could use another drink." Aunt Tilly tapped her foot on the Aubusson beneath her favorite rose-hued bergère. "Hudson will be here shortly."

Hudson, God love him, arrived almost immediately.

"Another round for everyone," she told him.

"Yes, ma'am." He disappeared into the kitchen to make our drinks.

As we waited, the EMTs rolled a still unconscious Mikey to the front door. His parents followed behind.

"Karli is going to ride in the ambulance," said Mike. "I'll follow in the car."

"Do you want us to come?" asked Clover.

"No. We'll call you when there's news." He slipped out the front door.

Aunt Tilly offered us a tight smile. "This is a Thanksgiving we'll never forget."

Jane winced and stood abruptly. "I'm going to find Earl."

When her mother left, Clover shook her head. "I've been telling them for months. That boy needed help. Would anyone listen to me? No. Mother told me to mind my own business. Mike refused to see the truth. And Karli? She called me names. This is the first time I've let the girls near their cousin since the Fourth of July."

"He's a regular user?" asked Anarchy.

Clover shrugged. "We haven't seen him since July, but he was stoned at the family picnic. His eyes were mere slits, and he ate a whole bowl of potato salad. Enough for ten people."

Mother and Daddy, both shivering, stepped inside from the balcony just as Jane returned to the living room. "Earl's not with the children," she said. "They haven't seen him."

"He must be here somewhere," said Clover.

"He's not. I checked every room."

"Would he leave without telling you?"

"Never."

An uncharitable thought glided across my brain. Had Earl supplied the pot that sent Mikey to the hospital? Was that why he disappeared? I stood.

"Ellison?" Anarchy looked up at me from a chair that didn't look sturdy enough to hold him.

"I need some air."

"And a coat," said Mother. "It's freezing out there."

"They're in the guest bedroom," said Aunt Tilly.

"I'll get it," said Anarchy.

While he was gone, Hudson appeared with our drinks, and I took a grateful sip.

"What do we do?" said Clover. "I know Mike said to go home, but they shouldn't be alone. What if—"

"Don't talk that way." Wyatt patted her knee. "Mikey will be fine."

Anarchy draped my mink around my shoulders, and together we stepped outside.

He wrapped an arm around my shoulders. "There's a plaid topcoat on the bed."

I dragged my gaze away from the lights. "Pardon?"

"A plaid topcoat. Rust and mustard. Is that something Wyatt would wear?"

"No." Wyatt worked for a large accounting firm. He wore navy or gray. Period.

"Mike had on his coat when he left, so the plaid coat must belong to Earl."

"He left without his coat? In this weather?" What possessed me to look down? Intuition? Bad luck? I didn't mind heights, but seventeen floors was a long way down. For whatever reason, I looked, and Aunt Tilly's Waterford glass slipped through my fingers and shattered against the concrete balcony.

"What's wrong?" Concern etched Anarchy's handsome face.

I swallowed bile, clutched the guardrail, and closed my eyes. "I found Earl."

CHAPTER THREE

Mother was not pleased. Not with me. Not with Anarchy. Especially not with Earl. She demonstrated her displeasure with pursed lips, narrowed eyes, and an icy stiffness in the set of her shoulders. "Ellison," she said as she rose from the rose silk fauteuil.

"Yes, Mother?" I barely contained a sigh.

"It's Thanksgiving."

That was indisputable. "Yes, Mother."

"We're at your Aunt Matilda's."

Technically, Tilly was my great aunt, but I wasn't about to quibble.

"And you found a body."

"Anyone might have noticed it," said Anarchy.

Mother turned her bone-chilling gaze his way. "Harrington and I were out there, and we didn't see a thing. But Ellison? It's like she's a beacon for corpses."

Anarchy's lips quirked.

Fortunately, Mother didn't notice.

He adjusted his tie, a red silk we'd bought on our honeymoon in Italy. "To be fair, Ellison finds only a small percentage of the murder victims in Kansas City."

Ice flowed from Mother's fingertips, turning Aunt Tilly's living room into a walk-in freezer.

"Hicks might have fallen." Wyatt pushed his glasses up his thin nose. "He'd had plenty to drink."

All eyes shifted to the balcony and its railing that reached four-and-a-half feet. No one fell over the railing.

"Or he jumped," he added, but his tone was doubtful.

Jane, who hunched on the sofa, lifted her tear-stained face from her hands. "Earl would never do that."

"How do you know?" Mother sounded genuinely curious.

Jane flushed. "I just know. We had so much to live for. We were happy and—" she glanced around Aunt Tilly's antique-packed living room, then lowered her head to her hands.

I tended to agree with Jane. Not because I believed he was deliriously happy. Not at all. I doubted he'd jumped because Earl had struck me as a slick operator, not the kind of man who'd take his own life.

"Well," said Anarchy. "If he didn't fall, and he didn't jump, someone murdered him."

Earl's widow gasped.

"I've already called the station. Peters will be here soon." Peters was Anarchy's irascible partner.

"You'll investigate with him?" Daddy stood at the entrance to the living room.

Anarchy gave a brief nod.

"Harrington," Mother stood. "I'd like to go home."

"I'm sorry, Frances, but you'll have to stay until Peters questions you."

She pressed her clasped hands to her chest. "Peters? Questioning me?" Mother and Peters were like oil and water, they didn't mix.

"He'll question everyone. Even me."

"It's a waste of his time. I didn't kill that dreadful man."

"I know, Frances." Anarchy's tone was placating. "But it looks like someone here did. And you may have noticed something important."

Jane let out a low miserable moan.

I couldn't blame her. I was one hundred percent sure my family was blameless. Which meant that one of her children or one of their spouses killed her husband. Or…she had.

Anarchy rubbed his chin. "We'll need to recreate the past hour. Aunt Tilly, may we use your office for interviews?"

"Of course, dear boy." She frowned. "But are you certain he didn't fall? He did drink rather a lot."

Anarchy's assessing gaze returned to the balcony. "I'm sure."

What a night this was turning out to be. Mikey on his way to the hospital, and a man murdered.

Peters, wearing a furious you-interrupted-my-turkey-coma expression and an irredeemably wrinkled raincoat, arrived a few minutes later. He and Anarchy asked Mother to join them, then they all disappeared into Aunt Tilly's study.

Fat tears ran down Jane's cheeks, and she rubbed her eyes, smearing her mascara.

Clover and Wyatt held hands.

Aunt Tilly shook her head as if the whole disastrous evening was a giant misunderstanding. "He fell. He must have. No one here is a killer."

I stood, eager to escape Jane's low sobs. "I'll check on the children. Karma, would you like to join me?"

She gave a grateful nod, and, together, we walked toward the TV room.

"I feel sick," she said. "Positively green."

"I know."

"You feel this way every time, don't you?"

The awful thing was…I didn't. I'd found so many bodies that I'd grown a protective shell. "It's always terrible."

She reached out and squeezed my hand.

"Still glad you moved here? I bet if you were in San Francisco, you'd be at some marvelous dinner in a fabulous house with a spectacular view of the bay."

She shrugged. "Maybe. But the company is better here."

We entered the TV room, where Gina huddled in the corner of a squishy couch. Her eyes were red-rimmed but dry, and her hands were clenched in her lap. Her cousins, Heather and Ivy, sat on the floor with their backs against the couch. Grace and Beau squeezed together in an oversized club chair.

"Gina, how are you?"

"How do you think?" she snapped. "My brother's dying, and my parents left me here." She swiped angrily at a tear.

I sympathized. I did. But there were problems bigger than hers. "Was Mikey taking anything?"

The question earned me a glare.

"Please, Gina. Knowing what's in his system may save his life."

She wrapped her arms around her knees. "He swiped a bottle of Mom's Valium."

"I see." I moved to the far end of the couch, picked up the telephone receiver, and dialed the operator. When she answered, I said, "Would you please connect me with St. Mark's Hospital? It's an emergency."

A moment later, I was on the line with a nurse in the emergency room. "This is Ellison Jones calling." I glanced at the ceiling, then added, "I'm Frances Walford's daughter." Mother was the board chairman, and dropping her name got immediate results.

"How may I help you, Mrs. Jones?"

"You have a patient, Mikey Kowalski. I've just been informed he may have taken Valium. I thought the doctor would want to know."

"He will. Thank you. Is there anything else?"

I lifted my brows and gazed pointedly at Gina. "Is there anything else they should know?"

"No."

Ivy's hand snuck around the side of the couch and she pulled out a half-empty bottle of bourbon. "He drank."

I eyed the level. "Half a bottle?"

"No," she replied. "Just a couple of swigs."

"He also drank bourbon," I told the nurse. "We're not sure how much."

"I'll tell doctor. Thank you, Mrs. Jones. Happy Thanksgiving."

"To you as well." I hung up the phone and said, "Thank you, girls, for telling the truth."

"You're not mad?" said Ivy.

"No."

"She's disappointed," said Grace. "That's worse."

"I assume the bottle is Aunt Tilly's?"

Heather and Ivy gave identical nods.

Gina stared into space. "You didn't ask how he was?"

"Giving information was more important than getting it."

She glared at me with you-couldn't-possibly-understand disdain.

"Beau, how are you doing?" I asked. The poor boy had been dragged into another family mess.

"I'm okay." His eyes were at half-mast. "Can we go home soon?"

"Anarchy and Detective Peters are asking everyone a few questions. When they're done, we'll go."

He nodded, yawned, and snuggled closer to Grace.

I glanced at the TV where Lucy pulled away the football just as Charlie Brown tried to kick it. Then I held out my hand for the bourbon bottle. "I'll take that." From the slightly glazed looks in Mikey's cousins' eyes and the level of bourbon left in the bottle, I strongly suspected he wasn't the only one who'd been tippling.

Karma and I returned to the living room at the same time as Mother.

She glared at me, and said, "They want to talk to you next."

I nodded, gave Karma the bourbon bottle, and headed into the study.

Like everything else in Aunt Tilly's house, her study was feminine and delicate and decorated with French antiques.

Peters looked slightly ridiculous sitting behind a gilt desk.

I smiled at him. Brightly.

He grimaced at me. "We need a timeline."

I took a seat. "I'm pretty good with the sequence of events, but I'm not sure about the times."

He grunted.

"Just tell him what you remember," said Anarchy.

"All the adults were in the living room when Grace came and got me. We knocked on the bathroom door. When Mikey didn't answer, I sent her to get Anarchy."

Peters made a note. "And then?"

"Anarchy and Mike arrived, and Anarchy sent me to get a screwdriver. They took the door off the hinges, then Mike went to call an ambulance. He must have said something as he passed through the living room because everyone crowded into the hallway."

"Everyone?"

I nodded. "I think so."

"You saw Hicks?"

I closed my eyes and recreated the chaotic scene. "No. I guess I didn't."

He made another note. "What next?"

"We sent the kids back to the TV room, and Wyatt offered to go downstairs and wait for the ambulance."

"Did anyone go with him?"

"I don't think so."

"After that?"

"The EMTs arrived. Quickly. They must have been parked nearby in case there was an emergency during the lighting ceremony. Then, everyone returned to the living room to get out of their way. That's when we realized Earl was missing."

"Did anyone besides Wyatt leave the group in the hallway?"

"I don't know. I was in the bathroom with Anarchy and Mikey. There seemed to be a lot of jockeying for position."

"Position?"

"A better view."

Peters nodded. People's fascination with tragedy no longer surprised him.

"When you told everyone you'd found Earl, how did they react?"

"Clover and Wyatt looked shocked. Jane collapsed."

"Sounds dramatic," Peters observed.

"It was. She pressed her palms to her cheeks, then she fell onto a couch and sobbed. But…"

"But what?"

"I didn't see any tears." Jane had covered her face with a handkerchief.

"Did you ever see her leave the crowd outside the bathroom?"

"I'm sorry. I don't know."

He grunted. "Tell me about them."

"What do you want to know?"

"What do they do? Do you like them?"

"Jane is a bookkeeper for a commercial builder. Mike sells plumbing parts. Wyatt is an accountant. Neither Clover nor Karli work outside their homes."

"Do you like them?"

I glanced at Anarchy. "Clover and Wyatt are okay."

"The rest are too blue collar for you?"

"Peters!" Anarchy sounded outraged.

"What? Your wife hangs out with the country club crowd, not bookkeepers or plumbers."

"That's not why I don't care for them."

"Then why?"

"Jane takes advantage of my aunt. Mike gives me the heebie-jeebies. And Karli is a mean drunk." I stood.

So did Anarchy. He dropped a kiss on my cheek, then said, "When you go back to the living room, would you please send in your dad?"

"Of course."

"We'll talk to him, then Karma, then Grace. After that, you all can go home."

"What about you?"

He grimaced. "I'll be late."

I lifted up onto my tiptoes and kissed his cheek. "I'll wait up for you."

"It could be after midnight."

I gave him a wry grin.

"What?"

"Our first Thanksgiving as husband and wife."

"And of course you find a body," Peters grumbled. He and Mother had more in common than either one would ever admit.

I gave him my best scowl and returned to the living room.

THE LIMOUSINE DRIVER TOOK US HOME. WELL, US WITHOUT Anarchy. He'd catch a ride with Peters when they finished questioning Jane and her family.

The kids and I went to the kitchen and let the dogs out in the backward. Max took off like a shot, burning with the need to protect the yard's perimeter from squirrels. Finn followed behind.

"Are you guys okay?"

Grace yawned. "We're fine."

"You're sure?"

Beau pushed a lock of blond hair away from his face. "I know we should feel sad, but we never saw Mr. Hicks. Never met him. It doesn't seem real."

"You never saw him?"

"Aunt Tilly sent us to the TV room," he explained.

"Wasn't he in the hall outside the bathroom?"

"Nope." Grace popped the "p."

What had Earl been doing while his family gathered round that door? Was he already dead?

One of the dogs scratched on the back door, and I let them in and passed out biscuits.

"Mom."

I turned to my daughter. "Yes?"

"Let's never do this again."

Find a body? I could make no promises. Despite my best efforts it kept happening. "What do you mean?"

"Aunt Tilly's on Thanksgiving. Next year, just tell Granna we're not going. We see the lights at least twenty times during the holidays. We don't need to see them on the busiest night. And we can go see Aunt Tilly another time when her other relatives aren't there."

"Done."

Her eyes widened as if I'd surprised her. "Just like that?"

"I spent my evening wishing I was curled up in front of the TV in the family room. If you two don't want to go, we'll skip it."

"What will Granna say?" Grace raised an excellent question. Mother would not be happy.

I'd deal with her displeasure. Easily said when it was a whole year away. "We'll stay home." Mother and Daddy could go without us. I glanced at the clock on the kitchen wall. "You two should head to bed."

Grace crossed her arms and tilted her chin. One of her brows lifted. "What about you?"

"I'll wait up for Anarchy."

"He could be hours."

"I'll make coffee."

Grace gave a slow nod, then she and Beau began their climb up the backstairs to the second floor.

"Grace," I called.

Her steps slowed. Beau's did too.

"Did any of the girls go off by themselves?"

"No," she replied.

Well, that was a relief. "Thank you."

They continued their climb, and I leaned against the counter.

The day had been endless. I'd prepared for our little dinner party (Aggie had done the cooking, but I'd set the table with the Francis I sterling and Spode Gloucester china I'd received on my first marriage). I'd arranged flowers. I'd made a run to the grocer for more butter. I'd taken the dogs for an extended run, so they'd be calm when Mother arrived. I'd argued with Grace over what she was wearing. I'd realized we were out of Daddy's favorite scotch and driven to three liquor stores before I found one open. I'd kept a nervous eye on my watch throughout dinner, because, if we were late to Aunt Tilly's, Mother would blame me. And I'd found a body.

Fatigue made my eyes gritty. Gathering the remains of my energy, I filled Mr. Coffee's reservoir with water, then gave him a fond pat.

Tired? Mr. Coffee was always solicitous.

"Exhausted." I spooned coffee grounds into the filter.

Holidays can be that way.

"I found a body at Aunt Tilly's. Someone at the party is responsible." I waited for Mr. Coffee's response, but I'd rendered him mute. Only the orange glow of his on button let me know he was thinking. And perking.

That's why you're waiting up for Anarchy. You want to talk about it. But he'd want you to go to bed. Get your rest.

Mr. Coffee was right on both counts. I did want to talk. One of Tilly's extended family members was a murderer. That required discussion. And Anarchy would want me to rest. But I didn't want to go to bed alone on our first Thanksgiving as husband and wife.

I poured myself a cup of coffee, added a jot of cream, and settled on a kitchen stool.

The dogs flopped onto their mats in the corner, dropped their chins to their paws, and closed their eyes.

Looks like it's just us.

"You won't find me complaining."

What happened tonight?

"Jane remarried. Her new husband fell from the balcony."

Fell? You made it sound like murder.

"He didn't exactly fall. There are guard rails. Either he jumped or someone pushed him."

You and Anarchy think he was pushed. Mr. Coffee saw things clearly.

"Yes."

Your mother was there?

"She was. She was even on the balcony before me." I stared into the depths of my cup. "I was the one who looked down and spotted the body."

I'm so sorry. Mr. Coffee got me. He understood the horror of looking down on a man who'd plummeted seventeen stories. He also understood the painful tension that tightened my neck and shoulders when I seriously disappointed Mother. And finding bodies made for serious disappointments. *Anyone could have looked down and seen him.*

"Anyone could have. I did." I was starting to sound like Mother.

Not your fault. How did your Aunt Tilly react to a murder at her party?

"She was resilient as always. When we left, she was comforting Jane." I swirled the remaining coffee in my cup and frowned. "She looks thinner." My great-aunt had always maintained a waspish figure, but tonight she'd looked almost gaunt. "She's amazing. She's in her mid-eighties and still plays golf." And she sported the Palm Springs tan to prove it.

More coffee?

"Thank you."

When my mug was full and I had resumed my perch on the stool, Mr. Coffee asked, *Why would someone kill Jane's husband?*

"I think Earl believed he'd found himself a rich woman."

Hadn't he?

"Jane's not rich. Not at all. Sometimes Aunt Tilly helps." Much to Mother's chagrin, Aunt Tilly had provided down payments on houses, and paid Clover and Mike's college tuitions, that sort of thing. "Maybe Earl thought Jane was Aunt Tilly's heir."

Is she?

"I don't know."

What does Jane do?

"She's the bookkeeper for a construction company. Aunt Tilly got her the job."

What did Earl do?

"He was a used-car salesman."

Mr. Coffee gave an amused gurgle. *I bet your mother was thrilled with that.*

I chuckled softly. Poor Mother. Being even shirttail related to a used-car salesman was enough to justify the one-hundred-and-forty calories for an extra scotch.

You think a member of Jane's family killed him?

"Earl and Jane got married in Vegas without informing her children." I thought back to Mike's grinding teeth.

Did any of them have an opportunity to throw Earl off the balcony?

"Mike was on the phone when everyone gathered round the bathroom door. He could have killed Earl before he returned to the bathroom."

Anyone else?

"Wyatt volunteered to go to the lobby and wait for the ambulance. He could have killed Earl before going downstairs."

Their wives?

"Anarchy will find out."

CHAPTER FOUR

I contemplated the unslept in half of our bed, wrapped the warm wool robe I bought on our honeymoon over my nightgown, jammed my feet into leather slippers, and went in search of coffee.

Having stayed up late waiting (in vain) for Anarchy, I needed a jolt of caffeine. Two jolts. Possibly three.

When I reached the kitchen, Mr. Coffee winked at me. *Aggie filled me up, just push the button.*

"Where's Aggie?" I pushed his button.

Shopping.

"That's right." Aggie and her sister got up at an ungodly hour the day after Thanksgiving, hit the stores (and the sales), and finished their Christmas shopping in time for brunch.

To me, it sounded like a close approximation of hell. Crowds of hungover shoppers fighting for deals? No, thank you.

I settled on the kitchen stool to wait for the beverage that would get me through my day, or at least my morning. "Did Anarchy come home?" It was possible he'd come late, decided not to disturb me, and slept in the guest room.

I didn't see him.

I lowered my head to my hands and stared at the countertop. I'd never say this to Mr. Coffee, but some mornings I wished he'd perk faster.

A literal horde on the backstairs had me turning on my stool, and Beau, with the dogs on his heels, burst into the kitchen.

"Good morning." I managed to smile for him. "Pie?"

"Yes, please." He frowned. "Where's Anarchy?"

"He's still investigating Mr. Hicks's death."

"He didn't come home?"

I swallowed a sigh but couldn't help the slump of my shoulders. "Not yet."

"You're sad." He wrapped his arms around me and squeezed.

Emotion clogged my throat, so rather than argue, I smoothed his blond hair. Long seconds passed before I asked, "Do you want whipped cream on your pie?"

"Yes!"

"Me, too." If I was standing in for Anarchy and eating pie for breakfast, I might as well go all out.

"Your coffee is ready." Beau nodded toward Mr. Coffee's full pot.

The clouds above my head parted, the angels sang, and I stumbled toward nirvana, splashing ambrosia into my mug and sipping without even taking time to add cream.

"You sure do love your coffee," Beau observed.

"I do."

I released my hold on the coffee mug and pulled leftover pie and whipped cream from the refrigerator. "How big a slice?"

"I'm hungry."

I cut a huge wedge and put it on a plate, then dipped a spoon into the whipped cream and dropped a dollop in my coffee. "How much whipped cream?"

"I love whipped cream."

"Tell you what." I pushed the bowl and the spoon over to him. "Help yourself."

He grinned. "I need my pie."

"Oh. Right." I picked up Beau's slice and set it in front of him. "You also need a fork."

"I can get it."

"It's right here." I opened the drawer.

"Starting without me?" Anarchy stood in the kitchen doorway wearing his clothes from last night. Stubble shadowed his jaw, and dark circles hung beneath his tired eyes.

"You made it!" Beau sounded absolutely thrilled.

"Hey, I wouldn't miss the start of a tradition."

My eyes filled with tears, and I turned my back so they wouldn't see me cry. This was a happy moment, not a weepy one. "Coffee?"

"Please." He came up behind me and dropped a kiss on my neck as I poured.

"I'll let you cut your own pie."

"Who cut Beau's piece?"

"I did."

"I like the way you cut."

"Fine." A smile took over my whole face as I cut a slice of equal size for Anarchy and watched as he took a seat next to Beau at the kitchen island. They dug into their pie like they hadn't had an enormous dinner the night before, like their stomachs were bottomless pits, like they were men who didn't need to count calories or watch their waistlines.

"You're not eating?" asked Anarchy.

I held up my coffee cup. "I added whipped cream."

"Not the same," said Beau.

"I'm happy with my coffee." Which needed to be refilled.

"May I please go skating with Joey this afternoon?"

Joey's parents belonged to a club that maintained an ice rink.

"Of course."

Beau grinned then forked another enormous bite.

Woof! Finn, who sat at Beau's feet, stared at him with soulful eyes.

"Ellison says I can't feed you from the table."

Sure, make me the bad guy.

Anarchy stood. "More coffee?"

It was as if he could read my mind.

He took the cup from my hands and poured. "This is a great tradition. We should do it the day after Christmas, too. What do you say, Beau?"

He looked worried. "Do you serve mince?"

"Pecan."

His face cleared. "I love pecan pie."

Ding, dong.

The dogs scrambled to their paws and raced to the front door, barking like lunatics.

"It's eight-thirty," I observed. "It can't be Mother." She wasn't an early riser, and, if she wanted access to our house, she simply barged in.

"Karma?" Anarchy suggested.

Ding, dong.

The dogs lost their ever-loving minds.

"Not Karma. She wouldn't ring twice."

"Libba?"

"Ha." Like Mother, she barged in.

"Are either of you going to answer the door?" asked Beau.

I sighed. "I suppose."

When I reached the front door, I scolded the dogs. "Quiet! Sit!"

In what was a holiday miracle, they both listened. Only then did I open the door.

Clover stood on the other side.

The poor woman looked like death warmed over.

I grabbed the dogs' collars and said, "Please, come in."

She slipped inside. "I'm sorry to come so early." And

without calling first. "But I needed to talk to you. Your husband and his partner think that Earl was murdered." She looked at me expectantly, as if she expected me to tell her Anarchy's thoughts.

"I don't discuss my husband's cases."

"But we're family."

I must have reacted—a tic near my eye, a wrinkled nose, a curled lip—because Clover's face flushed with sudden anger. "You think you're better than us."

Mother definitely thought that. Me? Not so much.

"No," I replied. "Not at all. But I wouldn't have much of a marriage if I compromised my husband's cases by discussing them." I discussed them with Aggie all the time. But Aggie was different. She really was family.

Clover snorted.

I forced a polite smile. "May I offer you coffee?" She looked like she needed a cup.

She sagged as if that small kindness had broken her. "Please." She raked her fingers through her already messy hair, and a mulish expression settled on her tired features. "Maybe you can't talk, but you can listen."

"Yes," I agreed. "I can listen, but I can't promise I won't tell Anarchy everything you tell me."

"I'm counting on it."

I held out my arm. "Let me take your coat."

She shucked out of a navy peacoat and gave it to me.

I led her to the living room. "I'll hang this up and get us some coffee. Make yourself at home."

When I returned, carrying a tray with two coffee mugs, a pitcher of cream, and a plate of cookies, Clover was slumped in a wingback chair picking at her cuticles.

"Cream?" I tried to sound chipper. Tried and failed.

"Black." She accepted the coffee and for long seconds she stared into the mug's depths. "I didn't kill Earl. Neither did Mike or Wyatt. That leaves Karli."

I was struck with the sickening certainty that Karli would soon be knocking at my door, equally eager to throw her sister-in-law to the wolves. "Why would Karli kill him?"

"I don't know. I just know I didn't do it. Neither did Mike or Wyatt."

When I'd gone to the kitchen for coffee, Anarchy had urged me to talk to Clover, certain I'd be able to get more information from her. This wasn't information, it was casting blame where it hurt the least. I tried a different tack. "What do you know about Earl?"

Her upper lip curled. "He was after Mom's money."

I raised my brows.

"I know. I know. She doesn't have any. But she told him she was Aunt Tilly's heir."

"Is she?" Mother would have kittens.

"She wants to be. She says your side of Aunt Tilly's family is already rich as Midas." Her gaze traveled my living room, as if my furnishings made her point.

"What else can you tell me about Earl?"

"He smoked too much, drank too much, and Mom paid for that trip to Vegas."

"A real gem."

"Mom can pick 'em. Do you remember her last boyfriend?"

"I can't say as I do."

"Vinny." She shuddered. "Turns out, Vinny got the money to take her out by robbing liquor stores. She visited him in prison. Regularly. She'd still be taking the bus to the pen, but he died."

"Died?"

"He started an argument with a man holding a shiv."

A story I prayed Mother never heard.

"The one before Vinny cleaned out her bank accounts and disappeared. Aunt Tilly had to pay all Mom's bills until Mom got a job."

"The bookkeeping job?"

"That's the one." She stared at the hands she had clasped in her lap. "We didn't like Earl. How could we? But he wasn't the worst man she'd been with. Wyatt and I didn't kill him. And it couldn't be Mike. My brother doesn't have a violent bone in his body."

I wasn't so sure about any of that. They'd all looked ready to wring Earl's neck. Tossing him off a building wasn't a stretch.

"It had to be Karli."

"I'm sure the police will figure it out."

She bit her lower lip.

"How's Mikey?" I asked.

"He'll be fine. When they release him from the hospital, Karli and Mike are sending him to a rehab facility. Aunt Tilly is paying for it."

Aunt Tilly paid for an awful lot. I kept that thought to myself. "I'm so glad he's better."

"I blame Karli. She can't be bothered to mother." Clover drained her coffee mug and stood. "I should go. The girls need me."

I rose from the settee. "I'm so sorry this happened to your family."

Clover pressed her palm to her lips and nodded. "It's been less than a day, and it's tearing us apart."

"Murder does that."

On that cheery note, she left.

I closed the door on her and returned to the kitchen, where Anarchy was putting rinsed plates into the dishwasher. "Where's Beau?"

"He mentioned ice skating and went upstairs to change. What did Clover say?"

I told him everything.

"Do you think your aunt made Jane her heir?"

"No idea. Why?"

"If she is Tilly's heir, one of her family might have killed

Earl to keep him away from the money. I should have asked your aunt about it last night."

"Why didn't you?"

"Your aunt looked tired and…frail. I decided to let her rest."

"That was kind." I studied my husband. "You look like you could use some rest, too."

He closed the dishwasher door. "I wish I could. I came home for pie with Beau and a shower." He glanced at his wrist. "I'm due at the medical examiner's office in an hour."

"You haven't slept."

He grimaced as he leaned against the edge of the counter. "I was present when someone was murdered. My captain wants this solved quickly."

In my experience, being exhausted and clear thinking did not go together, but I refused to nag. "Is there anything I can do to help?"

"If you talk to your aunt…"

I imagined that conversation. *Aunt Tilly, it's absolutely none of my business, but we think someone may have murdered Earl over your money. Who's your heir?*

"Does it matter who inherits?" I asked. "If Jane and her family believe they're the beneficiaries, does it matter what Aunt Tilly's will says?"

"Maybe. Maybe not. I'd still like to know." He studied my expression. "I'm not asking you to call her or go by her apartment."

I exhaled.

"But if you see her—"

"Of course."

A smile tugged at his lips. "Come here."

I went, melting into his chest as he wrapped his arms around me.

"Best Thanksgiving ever," he whispered against the shell of my ear.

"Earl was murdered."

"The first Thanksgiving that you're my wife. Of course it's the best."

I tilted my head and stared into his eyes. "How did I get so lucky?"

"I'm the lucky one."

Max nudged us, and Anarchy smiled at him. "You want in on the hug, buddy?"

Max wanted his breakfast.

I swallowed a sigh and left the comfort of Anarchy's arms. "Go take a shower. I'll feed the dogs then take them for a walk."

"And after that?"

"Beau's skating. Grace will hang out with her friends. I may paint."

He nodded. "I'll try to be home early."

I wasn't holding my breath.

CHAPTER FIVE

The right shade of green eluded me. Either there was too much yellow or too much blue.

"I give up."

Finn, who curled on his mat in the corner of my studio, gave his tail an encouraging wag. Max, who was on his own mat, didn't bother. He was too accustomed to my fruitless searches for the perfect hue. He even yawned, knowing that I'd find the right color tomorrow when I wasn't stressed about a murder.

"You're right."

My dog yawned again. He knew he was right. He was always right.

I washed my brushes in the sink, put them in a mason jar to dry, then, in search of coffee, descended the stairs to the kitchen.

Aggie, who wore a muumuu the exact shade of green I'd been hoping to mix (somewhere between split pea and asparagus), was dicing leftover turkey. The orange pom-poms on her cuffs bounced as she worked. "I'm prepping Turkey Tetrazzini."

"That sounds delicious."

"Coffee?" She nodded at Mr. Coffee's full pot. "I just made some."

"I'll help myself. How was your shopping trip?"

Max scratched on the back door. I opened it, and the dogs rushed out into the cold.

"Successful," she replied.

Brnng, brnng.

I picked up the receiver. "Jones's residence."

"Ellison." Mother's voice boomed through the phone line.

I winced. "Good afternoon, Mother."

Aggie put down her knife, poured me a cup of coffee, and put it in my hands. What would I ever do without her?

"I need you to go to St. Mark's immediately."

"Why? What's wrong?"

"It's your Aunt Tilly. She's been admitted."

"What happened?"

"She's not well."

I snuck a restorative sip of coffee. "Could you be more specific?"

"No. Now get down there before Jane and her brood descend like a pack of locusts. It's undoubtedly their fault she's there. I'm sure the stress of that horrid man going off the balcony is what put her in the hospital." Mother gave a martyred sigh. "I'd go myself, but I'm expecting ten for dinner."

I glanced at the kitchen clock. It was just after four, the kids would be home soon, and I hadn't seen them all day. "I'll go in the morning."

"Ellison." Mother's voice was honed to a don't-you-dare-argue edge. "Go see your aunt."

"Why is she in the hospital?"

"I already told you, I don't know. Hudson called. The poor man was beside himself with worry."

How would I feel, being in the hospital alone during the holidays? "Fine. I need to change clothes, then I'll go."

"Don't dally."

"Goodbye, Mother." I hung up the phone before I could snap at her.

"Everything okay?" Anarchy had slipped into the kitchen without me noticing.

I offered him an I-wish-I-could-stay-home-and-snuggle-on-the-couch smile. "Aunt Tilly is in the hospital. Mother wants me to go see her."

"I'll go with you."

If Anarchy didn't look so tired, I'd be tempted to say yes. But he looked wan, and his lips drooped in an uncharacteristic frown. "You should rest. If I go now, I'll be home for dinner."

"Leftovers?" he asked.

Aggie held up a wooden spoon. "Turkey Tetrazzini."

"I can't wait, Aggie. And I can't go looking like this." I waved my hands over my paint clothes, then headed upstairs.

Anarchy followed me. "I'm happy to take you."

I glanced over my shoulder at his tired face.

"You should nap."

We reached the bedroom, and Anarchy closed the door behind us.

"Did you learn anything at the autopsy?"

"No."

I heard a hesitation in his voice. "But?"

"Jane took out a fifty-thousand-dollar policy on Earl's life last week."

"What!"

"We found a copy of the policy among his things. In fairness, he insured her life for the same amount."

I toed off my sneakers. "What did Jane say?"

"She claims the policies were Earl's idea."

I perched on the edge of the bed and stared at the carpet. "Jane isn't my favorite, but..."

"You don't think she's a killer." Anarchy joined me on the bed, stretched his long legs, and rolled his shoulders.

I gave him a quick kiss on the cheek, stood, and shimmied out of my jeans. "I've been wrong before. Was she unaccounted for last night?"

He winced and rubbed the back of his neck. "The only people I'm certain had an opportunity are Mike and Wyatt. But the situation was so chaotic, Jane could have stepped away without anyone noticing."

I pulled a pair of gray wool slacks from the closet and paired them with a cream cashmere sweater. "Did Clover or Wyatt know about the policy?" Fifty-thousand dollars, especially when it was payable on a man they loathed, was a good motive for murder.

"She says they did not."

"Hmph." Jane was a mother, and mothers protected their children.

"Exactly."

I pulled the sweater over my head then studied my reflection in the mirror that hung above my dresser. I added a string of pearls. "Do you still want me to ask Aunt Tilly about her will?"

He made to stand. "I'll come with you."

"No. Rest. You've been up since seven yesterday morning."

"You're sure?"

I returned to our bed, rested my hands on his shoulders, and stared down into his tired eyes. "Positive. Take a nap. That's an order."

"Okay, boss."

I leaned forward, kissed his forehead, then headed for the door. "I'll see you at dinner."

"Ellison."

I looked over my shoulder.

"I have a bad feeling. I think I should come with you."

"You have a bad feeling because you're so tired you can't see straight." I pointed to the pillows. "Rest."

I parked in the visitor lot and entered the hospital through its main doors, which made for a nice change. Far too often, I arrived at the hospital via the emergency room.

The volunteer at the information desk, a woman whose white hair was looking distinctively lavender, peered through thick glasses and shuffled papers when I asked for Aunt Tilly's room number. "Here it is." She jotted the number on a piece of paper.

"Thank you. I wonder if you'd also give me Mikey Kowalski's room number."

After more shuffling, she added Mikey's room number to the paper. "Have a nice holiday weekend."

Too late for that. I wished her the same.

I rode the elevator to Aunt Tilly's floor then walked an oatmeal-hued corridor. Was there anything more depressing than a hospital during the holidays? Undoubtedly. But eyeing the string of construction paper feathers tacked to the nurses' station, I was hard-pressed to think of a sadder place.

The door to Aunt Tilly's room stood open, and I peeked my head inside. "Aunt Tilly?"

"Ellison!" She sounded delighted to see me. "You're just in time."

I stepped into the room, gave my great-aunt a kiss on the cheek, and said, "Good afternoon, Hudson."

Aunt Tilly's houseman held a silver cocktail shaker in his hands, and a black liquor suitcase stood open on the window ledge. He'd brought vodka, vermouth, olives, and glasses.

"You'll have a martini," said Aunt Tilly. A statement, not a question.

"What do the doctors say about martinis when you're in the hospital?"

Aunt Tilly, who wore a pink quilted-satin bed jacket to which she'd pinned a diamond brooch, wrinkled her nose. "What do they know?"

There was no point in arguing. Aunt Tilly would do exactly

as she pleased. I took the path of least resistance, and said, "I'd love to have a drink with you."

"This is why you're my favorite. You know when to pick your battles."

I accepted a martini glass from Hudson, settled on the Naugahyde chair next to Aunt Tilly's bed, shrugged off my jacket. "I'm your favorite?"

Aunt Tilly's cheeks flushed the same soft pink as her bed jacket. "Jane needs me, it doesn't make her my favorite."

I sipped, letting the vodka roll across my tongue as I took in my great-aunt. Her color was off, but her hair was perfect. Her eyes were tired, but her lipstick was expertly applied. A dark bruise peeked beneath her sleeve, but she'd covered it with a diamond wristwatch. "How are you feeling?"

"Right as rain." She offered up a bright smile.

"Now, Miss Tilly." Hudson's voice held a scolding tone. "You fainted."

My octogenarian great aunt rolled her eyes. "You worry too much."

"Aunt Tilly?"

"Earl's death came as a shock." She took a restorative sip of vodka. "It upset me more than I thought. To think, the man stumbled off my balcony."

I stared at her. Did she believe Earl tripped on his shoelace and fell over a four-foot railing? "Earl didn't stumble off the balcony, Aunt Tilly. He was mur--"

"Poor, poor Jane. She's a bad picker." Apparently, Aunt Tilly did not want to discuss murder.

"So I've heard."

Aunt Tilly shifted her gaze to Hudson. "You go on home. Be with your family. If I need another martini, Ellison can make it."

"I can stay," he offered.

She smiled at him. "I'll be fine, Hudson. Thank you for everything."

He gave a slow nod. "You take care, Miss Tilly."

"I will. I promise."

"Happy holidays to you, Miss Ellison." Hudson collected his coat from the small closet and slipped out into the hall.

Aunt Tilly took another sip of her drink. "What was I saying? Oh, yes. Jane's terrible taste in men. Earl came back from Las Vegas, called an insurance agent, and took out a fifty-thousand-dollar policy on her life. Who does that?" She swirled the liquor in her glass. "A man who might kill his wife, that's who. Well, I told her that she should take out a similar policy. I even offered to pay for it."

"Was the policy in force?" Fifty-thousand dollars was a strong motive for murder.

"I wrote the check for the yearly premium last week." With her free hand, she smoothed the blanket on her bed, and I couldn't help but notice a dark bruise near her wrist.

I swallowed. Hard. This was my chance to ask Anarchy's uncomfortable question. "Clover suggested that Earl might have married Jane for…your money."

Tilly chuckled. "Wouldn't that have sent your mother around the bend? If Earl Hicks ended up the beneficiary of my estate." She shook her head. "She doesn't have to worry now."

"I hate to ask this, but…"

"Who gets it all when I die?" Aunt Tilly looked amused. "The bulk of my money will go to a charitable trust. It will support the arts and children's organizations here in Kansas City."

"That's lovely."

"I named you and your mother co-trustees."

I choked on a sip of vodka. All this time, I thought Aunt Tilly liked me.

"Of course, I remembered Hudson. The man is a saint for putting up with me for all these years. Your mother and Sis get my homes and their contents. I figured Frances would want the family real estate and antiques to stay in the family." She wasn't wrong. "Jane gets seventy-five-thousand dollars. You get my jewelry." She patted the brooch she'd pinned to her bed jacket. "Marjorie, Clover, and Mike get twenty-five thousand each. My great-great nieces and nephews get five-thousand, and I've put another fifteen thousand in college funds for each of them."

"That's very generous of you."

"I suspect, of all my family members, you're the only one who'll think that. I'd appreciate it if you'd keep the details to yourself."

"May I tell Anarchy?"

She sank deeper into her pillows (Hudson must have brought them from home, because they were far too fluffy to belong to the hospital). "If you must."

I nodded my thanks. "You fainted?"

"I did." She pursed her lips in annoyance. "And Hudson over-reacted. I should be at home now, in the TV room with my feet up. Instead, I'm here." Her displeasure was palpable.

"Tilly?"

I turned in my chair and spotted John Milbank in the doorway.

His brows lifted as he took in the martini glasses in our hands. "Ellison, nice to see you." His voice was as dry as our drinks, and Hudson mixed an arid martini.

"Likewise." Why was John visiting Aunt Tilly? He was an oncologist. Surely fainting called for a neurologist.

"You brought cocktails?" He entered Tilly's room and picked up the chart that hung from the end of her bed.

"I arrived and was served a cocktail. It is five o'clock."

"It's also a hospital."

"Pish," said Tilly. "When a woman reaches my age, she should do as she pleases."

"Even if it affects her medications?" His gaze scanned her chart.

"Aunt Tilly?" My tone invited an explanation.

She gave a put-upon sigh. "Something else I'd like you to keep to yourself, dear. I have cancer."

My stomach sank. "No."

"Yes," John replied. "And she's declined chemotherapy." His disapproval was evident in the set of his jaw.

"Chemotherapy would buy me a year? Maybe two? Or it might kill me. I've had a marvelous life. I don't mind dying. Especially not when it's on my terms."

John huffed.

Aunt Tilly pointed at him. "That's enough out of you, doctor. I've made my choice."

"Fine, Tilly." He didn't sound happy. "How are you feeling?"

"Ready to go home."

"We need to run some tests."

She pursed her lips. "You and I both know there won't be any testing on a holiday weekend. Let me go home. I'll come back on Monday."

"Tilly, you blacked out. You're lucky you didn't hit your head or break a bone when you fell."

They stared at each other. Neither willing to cede an inch.

John blinked first. "I'll make you a deal."

"I'm listening."

"Stay the weekend, and I'll make sure you're first for testing on Monday."

"It's a good deal, Aunt Tilly."

"Fine." She wrinkled her nose at both of us, then drank. Deeply. "But, Ellison, you and that handsome husband of yours will bring me dinner tomorrow night. I want Winstead's. A steakburger with cheese and grilled onions, French fries, and a frosty malt."

"Done."

For a moment, I thought John might argue for healthier food, but he'd already won one battle. He wouldn't win a second. He seemed to realize that, because he gave an unhappy nod. "I'll see you when I'm on rounds in the morning." He nodded my way. "Ellison, always a pleasure."

"Likewise." I waited till he was gone to ask my aunt, "How long have you known?"

"Months."

"Aunt Tilly..."

"My terms, Ellison. I want to go on my terms. Do not tell your mother. She'll do nothing but treat me like an invalid." Aunt Tilly wasn't wrong. Mother would hover. And fuss. And manage. And Aunt Tilly would hate every second.

"I won't tell her. I promise."

"Thank you, dear." She held out her glass. "Would you top this off."

I added more vodka to her glass and swallowed a sudden lump in my throat. "How long have you got?"

"The doctors say a few months, but what do they know?"

"Aunt Tilly..."

"Don't," she said. "Don't. I went to Paris last month. I walked the streets George and I visited on our honeymoon. I sat on a park bench and watched the Bateaux Mouches on the Seine. I ate my favorite meal. Then I went to Palm Springs and played golf every day. And bridge with women I've held dear for more than half my life. I celebrated Thanksgiving with family—even if that despicable man did his best to ruin it—and I'm having unexpected cocktails with my favorite great-niece."

I lifted my glass and smiled at her over the rim. The smile was watery. God broke the mold when he made my great-aunt, I'd never meet anyone else like her again. "I'll miss you."

"Of course you will." She held out her free hand, and I took it in mine. "Ellison, if there's one thing I've learned, it's that one must seize opportunities. They don't always knock again. I've had a wonderful go, and my only regrets are things I didn't do. I didn't let George buy me that strand of Akoya pearls from

Cartier on our twenty-fifth anniversary. He wanted to, and I told him, 'no.' I didn't go on that spa trip your mother planned."

"Don't regret that." I had gone on that trip. With Mother, Aunt Sis, and my sister Marjorie. Mother bossed her daughters and bickered with her sister. Aunt Sis drank. And Marjorie sniped. At me. Endlessly. I'd come home exponentially more stressed than before I left.

Aunt Tilly laughed softly. "I'd have liked for us all to be together."

"Maybe I can..."

She held up a hand. "No, dear. Look at me. I'm spending the holiday weekend in a hospital bed. My days of traveling are over." She looked me dead in the eye, then drained her glass. "Remember, no regrets."

"More?"

She grinned. "Need you ask?" I poured, and she shooed me toward the door. "Go home and spend time with your husband. I'll see you tomorrow night."

"Are you sure? I can stay."

"Go."

I collected my jacket, kissed her cheek, and left without letting her see the tears in my eyes. Rather than heading immediately home, I descended a floor and poked my head into Mikey's hospital room.

The patient was propped up in bed with his nose in a book. His father sat in the Naugahyde chair next to the hospital bed.

"Good evening." I ventured.

"Ellison." Mike stood. "What are you doing here?"

Who said chivalry was dead?

"I thought I'd stop by and see the patient."

Mikey looked at me over the top of his book, then went back to reading.

"I'm glad you're feeling better."

"Yeah." Mikey sounded bored. And annoyed. And totally ungrateful.

"Ellison?" Mike nodded toward the hallway. "A word?"

"Of course."

We stepped out of the room.

"Any word on the investigation?"

"I can't comment on my husband's cases."

"So, it was murder."

"I didn't say that."

"Your husband is a homicide detective. If it's his case, it's murder." Mike made an excellent point. "It must have been Wyatt."

Interesting how Clover and Mike were so willing to blame their sibling's spouses. I shrugged. "I don't know anything."

He leaned against the wall and raked his hands through his hair. "I've been sitting in that chair all day, trying to figure out what happened. When we took the door of the hinges, everyone gathered around. Everyone. All of us on top of each other, right until Wyatt left to wait for the ambulance."

Not everyone. Why hadn't I seen it before?

CHAPTER SIX

"**A**narchy?" I called his name as soon as I set foot in the house.

The dogs raced toward me, their stubby tails working so hard their butts shook.

I offered pets and scratches behind ears and asked, "Where's Anarchy?"

Woof. Max trotted toward the back of the house.

I followed him through the kitchen to the family room where Anarchy was stretched out on the couch with his eyes closed.

Max flopped onto the carpet in front of the fireplace, and Finn snuggled next to him.

I chewed on my lower lip. Should I wake Anarchy? The man was exhausted, but...

"I can hear you thinking." His lids remained closed.

"I didn't want to disturb you."

He pushed up on his elbows and gave me a sleepy grin. "You never disturb me."

My knees went weak.

"How's your aunt?"

"May I?" I joined him on the couch and rested my clasped hands in my lap. "We need to talk."

"That sounds ominous."

"Maybe. Where are the kids?"

"Beau is spending the night with Joey, and Grace is out with her friends."

"Aggie?"

"On a date with Mack."

"Dinner?"

"Warming in the oven. There's a salad in the fridge." He studied me. "Do you want a drink?"

"Hudson brought Aunt Tilly's liquor case. I had a martini with her."

His brows rose.

"That was her doctor's reaction, too."

"I bet."

I squared my shoulders. "When we were in the bathroom, where were Aunt Tilly and Hudson?"

"In the kitchen. Hudson was doing the dishes."

"Why was Aunt Tilly there?"

"With all the hullabaloo, she needed a drink."

"Hullabaloo?"

"Her word."

"And she went to the kitchen?"

Anarchy frowned as he nodded. "Yes."

There were two call buttons in Aunt Tilly's apartment. One near her chair in the dining room, the other near her favorite chair in the living room. Each rang directly to the kitchen. If Aunt Tilly wanted a drink, she'd call for Hudson, not go to him.

"What if they killed Earl?"

He stared at me. "Why would they do that?"

"Let's assume Earl married Jane with the belief that she'd inherit Tilly's money."

His gaze sharpened. "Will she?"

"Aunt Tilly remembered her. Generously." Mother would have a fit. "But it's not the millions Jane is counting on."

"Who gets the money?"

"The bulk of her estate will go to a charitable trust." My shoulders sagged under the weight of being a co-trustee with Mother. "Back to Earl. No one ever saw him in the hallway outside the bathroom."

"They did not."

"That leaves him in the living room. Alone with Aunt Tilly. I know my great-aunt. She wouldn't leave a guest to fetch a drink, no matter how much she might dislike him."

"She disliked him?"

"She paid the premium for the policy Jane carries on Earl's life."

"So, Tilly and Earl are in the living room, then what?"

"They went out on the balcony to see the lights come on."

"Aunt Tilly pitched him over the edge?" He reached for my hand and squeezed my fingers. "I don't think she has the strength."

"What if they struggled?"

He shook his head.

"What if Hudson joined them on the balcony?"

Anarchy opened his mouth, then closed it as he sat back against the couch cushions. "That's possible. But why?"

"Aunt Tilly has a terrible bruise on her wrist. What if Earl tried to throw her off the balcony?"

"And Hudson came to her rescue?"

I nodded enthusiastically. "Exactly."

"Then they should have told us."

"Even after Aunt Tilly paid for a fifty-thousand-dollar life insurance policy?"

"Don't take this the wrong way, but your great aunt doesn't seem the type to worry herself over that amount of money. If that's what happened, she should have told us."

Everything was black and white for Anarchy. "There's something else."

Anarchy grimaced.

"Aunt Tilly is dying of cancer. No one knows, and she's refusing treatment." Aunt Tilly adored Hudson. She wouldn't want him to face repercussions when she was gone.

My husband pulled me onto his lap. "I know you're fond of her. I'm sorry."

"Me, too. What do we do?" In regard to Earl, not Aunt Tilly's cancer.

"Tonight, we have dinner and go to bed early. I'll talk to her tomorrow."

"I promised her we'd bring Winstead's."

"Sounds like you're coming with me. Now, Mrs. Jones--" he pulled me close and kissed the corner of my lips "--I want you to put murder and cancer and whatever is bothering you about Tilly's estate out of your mind."

Easy to do when his lips moved against mine. "And?"

"How hungry are you?" He nibbled on my earlobe.

Starving. "Not very."

I felt his smile against the curve of my cheek. "I was hoping you'd say that. Dinner can wait."

"Ellison! Anarchy! I'm so glad you're here." Aunt Tilly was in her hospital bed wearing a white satin bed jacket (again with a diamond brooch pinned near the shoulder) and a broad smile. "There's nothing duller than a hospital on the weekend. And you brought Winstead's! Thank heavens! The food here is abysmal."

Anarchy put the Winstead's bag on the table that spanned Aunt Tilly's bed. I deposited the frosty.

"You're wonderful. Both of you. Now sit." She'd somehow finagled an extra chair. The room was crowded but Anarchy and I both had a seat. "Tell me what you've been doing."

"Nothing exciting," I replied.

She wrinkled her nose as if she didn't care for my answer. "Your mother came to see me. And Jane."

"At the same time?"

"Sadly, yes." She reached for her frosty and the sleeve of her bedjacket rode up, revealing a bruise that matched her other wrist.

"Aunt Tilly, what happened?"

"I'm old. I bruise easily."

I tilted my head and pursed my lips.

"I'm fine, Ellison."

"It looks like someone grabbed you," said Anarchy.

"Is there a spoon?"

"In the bag," I replied. "Did Earl cause those bruises?"

Aunt Tilly put the frosty on the table and dug through the Winstead's bag for a spoon. "Life is short. Eat dessert first."

I winced but stuck to my guns. "Did he?"

"Aha!" She held up the spoon.

"I think you and Earl went out on the balcony to see the lights and he attacked you." I nodded toward her bruised wrists. "You struggled. Hudson, who was in the living room picking up glasses, saw you and came to your rescue. Somehow, Earl went over the edge."

Aunt Tilly spooned a bite of frosty.

"Am I right?"

"Ellison." Her voice held a warning.

"Jane's family is tearing itself apart."

She stared at me for long seconds before transferring her gaze to Anarchy. "You're half right. Hudson was never on the balcony."

"What happened?"

"We stepped outside to see the lights..."

Seconds passed as Aunt Tilly stared sightlessly at the oatmeal-colored wall.

"You stepped outside," Anarchy prompted.

"Earl told me I had a lovely home. I thanked him." She pressed a hand to her chest. "Then he grabbed my wrist." Aunt Tilly held out her right hand. "His grip was so tight. I told him he was hurting me. He didn't care. He said everyone had noticed how much I'd been drinking. No one would doubt that I fell off the balcony. He and Jane had talked, and they didn't want to wait for my money."

"Oh, Aunt Tilly." The tears in her eyes were at odds with the determined tilt of her chin. "Jane would never..."

She waved off my sympathy. "I know that now, in the moment, it broke my heart. I fought him, but he dragged me to the railing and leaned us both over the edge. I refused to die like that. I have my ending planned, and it's not splattered across the roof of a porte cochère. I linked my foot around his ankle and yanked. He lost his balance, then he was the one falling."

"What happened next?" asked Anarchy.

"I went to the kitchen and asked Hudson for a drink."

My husband dragged his palm across his chin, hiding a pained expression. "Why didn't you tell us?"

"I was in shock."

"And yesterday?"

"I was hoping you'd determine he fell."

Anarchy gave a slow unhappy nod. "How long has Hudson been with you?"

"Thirty-five years."

"He's like family."

"Hudson had nothing to do with what happened on the balcony." Aunt Tilly spoke quickly. Decisively. And I didn't believe her. "You'll never prove otherwise." She dug her spoon into her frosty like the frozen treat was responsible for the world's misfortunes.

"Even if he did, no charges would be filed. It was self-defense."

She stared at Anarchy with narrowed eyes. "I assume Ellison has told you my situation?"

"She has."

"Then you know I won't be here long."

Anarchy gave a tiny nod.

"Even if Hudson was on that balcony, which he was not, I wouldn't tell you. I won't be here to protect him from an overzealous prosecutor who charges a black man with throwing a white man to his death. I won't be here to defend Hudson's claim on my estate when Jane claims wrongful death. I won't do that to him." Her gaze shifted to me. "You know better than anyone in this family that there's more than blood. The family we choose can be more precious than the family we're born with. Hudson is family."

The expression in Anarchy's brown eyes was grave. "No one will believe you threw a man forty years your junior off a balcony."

"Adrenaline is an amazing thing. I was reading just the other day that a man picked up a car and pulled a child from beneath its wheels."

Anarchy leaned forward, resting his elbows on his knees. "You're certain about this Tilly?"

"I've never been more certain. This holiday is about gratitude. I've had a marvelous life, for which I'll be eternally grateful. I had the love of a wonderful man. I've had marvelous friends. I even have a few family members whom I adore." She winked at me. "And, I've had Hudson. Through thick and thin. He saw me through my husband's death, held my hand when the doctors told me about my cancer, and acted as my protector." She held out her hands. "Please. Let me give him this."

My breath caught in my chest as I stared at my by-the-book-homicide-detective husband.

He closed his eyes and laced his fingers together.

I didn't dare breathe. Didn't dare try.

Worry furrowed Aunt Tilly's brow.

"You're willing to swear an affidavit that Hicks was drunk and fell over the railing?"

"If that's what you want."

I exhaled. Loudly.

A tiny smile curled Anarchy's lip. "I'll come by tomorrow, and we'll write out a statement."

My heart overflowed with appreciation for the man sitting next to me.

We sat with Aunt Tilly as she ate her steakburger and fries and frosty, then I kissed her on the cheek, and we stepped into the hallway.

"Thank you," I told Anarchy. "I am forever grateful. But why?"

"Because your aunt was right. About everything. About what might happen to Hudson. About gratitude. About family."

"But justice?"

"A venal man tried to murder your aunt and died for his trouble. I'd say justice was served."

I raised up on my tiptoes and kissed his cheek. "Thank you. And since we're talking about gratitude, I am grateful for you. Every day."

"I feel the same way." He gazed into my eyes. "Will you make me a promise?"

I nodded. "Anything."

He leaned closer and whispered in my ear. "No bodies at Christmas."

I laughed softly. "That's a promise I can't make."

RICH GIRL

A COUNTRY CLUB MURDERS NOVELLA

CHAPTER ONE

September 1975
Kansas City, Missouri

Pansy barked. Along with counter-surfing and destroying the neighbors' landscaping, it was her favorite activity.

"You're lucky that you're pretty," I muttered as I approached the window where she hopped on her back legs like a deranged kangaroo.

She had her nose pressed against the glass. Outside, the lawn stretched to the street in emerald perfection despite the late-summer heat.

Woof!

"For the love of Pete. Stop bark—oh. Charlie, come here!" My voice carried through the house. "Something is happening at Ellison's."

A moment later, my fiancé joined me, his hair still mussed with sleep. "You know, Anarchy lives there, too." His voice was hard.

I glanced at him in surprise. Charlie never took that tone with me. But dark shadows hung beneath his eyes. Charlie was a cardiologist, and when he worked late, it was because one of his patients desperately needed him. "Never mind Anarchy. What's happening?" I'd run out of fingers counting the police cars parked in the driveway next door. Had Aggie made donuts? Because if she had, I wanted one—or six.

But I'd never known Ellison's housekeeper to cook for Anarchy's whole precinct. Something was wrong.

And if Ellison was in trouble, I was going over there. That's what best friends did. They showed up when you needed them, preferably with a pitcher of martinis. I checked my watch. Too early for martinis. Maybe Bloody Marys?

Charlie slipped a restraining hand around my waist. "Call her."

What a terrible idea. "She's next door. She needs me."

"She has Anarchy."

I rolled my eyes. "Not the same." Men were well and good. A few, like Charlie, were better than well and good. But a best friend of nearly four decades was irreplaceable.

"Libba, you'll be in the way."

I stiffened. I had never, not once in my entire life, been in the way. "Not possible."

Charlie sighed as he released me. I knew what he was thinking—that Ellison was fine, and I was just curious. That whatever was happening was none of my business. But Charlie was a smart man. Too smart to say any of that aloud.

I headed toward the front door.

"Libba!" The edge in Charlie's voice was sharp enough to pause my steps.

I glanced over my shoulder, daring him to argue.

"Sweetheart, you can't go in your nightgown. You'll get arrested for public indecency."

He had a point. The nightie was sheer. I kissed his cheek and headed upstairs. "I'll change first."

Ten minutes later, wearing a khaki skirt, a crêpe de chine camp shirt, and wedge-heeled espadrilles I'd picked up on sale at Swanson's, I cut across Charlie's lawn—a woman on a mission.

The grass was still damp from the sprinklers, and I regretted my choice of shoes. Espadrilles were never the same once the soles got wet.

A stolid officer stopped me at Ellison's drive. "Ma'am, you need to turn around. This is a crime scene."

Ma'am. I did *not* look like a ma'am. I was barely forty. I swallowed my irritation and forced a smile. "I'm Mrs. Jones's best friend."

He didn't budge.

"I'm worried about her."

"Mrs. Jones is fine."

"What's happened?" I waved at the collection of police cruisers.

"There's been a murder."

Given the plethora of police cars and worried expressions, that wasn't exactly surprising. "That's why she needs me."

He shook his head and crossed his arms over his chest. "I'm sorry, ma'am."

We weren't getting anywhere. Time for Plan B: infiltration via the backyard.

"What's going on?" The voice carried more authority than the president and the pope combined.

Frances Walford, Ellison's mother, stood a few feet away on the drive. She wore a linen pantsuit with sensible heels and pearls the size of marbles. She looked down her nose at the officer with the disdain she usually reserved for people who ate their dinner roll off the wrong butter plate.

When her gaze shifted my way, I was deeply grateful I'd taken the time to dress.

Frances and I held different opinions on everything from hemlines to hairdos (she wore a silver helmet). We'd never discussed politics or religion, and I suspected doing so would end with one of us (me) requiring medical attention.

If asked "Why did God put you on this earth?" Frances would launch into a dissertation about serving her fellow man (really, she just wanted to organize them according to her grand plan) and inspiring others by leading an exemplary life.

If asked the same question, my response would be one word: Fun.

We were Aesop's proverbial ant and grasshopper. Except this grasshopper had plenty saved for winter.

But we had one thing in common—we both adored her daughter.

"Well?" Her lips were pursed. Her arms were crossed.

"I don't know, Frances." She'd insisted I use her first name after I turned thirty-five. "This officer won't let me in."

"It's a crime scene—a murder scene." The sharpness in his tone suggested his patience was wearing thin.

"My daughter is in that house."

"I can't let you in, ma'am."

Steam exited Frances's ears, swirling around her perfectly coiffed head until it formed demon horns.

The angel on my right shoulder feared for the officer's well-being. The demon on my left rubbed its hands together in antici-patory glee. For once, I listened to the entity on the right.

"Frances, let's go back to my house and call her."

She lifted her chin another inch. "I already called. Several times. The line rings busy."

"We'll request an emergency breakthrough."

She huffed softly. A genteel huff. But a huff that conveyed deep displeasure. If she wanted to speak with her daughter, her daughter should answer the phone. If she wanted to march through a crime scene, the police should stand aside.

"Mrs. Walford, what are you doing here?"

Frances's shoulders visibly stiffened at the question, and I almost felt sorry for the man who'd asked—Detective Peters, Anarchy's partner. Almost. Peters didn't engender sympathy. He was a terrible grump, especially to Ellison (and, by extension, me—I'd even heard him mutter "boozehound" under the cover of his ridiculous mustache).

"What is happening here?" Frances completely ignored his question.

"What do you think?" His eyes glittered. "Your daughter found another body."

Frances paled and pressed a palm against her chest. "In her house? Are the children all right?"

I hadn't thought to worry about anyone's safety. The guilt pinched harder than I expected.

"The kids are fine. The body was on the back patio."

Which meant sneaking in through the backyard was off the table.

"I wish to speak with Ellison." A command, not a request.

Peters scratched his chin, clearly weighing the pros and cons of an out-and-out battle with Frances. "Fine," he ceded. "This way."

His grudging invitation didn't specifically include me, but I didn't care. I was going. With a condescending nod to the officer who'd blocked my path, I trailed after Frances.

Peters led us up the front steps.

Assured that she was getting her way, Frances shifted her focus. "Libba, when are you and Charlie getting married? Have you set a date?"

I choked on my own spit and stumbled over a non-existent rock.

"Keep up, dear." Was that a twinkle in Frances's eye?

We were in the foyer before I answered, "No date yet."

She shook her head. "Don't waste time. There are plenty of women interested—Charlie Ardmore is a catch."

And I wasn't?

Before I could craft a biting reply, we reached the kitchen, where Ellison slumped on a stool at the island. Her back was to us, but I'd have bet Charlie's firstborn that she had both hands wrapped around a mug of coffee.

"Ellison Russell!"

Ellison's shoulders lifted to her ears, and she turned toward us. Dark circles shadowed her eyes, and her hair was a mess. "It's Jones, Mother. Ellison Jones."

Frances flicked her wrist as if Ellison's married name was an annoyance, like rain at a garden party. "Explain to me what's happening."

"I let the dogs out and found a dead man on the patio." Simple. To the point. Concise.

Not good enough for Frances. "Well, who is it?"

"No idea. I've never seen him before."

I drifted toward the window, trying to catch a glimpse of the body. Too many officers blocked the view.

"I suppose that's a blessing," Frances said. "Does your husband recognize him?"

"No."

"Then why is he on your patio?"

"An excellent question, Mother. Perhaps you can identify him."

"Don't get smart with me."

I turned from the window, offering a placating smile. "We're both relieved you're okay."

Ellison shrugged as if "okay" was a stretch. "Coffee?" To my misguided friend, coffee was the cure for all ills. In truth, alcohol was the answer.

"Please," I replied.

"Mother?"

Frances patted her silver hamlet. "Do you have cream?"

"I always have cream." Ellison's voice was chock-full of exaggerated patience.

"Is it fresh?"

"Yes, Mother. It mooed at me this morning."

"There's no need for sass." When Frances was unhappy (and bodies made her extremely unhappy), she treated Ellison like a teenager.

In a bid to avoid the coming argument, I headed to the cabinet and grabbed two mugs.

"If you'd stop finding bodies, life would be much easier. I wouldn't have to worry so much." Because it was all about Frances, although she did have a point. Ellison found too many bodies.

Ellison closed her eyes and pressed her fingertips to her temples. "Imagine how I feel."

If this bickering kept up, I'd need to trade my coffee for something stronger.

I filled the mugs, added fresh cream to both, and offered one to Frances.

"Thank you, Libba."

"You're welcome." Curiosity drew me to the window, and I peered out into the backyard. The milling officers shifted, revealing the dead man's face.

The mug fell through my fingers, shattering as it hit the floor and splattering my legs with hot coffee. If it burned, I didn't feel it.

"Libba!" Ellison exclaimed. "Are you okay?"

No. Not even close. "I know him," I whispered.

"Who is he?"

I buried my head in my hands, hiding behind my fingers.

"Libba?" Ellison's voice was gentle.

I shook my head.

"Who is he?" she repeated.

There was no escaping this.

The dead man on the patio was a shameful secret I'd hoped to take to my grave. "My ex-husband."

"YOU WERE *MARRIED*?" ELLISON'S MOUTH HUNG OPEN.

"It's a long story."

"When?"

I winced and wrapped my arms across my chest.

"Libba?" She wasn't about to let this go.

"Twenty years ago."

"The man on the patio." Frances's voice was careful. "Did you have any reason to want him dead?"

Frances was *worried*. About me. "No." My voice came out small.

Frances pursed her lips. "Ellison, call Hunter."

"I don't need a lawyer."

Ellison ignored me and reached for the phone. Now she listened to Frances?

"Ellison—"

"It can't hurt." She stuck her finger in the dial and spun clockwise. Of course, she'd memorized his number. If I found bodies as often as she did, I'd have my lawyer's number memorized, too.

"This isn't necessary." My voice shook.

"When did you last see him?" she asked.

"It's been twenty years."

"You recognized him instantly." She kept dialing.

His features were seared in my memory. "He has a distinctive face. Do I really need Hunter?"

Her expression was sympathetic. "Trust me. It's better to be prepared."

"It's just that he's so—"

"Perfect." Frances had nurtured hopes for Ellison and Hunter. She wasn't yet over her disappointment.

"He's been divorced three times, Mother."

"Your point?"

"He's not perfect."

Frances muttered something about pots and kettles and the color black.

Ellison ignored her. "As soon as I hang up, you can call Charlie."

Charlie.

I had never mentioned my first marriage to my fiancé. Charlie saw me as smart, confident, and desirable. The story of my first marriage would change that. "I don't want to tell him."

"Libba—"

"This murder has nothing to do with me. I haven't spoken to Ghislain in decades. It's all a huge—" What? A mistake? A coincidence? His body was on Ellison's patio. Someone had killed him. I swallowed a lump in my throat. "There's no reason to bother Charlie with this."

"Hunter, it's me." Ellison wrapped the phone cord around her right ring finger. "I found a body on the back patio."

"Tell him to come to the house," Frances instructed.

Ellison waved her off. "No, I don't know him. But Libba does. She needs you."

I didn't.

"Thank you." Ellison nodded and hung up. "He's on his way. Do you have any cash on you?"

"No."

"I'll get my billfold. Once you give him a retainer, anything you say is privileged." She hurried up the back stairs without waiting for my reply.

Frances refilled her coffee, fetched the cream from the fridge, and sniffed the carton before adding a jot to her mug. "More coffee?"

"I should clean this up." I opened the utility closet and grabbed rags and the broom.

"When were you married?" Frances asked.

I dropped a rag on the floor and pushed it around with my foot. "Twenty years ago."

"Before Ellison married Henry?"

"Yes." I bent and picked up the sodden rag, carried it to the laundry room.

"Your parents?" she called.

I returned and swept the shards into a pile. "They were horrified."

"Your mother never said a word."

"I don't imagine she did." Even now, her disappointment stung.

Frances held out her hand. "Give me the broom. You hold the pan."

I was dumping the shards when Ellison returned and handed me a twenty.

I eyed the bill. "I think Hunter costs more than this."

"Too true, but you can afford him. Besides, it's just a retainer. More coffee?"

Coffee wouldn't solve this problem. I needed something stronger. A double shot of bourbon? "Please." I turned away from the window and its horrific view. "How did he die?"

"Stabbed." She offered me a fresh mug.

My hand was shaking too hard to take it. "Stabbed?"

"There's a knife in his side. You can't see it from this angle."

Frances sniffed her displeasure. "Dear Lord, Ellison. There's no need to be gruesome."

"Murder is seldom pretty, Mother."

Frances scowled at her. "Why was he at your house?"

"I don't know, Mother. We've been over this."

Frances shifted her scowl my way. "Was he looking for you, Libba?"

My knees wobbled, and I grabbed the edge of the island. "Why would he do that?"

"You tell me."

"Mrs. Jones?" A uniformed officer appeared in the doorway. "There's a man out front. Says he's your lawyer."

"Please let him in."

A moment later, Hunter strode into the kitchen. He kissed Ellison's cheek, told Frances she was looking lovely, then turned to me. He had the kind of face that gave nothing away—useful in a lawyer, unsettling in a friend. "Libba."

"Hunter. Thank you for coming."

He crossed to the window and studied the activity outside.

"The body," Ellison said. "It's Libba's ex-husband."

His shoulders stiffened. "I wasn't aware you had one."

"I never told anyone."

His gaze cut to Ellison. "Can't wait to hear the story."

I handed him the twenty. "I guess I should give you this first."

He folded the bill and stuck it in his pocket. "Ellison, may we use the study?"

She nodded.

"Ellison comes with us." I looked at Frances, silently pleading with her not to intrude. This would be hard enough without her judgmental sighs.

She pursed her lips and extended her hand, examining her manicure. "I'll wait here."

Whether she'd taken pity on me or was simply uninterested in my sordid past, I couldn't tell. Either way, her easy capitulation came as a relief.

We walked down the hall to Anarchy's study. Hunter took the chair behind the desk; Ellison and I settled into the club chairs facing him.

A minute ticked by as I gathered my thoughts. Then, another one.

Ellison reached for my hand and gave my fingers a quick squeeze. "Libba?"

I took a breath. "We met when I was twenty. I was studying at the Sorbonne."

I'd been in Paris for less than a month and still saw the city with awestruck eyes—the elegant ladies walking Afghan hounds down tree-lined avenues, the chic girls who transformed their whole look with a new knot in their Hermès scarves, the bird-like older women with beady eyes and rare smiles.

But the men worried me. They were too charming, too hand-some, too outside my experience.

The afternoon we met, I sat alone at Les Deux Magots, drinking red wine and wondering if I could slip the ashtray into my handbag without the waiter noticing.

The man at the next table had salt-and-pepper hair, sad eyes, and a debonair mustache. His hand trembled as he lifted his espresso to his lips. A hero in the war? A broken heart? I was inventing his history when a shadow fell across my table.

"Pretty women should never drink alone."

I looked up. Piercing blue eyes. Cheekbones that could cut glass. Dark hair, sensuous lips, and an accent that should have been illegal.

"May I?" He pulled out a chair and sat.

"What if I said no?"

"*Bof.*" He raised his shoulders, opened his palms, let his eyebrows lift as his mouth puckered. A perfect Gallic shrug. A shrug that said no one—especially not a naïve American girl—could refuse him.

Butterflies swarmed in my stomach. "I'm Libba."

"Ghislain de Fevre." A *de* in his name—nobility. "You're American."

Why would a French nobleman approach a girl at a café? "Yes."

"Do you speak French?"

"*Un peu.*" More than a little, but I understood a basic truth: a Frenchman speaking English was swoon-worthy. An American speaking French made the natives cringe. I wanted him to linger. I wanted to flirt. And when he was gone, I'd write Ellison about how daring I'd been.

"What brings you to Paris?"

"My studies." I swirled my wine, searching for something sophisticated to say. Something Audrey Hepburn might say. "Do you live nearby?" I barely resisted planting my face in my palms.

"Not exactly—the Sixteenth Arrondissement." An elegant neighborhood—one of my father's business associates kept a house there. "Where are you staying?"

"I live with a French family in Place Maubert." The husband passed his days smoking and muttering over *Le Figaro*. His wife worked two jobs and took in boarders to make ends meet.

"How do you find the city?"

"Marvelous." There. That sounded like Audrey.

"Your favorite place?"

"Sainte-Chapelle on a sunny day. The Musée Rodin."

His eyebrows rose. "Not the Louvre?"

"It's crowded."

"It has the *Mona Lisa*."

"Would she be famous if she hadn't been stolen?" Ellison's theory, not mine, but Ghislain smiled, and the skin around his eyes crinkled. I bit my tongue and let him think I was clever. "What's your favorite painting?"

"*La Liberté Guidant le Peuple*," he said. "If you like, I'll take you."

The butterflies in my stomach migrated to my throat. "That would be nice."

"Nice?" He was teasing.

"Interesting," I allowed.

"Tomorrow? The museum in the afternoon, then dinner?" A date. He'd asked me out on a date.

My cheeks warmed. "I'd like that."

"Where should I pick you up?"

I wasn't ready to give a stranger my address. "I have an afternoon class. May I meet you there? The south entrance?"

His lips quirked. "Three o'clock?"

The man with the shaking hands lit a Gauloise, and I wrinkled my nose.

Ghislain noticed. "Come. Let's walk."

"I haven't paid." Or pocketed the ashtray—I wanted a souvenir.

He tossed a few francs onto the table.

I slipped the ashtray into my handbag and took his hand.

He laced our fingers together and led me toward the Seine.

"Is this something you do often?" I asked. "Pick up American girls in cafés?"

"You are the first."

"Why me?"

"You're beautiful."

I rolled my eyes.

"You are. But also—there is wonder in your eyes. As if you are seeing everything for the first time."

"You're saying I'm naïve."

"I'm saying you're a chance for a jaded man to see the world afresh."

"You're too young to be jaded."

"The war took much from my family."

I squeezed his hand.

We walked along the Seine. It wasn't a pretty river—brown and dirty—but the city that flanked its banks was magical.

"Everything seemed easy after that." I clasped my hands in my lap, remembering the feel of his fingers around mine. "Almost as if we were meant to be."

Ellison made a sympathetic noise. If we'd been meant to be, we'd be together.

"We took walks by the Seine, had picnics in the Bois de Boulogne. He kissed me when I speared the brass ring on the carousel in the Jardin du Luxembourg. We sipped wine in tiny cafés and danced cheek-to-cheek in nightclubs. He made me feel sophisticated. Beautiful. Desirable." I studied my hands. "We'd only been together for six weeks when he said he loved me."

We were dancing, my body pressed against his, when he whispered, "*Je t'aime.*"

I looked up at him and murmured, "I love you, too."

Even now, knowing what came after, that moment was perfect.

"This is the mystery man you wrote about?" Ellison asked. "I thought you broke up with him."

"That was easier than the truth."

"What happened?"

"He took me to meet his mother."

His mother was dreadfully thin, but she made boniness look elegant. She wore a black dress, very chic, very French.

I was grateful I'd worn simple black pants, a camel sweater, and pearls. Simple. Classic. Appropriate armor for meeting Ghislain's mother.

She studied me for a long moment. I resisted the urge to fidget.

"I am delighted to meet the girl who has made my son so happy." Then she coughed—deep and dry, rising from her toes.

She wasn't thin because she ate like a bird. She was sick.

Ghislain led her to a chair covered in faded pink silk. "Sit, Maman. I'll get your pills."

When he'd gone, she wiped her lips with a handkerchief and waved me to the chair opposite. "My son loves you."

My cheeks heated, and I glanced at the parquet floor.

"Do you love him?"

I met her gaze. "I do."

"Then you will be married."

My jaw dropped as I thought of the reasons not to get married. I was too young. Ghislain hadn't met my parents. He hadn't asked me.

She glanced toward the kitchen and lowered her voice. "Ghislain refuses to see the truth. He thinks I will recover." A Gallic shrug, followed immediately by a harsh, dry cough. "He is wrong. I am not long for this world. My son needs a woman in his life, and he has chosen you."

"She was dying." I kept my voice flat. "She wanted her son happily married before she passed."

We exchanged vows three days later—in her hospital room. No time to wait for my parents. Not when she'd run out of time.

"Except she wasn't dying." I stared at the ceiling. "It was a ploy to trap the naïve American heiress before her parents could intervene."

The room was silent.

"Of course, I didn't know they'd trapped me. I called home. My father arrived two days later with his checkbook." I swiped at my eyes. "They negotiated. How much to give my daughter an annulment?" I swallowed past the lump in my throat. "Twenty thousand dollars."

The price to break my heart—to break me.

"He was a con man," Hunter said flatly.

Ellison cut him a look but held her tongue.

I *appreciated* the lack of pity in Hunter's voice. "Not entirely. He really was a count. Just broke. Not two francs to rub together."

He made a note. "What happened after your father paid him off?"

"Father sent me to a convent. The idea was to finish the semester there." I sank deeper into my chair, wishing it would swallow me whole. "I'd only been there a few weeks when I got a call. My father's heart gave out. I flew home." I'd sat by his bedside, knowing how deeply I'd disappointed him, and cried my apology.

Too little, too late.

He died.

My mother never said she blamed me. She didn't have to.

"I haven't seen Ghislain since my father handed him that check." The shock, the deep sense of betrayal, the shame—they were old wounds, but the scars remained. Self-doubt, guilt, and rage—so much rage. They all lingered.

Ellison knelt next to my chair and gazed at me with eyes that said she understood—all of it: my feelings, my silence, my secrets.

I glanced away, looking out the window. I couldn't see the patio from here, but I knew Ghislain was out there—ready to upend my life a second time.

CHAPTER TWO

S omeone tapped on the study door, and Ellison called, "Come in."

Anarchy pushed open the door and froze when he spotted Hunter seated in his chair.

Hunter stood, immediately stepping out from behind the desk as if he'd been caught doing something wrong.

"Problem?" Anarchy's gaze traveled between the lawyer and his wife.

Ellison smiled brightly. So brightly she might as well have pointed a cartoon arrow at me. "Libba retained Hunter."

Anarchy rubbed his palm across his chin. "Did she?"

"I know—knew—the man on your patio."

Everything about him sharpened. His gaze. His stance. His expression. "How? Who is he?"

"Ghislain de Fevre."

"Ex-boyfriend?"

"Something like that."

Anarchy's gaze could cut glass. "Are you sure?"

"Pretty sure." There was a time when I'd regularly daydreamed about staring down at Ghislain's lifeless body. That first year home, every memory had rankled. Even the little ones. He'd called me, "ma puce." Of all the endearments available—mon amour, ma belle, ma chérie—he'd chosen to call me his flea. That should have been my first warning. Not that I'd paid a bit of attention to any of the warning signals. Too young. Too naïve. Too in love.

"Do you need a closer look?"

If I'd spilled my secrets over a case of mistaken identity... That would be awful. Of course, being right wasn't any better. "It can't hurt."

I followed Anarchy through the kitchen and out onto the patio, where police officers side-eyed me before they stepped aside.

Ellison's patio was dotted with wrought-iron furniture, colorful cushions, and pots overflowing with geraniums. I'd sat out here countless times, sipping martinis, trading gossip, commiserating about Henry, her dead husband.

We stopped by the body, and a breeze brushed across skin suddenly pulled taut. I didn't need Hunter, or Ellison, or Frances to tell me this situation might go poorly. The anticipatory prickle of a hungry guillotine whispered across my neck.

I recognized the dark hair worn slightly too long, the bump on his patrician nose, and the tiny scar on his hairline.

The breeze blew a handful of white petals into the pool of blood, and I averted my gaze. "It's him."

"What can you tell us about him?"

"As I said, his name is Ghislain de Fevre. He's French." I couldn't help but look at the body—a knife protruded from his ribs.

"Any idea why he'd be in Kansas City?"

"None."

"Why did you call Hunter?"

"Because your mother-in-law told me to." I met Anarchy's gaze, daring him to find fault with that logic.

His lips twitched, almost as if he were battling a smile. "Why did Frances think you needed a lawyer?"

"You'd have to ask her."

He tipped his chin. "I'll do that. What else can you tell me about him?"

"Not much. It's been decades."

"Next of kin?"

"A mother. Not sure if she's still alive."

"We found a room key for the Alameda."

The Alameda was the newest hotel on the Country Club Plaza, and rooms didn't come cheap. Ghislain must have found himself another heiress. My gaze strayed to his bare left hand.

"How did you know him, Libba?"

"We met when I spent part of my junior year in France. Haven't seen him since."

I'd imagined Ghislain coming to Kansas City and explaining why he'd done what he had. Those musings always ended up the same way—he begged for forgiveness, and I told him to go to hell. Silly, really. Ghislain wasn't the type of man who'd apologize. And I wasn't the kind of woman who'd forgive him.

"Would he come to see you? Because Ellison and I have never laid eyes on him, and you live next door. It makes sense that he approached the wrong house."

At a loss for words, I shrugged and asked, "How long has he been out here?"

"We let the dogs out at ten."

"Where are the dogs?"

"Locked in a guest bedroom."

"Max won't like that." Max, their Weimaraner, was the smartest dog I'd ever met. And when he was unhappy (locked in a room), he used that intelligence for evil. Their other dog, an Airedale, was as dumb as a box of rocks, and he'd follow Max's lead. When Ellison and Anarchy opened that door, they'd find a shredded bedspread, feathers from the pillows the dogs destroyed covering every surface, and chew marks on the furniture.

"Ellison's been wanting to redecorate."

I chuckled as I nodded toward the body. "What time did she find him?"

"Six. Can you account for your whereabouts last night?"

"I was at Charlie's."

"With Charlie?"

"Mostly. He got home from the hospital around midnight."

Anarchy grimaced. "Don't answer any more questions without Hunter present."

Anarchy's advice hung in the humid air, the implication clear. I was a suspect. Already. And Anarchy didn't even know the details. My heart sank to my espadrilles.

"Libba!"

We both turned toward the kitchen door where Ellison stood.

"Come on. I'm taking you out for breakfast."

"I'm not hungry." How could I be? There was a corpse at my feet.

"Then we'll shop."

"I don't need anything."

"When has that ever stopped you?" She wasn't wrong.

"I—"

"No excuses." Her eyes gleamed with steely resolve. "We're going."

"It's best not to argue when she takes that tone," Anarchy observed.

She'd hate me for saying so, but it was a tone very similar to the one Frances used—used to use—when she bullied her daughter into chairing a gala, attending a luncheon, or attending Sunday dinner. Ellison had finally mastered a simple, two-letter word—no—and Frances had been forced to change tactics.

With a last glance at Ghislain, I headed into the kitchen where Ellison waited.

"It's him?" she whispered.

I nodded.

"I was thinking Putsch's Café for breakfast, but you look like you need a drink."

"I wouldn't say no to a Bloody Mary." Or three. "I should grab my handbag and tell Charlie where I'm going." I had to tell him more than that. I had to tell him about Ghislain. The mere thought made me groan.

"Charlie took Pansy for a walk. I saw him leave a few minutes ago."

I frowned. Charlie seldom walked Pansy. He paid a neighborhood girl to do it. Twice around Loose Park for two dollars.

But I'd gladly take the reprieve.

Revealing my most humiliating secret hadn't factored into my plan for the day. I needed time to frame this mess—my failed marriage—correctly. *Darling, I have an ex-husband. He married me for my money, and my father paid him to divorce me. At any rate, he was murdered in Ellison's backyard.* Blunt. Shocking. Potentially engagement-ending. *Also, I'm a suspect in his murder.*

Poor Ellison, how did she deal with this on an almost weekly basis?

"Come on." She grabbed my wrist and tugged. "Let's fetch your handbag before you get stuck making long explanations." Having a best friend who gleaned my reluctance to share the most humiliating thing that ever happened to me was a gift beyond measure.

I'd kept this secret for decades. Waiting a few more hours to tell Charlie wouldn't hurt.

Minutes later, we were in Ellison's car on our way to the Country Club Plaza.

"Vodka or shopping?" she asked.

I glanced at my watch. Barely ten. Early for a drink—even

by my standards. Also, if I started drinking, I wasn't sure I'd stop. "Shopping." The responsible choice.

"Shall we start at Swanson's?"

To my mind, Swanson's was the best store in Kansas City. Beautiful handbags and shoes. Gorgeous clothes. Saleswomen who kept diaries about their clients' likes and dislikes. "Where else?"

Ellison pulled into the parking lot and found a spot near the store's glass double doors. "Do you want to talk about it?"

It. Did she mean my marriage or the murder? Either way, the answer was no. "I'd rather have a root canal."

She barked a laugh and exited the car. I followed her. Together, we entered the store.

"What are we shopping for?" Her face lit with enthusiasm. Ellison was a world-class shopper.

"Let's start with shoes."

She nodded as if I'd said something wise, and we headed to the shoe department.

My steps slowed. "Is that Martha DuPuy?" The Dupuys were Charlie's other next-door neighbors. Martha and her husband Linus were...contentious. They let their dog wander the neighborhood, then complained about Pansy. In June, Martha had tripped on a crack in the sidewalk in front of the Tysons' house and threatened to sue them. It didn't help that Linus was a litigation attorney. And arrogant? The man thought the sun rose and set just for him. Martha agreed.

"Let's go upstairs and—"

"Ellison!" Martha had spotted us. "What is happening at your house?"

"Aggie made donuts." The words slipped through my lips, and I suppressed a wince.

Martha's already sour expression tightened. "I believe I'm owed an explanation."

Owed?

"It's an ongoing investigation, Martha. I'm afraid I can't comment." Ellison wasn't bound to silence like her husband. But Martha didn't need to know that.

"Did you find another body?"

"Not at liberty to comment."

Martha stood, nearly upending the salesperson who knelt at her feet. "That's as good as a yes."

"Think what you like, Martha." Ellison's calm in the face of Martha's ire was impressive. Then again, she'd grown up with Frances. Dealing with Martha was probably akin to swatting at a mosquito when she was used to fending off an Andean condor.

"We should sue."

My hands clenched. "Over what?"

"Eventually, all these corpses are going to affect property values."

Ellison laughed softly. "Good luck with your suit, Martha." Not a mosquito, a gnat. "Libba, there's a dress I've been considering upstairs. I'd love your opinion." She turned on her heel, leaving Martha speechless.

I offered up an acid smile. "Lovely to see you, Martha." Then, I followed my best friend.

I caught up with her on the escalator. "Is there a dress?"

"There's always a dress. Let's buy it and find a Bloody Mary."

We perused separately, but Ellison joined me as I considered a Rive Gauche pantsuit. "You should buy it."

As if I needed encouragement.

Esme, our usual saleswoman, rang up our purchases, and I checked my watch. "It's eleven."

"So?"

"Nabil's is open for lunch." And Bloody Marys.

Ten minutes later, we were seated at a table in the corner. The restaurant was intimate and popular (probably due to its chicken in lemon and caper sauce and dim lighting).

"You were married." Ellison swirled her Bloody.

"For less than a week."

Her eyes crinkled with concern. "How?"

"He swept me off my feet. This handsome, older French count, surrounded by sophisticated friends and wrapped in centuries of privilege. He wanted me. At least I thought he did. He was irresistible, right up until I discovered he only wanted my money." I tried for a self-deprecating laugh, but it came out flat.

"How did he know you were rich?"

"My father investigated that. Ghislain had a friend at the school I attended who provided him with a list of the well-to-do girls."

"He targeted you."

I took a healthy sip of Bloody Mary and shrugged. "I was the second girl on the list. The first one shot him down." Which somehow made everything worse.

"You never said a word."

"I was embarrassed. Humiliated. A trusting, lovesick idiot. And then my father..."

Ellison waved at the waiter, ordering a second round.

When the fresh drinks arrived, she asked, "So, who would want him dead?"

"Maybe he tricked another heiress."

"Which doesn't explain why he was in my backyard."

I pushed a strand of hair away from my face. "I have no idea."

"Tell me about him."

"Like I said, charming, aristocratic, connected." I winced at that.

"There. What was that?"

"His friends. We'd go to dinner with his friends. None of them realized I was fluent in French. They saw a silly American, and they weren't shy about mocking me. The worst was Ghislain's best friend. Pierre de Chabot." He'd called me a bêtise—foolish, nonsensical, inconsequential. And, because I'd lied about my fluency, I'd had to pretend I didn't understand.

"Another count?"

"A marquis, that's the level above a count. He had the most unusual blue eyes I've ever seen and a permanent sneer."

"Tall?"

I nodded.

"Dark?"

"Yes."

"Handsome."

"If you like aristocratic Frenchmen."

"Those eyes? Light blue with a dark rim?"

I stared at her over the rim of my glass. "How did you know?"

"Because he's sitting two tables over."

CHAPTER THREE

With courage born of drinking two Bloody Marys on an empty stomach, I rose from my chair.

"Libba?" Ellison's voice stopped me—for a half-second.

I offered her a grim smile and approached Pierre. "What are you doing here?"

He looked at me with the same superior sneer he'd always worn.

The urge to grab his water glass and dash its contents in his smug face was overwhelming. I clenched my hands and bit my tongue. I would not fill the silence. I'd asked a question; he could damn well answer it.

Seconds passed before he shrugged—a Gallic shrug, of course. "I decided to visit America."

"The country you described as a cultural wasteland? Filled with people too loud and too ignorant to ever understand la politesse?"

"Why not?"

I sensed Ellison beside me, but I kept my gaze fixed on Pierre. Smart women didn't look away from predators. "And rather than New York or San Francisco or Los Angeles, you came to Kansas City?"

"I find it charming."

I ground my teeth. "And Ghislain?"

A shadow passed over his eyes. "You've spoken?"

"We have not."

"He has a matter to discuss with you."

"Quite impossible."

"He will insist."

No, he would not. "It's been twenty years, what could he possibly have to say to me?"

"I will leave that to him."

"Ellison, please call Anarchy and ask him to join us."

Without hesitating, she hurried to the maître d's station, picked up the receiver, and dialed.

"Anarchy?" Pierre's eyebrows rose.

"My friend's husband."

We eyed each other with dislike.

"How long have you been in Kansas City?"

"Since yesterday." His gaze shifted to my left hand, where my engagement glittered brightly. "You are married?"

"Engaged."

His answering smile sent a shiver down my spine. "A lucky man."

"Really? You don't think he's saddled himself with a bêtise?"

He blinked. Twice.

"I've been fluent in French since I was ten. I understood every cut, every insult."

He steepled his long fingers, and his signet ring caught the light. "You understood, and you still married him."

"Ghislain never insulted me."

"He never defended you."

I hated that Pierre was right. Yet another warning that I'd blissfully ignored.

"He'll be here in ten minutes." Ellison stood immediately behind me.

"You're not going to introduce us?" Pierre's voice was mocking.

"Ellison Jones, meet Pierre de Chabot." I purposefully omitted his title.

He stood; a courtesy he'd not extended to me. "Charmed."

"Likewise." She couldn't have sounded less charmed.

"Have you known Libba for long?"

"She's my oldest friend."

He steepled his fingers. "Then she told you about me?"

"Why would she do that?"

Something ugly flickered in his eyes. "I'm her husband's oldest friend."

"Her ex-husband," I corrected.

Again, a shadow passed over his eyes. "Of course."

That flicker. I was missing something. And whatever it was, it was bad.

"Please." He waved at his table. "Join me."

If it meant keeping him here until Anarchy arrived.

I pulled out a chair.

Ellison claimed the one next to mine and nodded to the waiter.

He shifted our drinks from one table to the other, and I downed the last sip in the glass before tapping the rim.

He nodded his understanding.

"A bit early in the day, n'est pas?"

My shoulders stiffened at his judgmental tone. "It's been an eventful day."

"Oh?"

I didn't care for his smirk.

I'd be the one smirking when Anarchy took him in for questioning.

"What are your plans while you're in Kansas City, Pierre?" At least Ellison was trying to make polite conversation.

"No plans," he replied.

"Our art museum is fabulous."

His customary sneer deepened. "I live in Paris." As if all things French were intrinsically better.

This awful man had been Ghislain's best friend. That alone should have served as a warning. "The Louvre doesn't have an exclusive on good art."

"I'm sure your little museum has an impressive collection of American art, but the Louvre is the Louvre."

Ellison shrugged. I loved her for it.

His lips thinned. "The Louvre has the *Mona Lisa.*"

She scoffed. "Famous for being stolen."

"It's still a da Vinci."

She opened her mouth, and I anticipated her scathing retort. For all his sophistication, Pierre was remarkably uncultured. She'd eviscerate him.

"Ellison. Libba."

I glanced up at our friend Jinx.

Great. Just great. Jinx was the biggest gossip in Kansas City. To her credit, she didn't repeat a story unless it was true. Unfortunately, my story was true. I'd been married and kept it a secret for twenty years. She'd dine out on that for weeks.

Pierre stood.

Again.

For any woman but me.

Then he extended his hand. "Pierre de Chabot."

Jinx giggled. "I adore your accent. You're French?"

"Very."

She tore her gaze away from the handsome Frenchman and looked at Ellison and me, obviously expecting an explanation.

Not that I'd give her one. If I could get through this day without the whole town knowing how foolish I'd been, I'd come clean with Charlie. He deserved to hear all of this from me.

"Would you care to join us?" Pierre asked.

"I can't." Jinx's regret was tangible. "I'm meeting a friend for lunch. In fact, she's already seated." She nodded toward a table on the opposite side of the restaurant, where an older woman in a sharp suit waited. She had cat-eye glasses perched on her nose, and she frowned as she perused the menu. "A pleasure to meet you, Monsieur de Chabot."

"The pleasure was all mine."

Jinx tittered and, with a lingering glance, left us.

"Another old friend?"

"Yes." Where was Anarchy?

Pierre resumed his seat.

I glanced at Jinx. She and her friend were gazing at us with avid interest.

"Are you staying on the Plaza? The Alameda is quite lovely." Anarchy must have told her about the key in Ghislain's pocket.

Pierre sniffed. "If one likes a Spanish influence."

He really was insufferable. "You'd prefer French?"

"Bien sûr."

My gaze traveled to the entrance. Was that Anarchy? Finally?

Ellison's husband made his way to the table. I took in his chilly smile and was grateful he was on my side.

"You must be the famous Anarchy." Pierre sounded snide.

"Guilty. Although famous is a stretch. You must be Mr. Chabot." A "chu" instead of a "shu." Had Ellison failed to mention his title or had Anarchy ignored it?

Annoyance flashed across Pierre's face. He'd been denied his title *and* that stuffy little de before Chabot, and Anarchy had mispronounced his name.

I couldn't help but grin.

"What brings you to Kansas City?"

"Why do you ask?"

"Because I'm a detective."

Pierre froze for an instant. "Do you interrogate every visitor?"

"Only those associated with Ghislain de Fevre."

"And why is that?"

"Because he was murdered."

Pierre's face went slack, and he swayed in his chair.

Anarchy watched him intently.

Pierre reached for his water glass and took a drink. "Sophie?"

"Who's Sophie?"

I knew. Even as Ghislain wooed me, Sophie Clemenceau was there. Pretty. Witty. And when she looked at me, her eyes filled with disdain. She'd had a thing for Ghislain. At first, I'd worried he had a thing for her, too. But he'd convinced me otherwise.

Because I loved him, I ignored their lingering glances, the way they stood too close together, their private jokes.

Also, Ghislain swore, with his hand pressed to his heart, that there was nothing between them.

Of course, he was telling the truth.

He had to be.

What kind of woman would stand by as her lover romanced another woman?

But Sophie knew something I didn't.

I meant nothing to him.

She was the one with an aristocratic pedigree She was rich—or she would be when her father passed.

Too bad for them that her father forbade her from marrying an impecunious count.

And Ghislain couldn't wait for her father to die.

Of course, I learned that too late.

"What did Ghislain want to discuss with me?" I asked. His answer suddenly seemed important

Pierre whispered, "Mon Dieu."

"I doubt he came all the way to Kansas City to discuss religion."

Anarchy side-eyed me and repeated his question. "Who is Sophie?"

"Sophie Clemenceau," I told him.

"She is Ghislain's fiancée." Pierre's gaze lifted from his glass to my face, as if he expected his words to wound me.

I might have been a naive girl but I'd seen the way Pierre looked at her. He couldn't be happy about this.

"Her father finally died?" Silly question. Ghislain and Sophie were too mercenary for there to be any other explanation.

Pierre nodded.

"When did you last see her?" asked Anarchy.

"Last night. After dinner last night, Ghislain said the jetlag was getting to him. He went upstairs. Sophie and I had a nightcap in the hotel bar.

Ellison and I exchanged a loaded glance. We knew where to find Ghislain, but where was Sophie?

CHAPTER FOUR

Something was wrong.

I knew it the moment I walked through the door. The house felt different—expectant somehow, as if it were holding its breath. The air was too cold, almost frigid, and I smelled… dust.

"Charlie?"

No answer, but a strange droning came from the living room. I set down my shopping bags and followed the sound.

The cleaning lady came on Wednesdays. Today was not Wednesday.

Charlie ran the Hoover over the rug with grim determination. Morticians looked happier than Charlie. Morticians, and corporate lawyers who'd just lost their biggest client, and airline pilots with faulty engines. "Charlie?"

He startled, then switched off the machine. "You're back."

"And you're...cleaning."

"Pansy's shedding."

Pansy was always shedding. It had never inspired Charlie to vacuum before.

I'd once left his dirty socks on the floor just to see how many times he'd walk over them without picking them up. Seventeen times. The man had many wonderful qualities. Domesticity was not among them.

"What's wrong?" Had he somehow heard the story without my telling him?

"Nothing's wrong." He wound the cord around the vacuum with more attention than the task required. "Can't a man clean his own home?"

"A man can. You?" I clasped my hands and studied his face. There was a tightness around his mouth that concerned me.

"Charlie?"

"What happened at Ellison's?"

I sank onto the sofa. "It's a long story."

"I have time."

Where to begin? At the beginning, I supposed. My heart skipped a few beats and I clenched my hands into fists. I'd never intended to share this story. Never. And now I didn't have a choice. "When I was a girl in Paris, I met someone. A French count." I forced myself to meet Charlie's eyes. "I married him."

I watched his face, bracing for shock, or hurt, or anger, or any of the hundred emotions a man might feel when his fiancée admits she's been hiding a failed marriage. I'd lied by omission.

What I saw was…odd. A bright flare of curiosity before he schooled his features into polite surprise. Somehow, some way, he knew. "You never told me."

"I never told anyone."

"Not even Ellison?"

"Nope. The marriage lasted less than a week. I was young and stupid, and he was after my money. My father paid him off, and I came home." The scents of café au lait and Gauloises teased my memory, and I reached for his hand. "I'm sorry. I should have told you."

"Why didn't you?"

My cheeks warmed in the cool air. "Because I was embarrassed. Because I'd spent twenty years trying to forget it happened. Because—" I looked down, unable to hold his gaze. "Because I didn't want you to look at me differently."

He squeezed my hand, but the gesture felt mechanical, almost as though he was distracted. "What does this have to do with the police at Ellison's?"

"The body on her patio." I lifted my gaze. "It's him."

The color drained from his face.

"Charlie?" I squeezed his hand. "I know this is a lot to take in. I wish I'd told you sooner."

He didn't respond. His gaze had gone somewhere far away.

I'd never felt so alone. "Charlie?"

He pulled his hand from mine and stood, walking to the window. For a long moment, he stared out at the lawn, at Ellison's house.

"He came to see me." Charlie's left hand grabbed the drapes, wrinkling the velvet. "Yesterday. At the hospital."

The words didn't make sense. "Who came to see you?"

"Your husband. He knew who I was. Knew about our engagement." Charlie turned to face me. "He said you two were still married. That the divorce was never finalized."

The room tilted. "That's not possible."

"He had documentation, Libba. Something about paperwork that was never filed in France. He said he'd make it go away—for a price."

I'd sat in the avocat's elegant office and signed papers without looking at them, my heart too pulverized to care what became of me. My father supervised, stone-faced and silent—but I knew what he was thinking. Impulsive. Foolish. His daughter couldn't be trusted to take care of herself. And I'd been right. He sent me to a convent to wait out the scandal.

And then he died.

If something had gone wrong with the filing, if there'd been a problem...

Mother and I would have missed it. We'd been drowning in grief, in estate matters, in learning to live without him. A letter from a French lawyer would have been easy to overlook. Or ignore.

"How much?" My voice came out strange, thin.

"Twenty thousand."

I closed my eyes. Twenty thousand dollars. That's what Ghislain thought I was worth—the same amount my father had paid to make him go away.

"You paid him?" Why hadn't he mentioned this earlier, before I blithely forced my way into a crime scene?

"I offered to write him a check. He declined. He wanted cash. I told him the bank was closed. I'd get him his money this morning."

Ghislain died before Charlie could get to the bank. Except... Charlie kept cash in his safe. Charlie had lied. Steady-Eddie, straight-as-an-arrow Charlie had lied. "Did you pay him?" I asked again. This time, my voice was barely a whisper.

"I told him I'd meet him by the tennis courts in Loose Park at nine-fifteen, but he didn't show."

He'd been splayed out across Ellison's patio.

"What else was I supposed to do, Libba?" His voice was quiet. "I love you. I want to marry you. And I've been through one ugly divorce—I wasn't about to let him drag you through one, too. Twenty thousand dollars to make that happen? That's not a hard decision."

I couldn't argue with his logic. "I would have paid it."

He snorted softly. "I don't give a damn about the money. I care about you."

Tears stung my eyes, and I quickly swiped at them.

"Hey." Charlie crossed the room and knelt in front of me, taking both my hands in his. "We'll figure this out."

"Thank you," I said. "For wanting to protect me."

"Always."

He pulled me close, and I let him. I blinked back another tear before lifting my gaze. "I'm a suspect in his murder. I hired Hunter."

Charlie's hold on me tightened. No man likes to hear that his fiancée stabs people in the middle of the night. "You didn't kill him."

I wished he sounded more certain. "He died between ten and six. I don't have an alibi."

"We were together."

"You didn't get home till midnight." I wiped beneath my eyes, hoping I didn't look like a raccoon. "Also, his fiancée is missing."

"His fiancée?"

"Someone else I met in Paris." Sophie had waited for Ghislain for twenty years. And rather than collecting a quick signature from me, he'd chosen extortion.

Had the twenty-thousand been the first of many demands?

Had Ghislain rubbed his hands at finding a golden goose?

Did Sophie know?

I doubted it. She was too aristocratic, too perfect, to stoop to such tactics.

But perhaps she'd grown tired of waiting. I imagined Sophie sneaking through the shadows in our backyard. In my mind's eye, she wore a Julie Newmar catsuit (but more chic), her dark hair was sleek, her lips were ruby red, and, in her hands, she clutched a dagger.

A villainess.

A convenient villainess.

The doorbell rang, unnaturally loud in the silence hanging between Charlie and me.

Pansy barked, and the sharp sound of her claws hitting the hardwood echoed from the front hall. She was racing for the door, ready to plant her paws on the visitor's shoulders.

Charlie moved back to the window and peered outside. "It's Martha DuPuy."

"We could ignore her."

He winced. "She's spotted me."

"Ugh."

"Awful woman. I'll grab Pansy." He dragged her to the kitchen, her claws scrabbling for purchase as she barked her displeasure and whined to be set free.

But I had a worse job. I had to deal with Martha.

A moment later, I opened the door wide enough for a quick chat, not wide enough to suggest that she enter our home. I even kept my hand on the knob. This exchange would be quick.

"Your dog destroyed my petunia bed." No hello. No good afternoon. Just an accusation.

"Are you sure it was Pansy?" As a rule, when Pansy ruined someone's landscaping, she also tracked mud through the house.

"Who else?" Martha's eyes narrowed as her lips thinned. "Charlie will need to reimburse me."

Poor Charlie. It was almost as if he had an "easy mark" tattooed across his forehead.

"Certainly." I kept my voice pleasant. "Just provide us with a bill for the replacement cost and proof that Pansy did it."

"My flowers are trampled."

"How can you be sure Fritz didn't trample the flowers?" Fritz was the DuPuys' standard poodle. Who gave a French dog a German name? Why not Louis, or Gaston, or Jules?

"It has to be Pansy."

"Has to be?"

"She's dug up flowerbeds all along the block."

"You just said the flowers were trampled." I tapped a nail against my bottom lip, and the little demon on my left shoulder danced a jig in anticipatory glee. "Maybe the killer trampled them."

Martha gasped.

"We should probably tell Anarchy. You won't mind a dozen officers in your backyard, will you?"

"What!"

"It is a murder investigation, Martha," I spoke slowly, as if she might have difficulty grasping the concept. "The killer might have left a clue."

"Don't you dare call the police!"

"The police?" Charlie had joined us, and, sadly, he opened the door wider.

Martha inched forward.

"The killer trampled Martha's petunias." That stopped her.

"Your dog is responsible," she snapped.

"Pansy doesn't trample, she digs." Charlie spoke with the certainty of a man who'd replaced multiple flowerbeds, at least three boxwoods, and an untold number of tomato plants.

"I should call Anarchy and tell him about this." The satisfaction I got from Martha's stricken face probably said bad things about me. But she'd come to extort Charlie for the cost of annuals at the end of the summer. It was her own fault that I held no sympathy for her now. "He'll probably want to question you and Linus."

Martha pressed a hand to her chest.

All this for a few petunias—unless I was right. Had Sophie, wearing her black Catwoman suit, crouched in Martha's petunias, watching, waiting, planning?

I laughed—the very idea was ludicrous. Sort of. Sophie as Catwoman was ridiculous. Sophie committing murder? Not ridiculous.

Anger flamed in Martha's eyes, as if she suspected I was laughing at her. "You and Ellison, you think you're so smart. She's been nothing but trouble since Henry, God rest his soul, died. *He* was a decent neighbor."

Henry, who got himself murdered by blackmailing one of

Ellison's friends, might have been a decent neighbor, but he'd been a terrible man.

Charlie sighed. "What will it cost to replace the flowers, Martha?"

"No!" I blurted. "Absolutely not."

Charlie stared at me. So did Martha.

"We are not paying for her flowers. Pansy didn't destroy them."

Charlie had a clear choice. Either he upset me, or he upset Martha. He scratched the side of his face and grimaced. "Sorry, Martha."

Smart man.

Her expression, already sour, tightened. "You'll be hearing from Linus."

"Is that a threat?" Linus was a corporate lawyer, one who (according to Jinx) had recently lost a major client. He didn't have time to litigate a flowerbed.

"Take it as you will." She spun on her heel and marched off.

CHAPTER FIVE

After our abbreviated lunch at Nabil's, Ellison and I had made plans for cocktails. The hours between Martha's departure and Ellison's arrival stretched like the last two minutes of a football game. Two minutes meant twenty. Or thirty.

I was restless. Worried. My skin felt too tight.

Charlie watched me pace, and then, without a word, retreated to his study.

I took a bath so hot my skin turned pink, then stood in my closet for twenty minutes, staring at clothes I didn't want to wear. I finally chose ivory slacks and a silk blouse. Simple. Put-together. The kind of outfit that said everything was fine. Nothing was fine.

When I came downstairs, Charlie was polishing glasses at the bar cart. He'd changed into a fresh shirt, and his hair was still damp from the shower.

"I'll make martinis." Charlie's were never strong enough. I reached for the gin, and our hands touched.

Charlie flinched. "I'll get ice."

We moved around each other like strangers—painfully polite, careful not to touch again.

"Charlie." I hovered a bottle of dry vermouth above the pitcher and swallowed a hard lump of dread. "When Anarchy asks about Ghislain—"

"I'll tell him the truth."

Which version? I wanted to ask, but the doorbell rang. And the opportunity passed me by.

Anarchy and Ellison stood on the stoop, and I accepted a nut-studded cheeseball with a smile. "Aggie?" It was a sure bet Ellison hadn't made it.

"Who else?"

She could have bought it.

I led them to the living room, where Charlie waited by the bar cart. "Ellison, what can I get you? Libba made martinis."

"That sounds lovely."

Charlie picked up a martini glass. "What about you, Anarchy?"

"Club soda." Anarchy didn't drink when he was investigating a murder.

I'd make a terrible detective—death and venality and corpses made me thirsty. For gin. Or vodka. Or, in a pinch, wine.

I waited until Charlie handed them their drinks. "Did you find Sophie?"

"Not yet." Frustration gave Anarchy's voice an edge.

"What about Pierre?"

"He voluntarily surrendered his passport." Anarchy sank onto the couch. "Libba, can you think of any reason de Fevre might visit you?"

I glanced at Charlie, took a sip of my martini, and perched on the edge of a flame-stitched wingback chair that I'd insisted Charlie buy. Ellison sat in its twin.

Anarchy's gaze sharpened. "Libba?"

I brought the glass to my lips. "We were married."

From the look of surprise on his face, Ellison hadn't told him. "When?"

"I was twenty. Foolish. Naïve." I drained half my glass. "We were divorced after a week." I glanced at Charlie. "At least I thought we were. There may have been a problem with the paperwork."

Ellison gaped at me over the rim of her still-full glass. "You've been married all these years?"

I grimaced and tried for humor. "You were best friends with a comtesse, and you didn't even know it."

My joke thudded on the floor like a lead weight.

"If your husband is dead, who inherits the title? Are you still a countess?" Trust Ellison to get to the important issues. Issues I hadn't even considered.

"I have no idea."

"How did you find out about this? This morning, you told us you were divorced."

I polished off my drink, and Charlie, God bless him, claimed my glass and poured me another.

Charlie's back was to us as he said, "He came to the hospital and demanded money."

"When?" Anarchy's voice was sharp.

"Yesterday afternoon."

"And you're just telling me?"

"I didn't know de Fevre was dead until Libba got home from lunch." Charlie handed me the martini glass.

I wrapped my fingers around the stem and then forced myself to relax. Breaking the glass wouldn't make me look any less guilty. My husband shows up after twenty years and dies at my next-door neighbor's house. It looked bad. For me. Except I hadn't known Ghislain was in Kansas City until I saw his body.

"Did you pay him?" Anarchy's fixed a gimlet stare on Charlie—fitting since he'd returned to the bar cart.

Charlie tried for a nonchalant shrug, but I didn't miss the tension in his face. "The banks were already closed. I told him he'd have to wait for his money."

"How much did he want?"

"Twenty thousand."

"He didn't adjust for inflation." The words slipped past my lips.

Anarchy frowned at me. "What does that mean?"

I lifted my chin and ignored the sudden warmth on my cheeks. "It's how much my father paid to get rid of him the first time."

Anarchy's expression softened for an instant before he returned his attention to Charlie. "What time did he come to the hospital?"

"Around five. I was doing rounds."

"How long did you talk?"

"Ten minutes. Maybe fifteen. He showed me a copy of a marriage certificate and claimed the divorce papers had never been filed. I told him I'd need further proof. He pulled out a decree, signed by Libba, but not him."

How had that happened? I thought back to the avocat's office —the overwhelming smell of tobacco and old leather, the lemon light pouring through floor-to-ceiling windows, the feel of the pen in my sweaty hand. I'd signed, and our lawyer had assured us he'd collect Ghislain's signature and file the decree with the court.

Obviously, he hadn't.

I should sue for malpractice. Although, the man who'd handled my case was probably long since dead—he'd had a Gitanes surgically attached to his lips.

"We arranged to meet this morning. I'd watch him sign the decree and give him the money. After that, my plan was to surprise Libba with a trip to France. While I was there, I would have found a lawyer to file the paperwork."

Anarchy nodded. Slowly. "You worked until midnight?"

Charlie plinked a single ice cube into an old-fashioned glass and poured himself two fingers of scotch. "No. I left the hospital around ten."

"Where did you go?"

"I went for a walk." He gazed at the amber liquid in this glass. "I needed to think."

"Did you see anyone? Talk to anyone?"

"No."

Guilt sank its talons deep into my psyche. If I'd told Charlie my history—my whole history—he wouldn't have been blindsided. Instead, he'd needed to think. He'd taken a walk. Alone. As a result, he had a strong motive and a weak alibi.

"Charlie would never hurt anyone. He spends his time helping people. Healing them." My voice was too loud. "He'd never commit murder."

Anarchy acknowledged my outburst with a tiny nod then returned his attention to Charlie. "This morning, you went to the bank?"

A wince creased Charlie's face. "Not exactly."

Anarchy's eyebrows lifted. "You decided not to pay?"

"I took the money from my safe."

"I see. Where's the money now?"

"I put it back when de Fevre didn't show."

I could almost see the wheels turning in Anarchy's head. Charlie claimed that he and Ghislain hadn't met last night. But what if he was lying? Charlie left the hospital at ten; he could have easily killed Ghislain before arriving home at midnight. Anarchy rubbed his palm against his chin. "Why didn't you—"

"Was Ghislain killed on your patio or did he just die there?" I blurted. It was a good question. One I should have asked sooner.

"There's significant damage to the hedge between our properties, almost as if de Fevre collapsed on it before dragging himself to our back door."

My heart sank.

"It appears he may have been in your backyard first."

He'd articulated my worst fear. "Pierre was in love with Sophie."

Anarchy blinked at my sudden change of topic, but if someone needed to be thrown under a bus, Pierre was my top pick. Or Sophie. I'd happily throw Sophie under a bus.

"Head over heels. But Sophie had a thing for Ghislain. A classic love triangle. Those never end well." Especially not for me.

Ellison choked on her martini.

"Why would Sophie or Pierre be in your backyard?"

"No idea." I waved away his question. "No idea why Ghislain would be here."

"Twenty thousand dollars."

I glanced at Charlie, who'd gone pale beneath his late-summer tan. "We didn't kill him."

"I'm not saying you did." Anarchy sipped his club soda. "But let's assume Ghislain came here to collect the money."

I scoffed. "Charlie told him he couldn't get it until the next day. There was no reason for him to come to our house."

"To talk to you?"

"Pigs might fly before I talked to him."

"Still, someone stabbed him. Then, with a knife buried in his side, he crossed two large yards to get to our house. Why didn't he knock on your door, Libba?"

There was no point pretending I was an altruistic woman with the ability to forgive and forget. "He knew I wouldn't lift a finger."

Anarchy frowned. "I believe you, but any other detective would assume he was escaping the person who'd stabbed him."

No forgiving. No forgetting. But that didn't mean I'd commit murder.

"If I'd stabbed Ghislain, I'd have made damned sure he was dead before I went to bed."

"Libba!" Ellison sounded exactly like her mother.

"What? It's true." I didn't add that, given the trouble he'd brought to our doors, I wished I had stabbed him. If ever a man deserved a knife to the gut, it was Ghislain de Fevre.

CHAPTER SIX

Ellison finished her drink and stood. "We should head home."

I hated to see her go. Without even trying, she offered me a lift of confidence. She'd been in trouble so many times, and each time, despite insurmountable odds, things had turned out. It gave me hope.

Anarchy rose from his chair and escorted her to the front door. His hand hovered near her lower back, and, when he glanced down at her, the expression in his eyes softened. He had it bad.

Ellison gave me a brief, tight hug. "It'll be okay," she promised. "I'll call you in the morning."

I blinked back unwelcome wetness in my eyes and closed the door behind them.

Their departure left an unnatural quiet, and Charlie and I searched for something to say to each other.

"Dinner?" he blurted. He meant where should we go, not what are you cooking. I didn't cook.

My hand lingered on the front door's handle. "The Pam Pam Room?"

His eyes narrowed. As a rule, I didn't suggest restaurants within hotels. "Wasn't your late husband staying at the Alameda?"

"Yes." I lifted my chin, daring him to argue.

Charlie raked his hands through his hair. "Anarchy will catch the murderer." Despite his assertion, there was a slight hesitation as he spoke, as if he wasn't wholly convinced. "Or Ellison. She's good at identifying killers."

True enough. Ellison caught killers. It was also true that I'd helped her. More than once. "I'm not going to sit at home and twiddle my thumbs. We're suspects." And suspicion grated. I finally understood Ellison's need to clear her name when her husband was murdered. It hadn't been for Henry's sake. It had been for her. So she could walk into the club with her head held high. So her daughter Grace wasn't hounded by whispers. So Frances gave her room to breathe. "I refuse to live under a cloud of suspicion."

"Fine." Charlie's easy capitulation surprised me. He was a man who colored within the lines, not a guy who poked around luxury hotels looking for murderers.

"Fine," I replied.

We stared at each other.

I had anticipated an argument. Now, surprise tied my tongue.

The tick of the grandfather clock amplified the silence.

Seconds passed. We stood there. Mute.

Charlie cleared his throat.

"I'll grab my purse."

He nodded, pulled his car keys from his pocket, and dangled them from his index finger.

We drove to the Alameda in charged silence. We were doing this—interfering with Anarchy's investigation. Although, I'd argue that dining at the Pam Pam Room hardly rose to the level of interference.

But the night was young.

Charlie pulled into the Alameda's circle drive.

A bellman opened my door, and a valet took the car.

Charlie claimed my hand, and we stepped into the lobby and turned right. My heels clicked too loudly against the terra-cotta tiles. And my gaze scanned the Spanish-inspired lobby.

A woman with perfect posture, dark hair, and a haughty nose lingered outside the entrance to the restaurant. She checked the delicate gold watch on her wrist and frowned.

"Marie?"

The woman turned and, when she saw me, her eyes widened. "Libba?"

"Pierre didn't mention that you'd come, too." Her brother was supremely protective. I wasn't surprised he'd tried to keep her off the police's radar.

She stepped forward, brushing an air kiss against my right cheek, then my left. Two kisses, never three. Three was plebian. And Marie was aristocratic. She was also the only one of Ghislain's French friends who'd ever been kind to me. "You have not aged a day."

I studied her face—pretty brown eyes, slightly hooked nose, and sharp cheekbones. "You're the one who hasn't aged. You still look like a girl."

We were both liars.

"Charlie, this is Marie de Chabot. Is it still de Chabot?"

She shook her head and her lips pursed into an unhappy moue. "Marie de Clermont."

"Marie, my fiancé, Charlie Ardmore."

Marie extended her hand, and Charlie froze as if he wasn't sure if he should kiss it. A few uncomfortable seconds passed before he grabbed her fingers and gave her a firm shake. "A pleasure."

The curve of Marie's lips was gentle, nothing like her brother's cruel smile. "Likewise."

Charlie grinned at her. "We're headed in for dinner. Would you care to join us?"

"For a drink. I'm dining with Pierre, but, and this comes as no surprise, he is late."

"Is Sophie joining you?" I had questions for Sophie.

Marie turned her gaze from Charlie to me and shrugged. "Sophie is…missing."

Still? Sophie wasn't the type of woman to go missing. She was supremely confident, positive that the world danced to her tune ("La Vie en Rose"—the Edith Piaf version). I'd ask for more information after we were seated. For now, I settled for requesting a table for three near the windows.

A moment later, the three of us stared at the view of the Plaza.

I waited until a waiter took our orders—gin and tonic for Charlie, martini for me, and a glass of Sancerre for Marie—before saying, "I'm sorry about Ghislain. I know you were fond of him."

Marie lifted her left eyebrow. "I should offer you condolences. He was your husband."

"In my mind, we've been divorced for twenty years."

"But you weren't. You're a widow. The Comtesse de Fevre."

"Surely the title goes to a cousin."

"Ghislain had no relatives. You inherit."

"I inherit a title. Nothing more." Ghislain wouldn't have extorted money from Charlie if he had any assets.

"There is a moldering château." She nodded her thanks to the waiter and lifted her glass. "Santé."

I did not feel like toasting a money pit but I felt obligated to raise my martini glass. "Santé."

Charlie clinked his glass against ours and drank. Deeply. "You're a countess?"

"She is," Marie confirmed.

"Where is this château?" he asked.

"The Loire Valley."

"Can I give it to the state?" That was the easiest answer.

"Bof. The French government doesn't need another château."

"Then I'll sell it."

"Ghislain's mother is rolling in her grave."

Good.

"I still don't understand how this happened. Why didn't Ghislain sign the papers twenty years ago?"

Marie winced. "I believe he reached out to your father for additional funds."

"My father died shortly after my divorce."

She pulled a face. "I'm sorry. For whatever reason, Ghislain didn't sign the papers. Then, when Ghislain and Sophie decided to marry, the papers you signed were too old to be filed. He had a new divorce decree drawn. We came to get your signature."

That made sense. Sort of. What didn't make sense was Ghislain demanding money from Charlie. How had he even known about Charlie? Had he hired an investigator? What else had he known?

The spot between my shoulder blades tingled.

"Are we ready to order?" The waiter had returned.

"Please give us a few minutes." Charlie eyed my glass. "We'll need another round."

There was a reason I adored him.

I waited until the waiter left us. "When did Sophie's father die?"

Marie's gaze turned sharp. "In February. The estate settled last month."

Our gazes caught, and we held a silent conversation. Her gaze said Ghislain hadn't been worth Sophie's twenty-year wait. My gaze agreed.

"When did de Fevre realize he needed new documents?" asked Charlie.

"Last month," Marie replied. "We planned a trip to the States."

"I don't understand why Ghislain asked Charlie for money."

Surprise flashed across Marie's face. "He asked for money?"

"Twenty-thousand dollars."

She clicked her tongue in disapproval. "Perhaps Sophie's inheritance wasn't what Ghislain was expecting."

"Where is Sophie?"

She shook her head. "I haven't seen her since dinner last night."

"Could she have killed de Fevre?" Charlie's question was shockingly blunt.

Marie's hand trembled, and she thrust her fingers into her purse (a sac à dépêches from Hermès). She withdrew a pack of cigarettes and a small gold lighter. Still trembling, she put a cigarette between her lips, handed the lighter to Charlie, and leaned forward.

Charlie lit her cigarette.

She leaned back against her chair and blew a delicate plume of smoke. "Impossible."

"Why?" I asked.

"She'd spent half her life waiting. Why kill him now?"

"Ghislain could have contacted me through a lawyer. Instead, he traveled thousands of miles. All he needed was a signature. Instead, he asked for money. Not the actions of a man who can't wait to marry the love of his life." I sipped my martini. Had Sophie murdered Ghislain? A crime of passion? Surely not. Sophie was too calculating, a woman who considered every angle. If she murdered someone, the death would be well-planned, not a knife to the ribs in a fit of pique. Then again, I hadn't seen her in twenty years. People changed. And patience had its limits.

"The grieving widow." Pierre had snuck up on us.

A retort poised on the edge of my tongue. I swallowed it, telling myself that Pierre wasn't worth the effort.

"And this must be your fiancé." He looked down his nose at Charlie.

Charlie stood and extended his hand.

For a moment, I feared Pierre wouldn't take it, but the two men shook, then Pierre's hand fell to his sister's shoulder. His long fingers wrinkled the fabric of her dress as he squeezed. "We have dinner plans."

With whom? "Sophie?"

A pained look flashed across Pierre's face. Rather than reply, he sneered at me.

"It's odd, don't you think?" I smiled sweetly. "That Ghislain was murdered, and Sophie has gone missing."

His face froze, and malice flashed in his dark eyes.

I couldn't help but wonder what he was hiding.

Marie shook off his hold and stood. "Libba, it was lovely to see you."

"I agree. Although, we hardly had a chance to catch up. Lunch tomorrow?"

Marie glanced at her brother.

He glowered. No surprise there.

"Just us." I wrinkled my nose as if I'd smelled something bad. "We'll leave the men to their own devices."

She lifted her chin, ignoring Pierre's death glare. "I'd like that."

"I'll pick you up at noon." I still had questions that needed answering.

CHAPTER SEVEN

I pulled into the Alameda's drive at five minutes to twelve.

A valet hurried to the car door, and I rolled down the driver's side window. "I'm picking up…" Was Marie a duchess, a marquise, a comtesse? "Madame de Clermont."

"Yes, ma'am." He waved me toward a spot at the curb.

I ground my teeth over the "ma'am" (it was becoming a trend) and pulled over.

I parked the car a few feet from the curb and smoothed my dress (a navy blue Diane Von Furstenberg wrap) before striding into the lobby.

Marie waited for me inside, and we exchanged les bises, careful not to leave lipstick on each other's cheeks.

"So chic." Marie waved at my dress.

"Thank you." I'd taken a solid hour deciding what to wear. "You as well."

Marie wore a simple sheath, and she'd tied an Hermès scarf around her neck. A pair of oversized sunglasses perched atop her head.

"What are you in the mood for?" I asked.

"What are my choices?"

"Mexican—although we might be overdressed for Ponak's. We could go to Annie's Santa Fe. Winstead's. Fair warning it's a burger place, so no wine list. Plaza III, Putsch's, Houlihan's Old Place?"

"You pick."

"We'll go to Houlihan's." If Pierre followed us, he'd be so appalled by the kitschy decor that he'd never make it past the front door.

Ten minutes later, we were seated in a high-backed booth with a bottle of wine chilling in a bucket stand next to the table.

I sipped and wished for something stronger. "You're married."

Marie's expression hardened. "I am."

"Children?"

A gentle smile erased the hardness. "Three. A girl, Claire, and two boys, Aristide and Oliver."

"How old?"

"Claire is sixteen. The boys are fourteen and twelve."

"Your husband?"

"Jacques."

I didn't miss the tightness around her eyes. "How long have you been married?"

"Nineteen years."

"Did I meet him?"

"No. We met after you returned to the States. When I met Jacques, I still saw la vie en rose. So hopelessly in love. So…young."

"And now?"

"I am no longer young." And, by the look on her face, no longer in love.

"We already established that neither of us have aged a day."

She laughed softly. "If only that were true. Although, the lines on my face are the price of wisdom."

I'd always thought the lines on my face were the price of too much sun and too many martinis. I kept that thought to myself. "What have you learned?"

"Another person can't make you happy, but they can make you miserable."

I pulled a face. "Your husband?"

She took another sip of her wine and lit a cigarette. "I'm hardly unique."

"Why not divorce?"

"He'd never allow it. It's better now. We lead separate lives."

"The children?"

"Spend summers with him. He takes them on fabulous trips, lets them eat Nutella crêpes for dinner, and stay up long past their bedtimes. I stay in Paris, make them go to school, and insist that they eat their vegetables."

"I'm sorry." I'd never had to be the responsible one—grasshopper—but it didn't sound like much fun.

"They adore him."

"I'm sure they adore you, too."

She shrugged. "I tried to get full custody, but Jacques is a marquis. His title is ancient. He has influence, money, and an iron will."

"Pierre couldn't help?"

"No."

Had he even tried? "I was surprised to see your brother here in the United States."

She tipped her head back and blew smoke at the ceiling. "I was surprised when he asked me to join him."

"Why didn't Ghislain have a lawyer contact me?" It would have been easy. A signature or two.

Marie tilted her head and stared at me as if I'd asked something foolish.

The light dawned. A lawyer wouldn't have extorted money from Charlie. And Ghislain had been looking for another payday.

"What has Ghislain been doing for the past twenty years?"

"He wrote a book."

"Impressive."

"It sold a hundred copies."

I couldn't hide my grin. "What else?"

"He got a job in publishing. An editor. But he was fired for making his authors cry. Then he landed a job with the government. Something to do with promoting French culture. It paid his bills and let him feel superior. If one must work, those are the two aspects one must consider."

"Not always." Charlie worked because he cared about healing people.

"Your glasses still have a rosy hue."

It was my turn to shrug.

"What have you done with your life?" she asked.

"I traveled. I dated. I played cards. I'm a surrogate aunt to my best friend's daughter. Her son, too." It sounded empty when I said it aloud. What had I accomplished? Had I made a difference? My lips pinched, a furrow settled between my eyebrows.

"What's wrong?" Marie asked.

"My best friend's mother is wearing off on me." There weren't words to adequately describe Frances or how much I did not want to be like her. "She's very comme il faut."

Marie's eyes crinkled. "And she does not approve? We can't have that. Tell me about your fiancé."

"We knew each other in high school. It's only been in the past year that we… reconnected."

"You love him. I see it in your face."

"I do."

"I hope it lasts."

"I think it will. We're well suited."

"That is no guarantee."

I would not be asking Marie to make a toast at my wedding. "What has Sophie been doing since I left Paris?"

"Waiting for her father to die."

I winced.

"That was unkind." Marie shifted her gaze to the menu. "She works for a small couture house, managing the business."

"I imagine she's good at that."

We exchanged knowing smiles. Fashion. Money. Bossing people around. It was Sophie's dream job.

"Do you work?" I asked.

"No. Jacques wouldn't like that."

"But you live separate lives."

"I'm still his marquise."

There were so many possible responses. I settled for the easy one, uttered with the healthy dose of derision. "Men."

"You're the one getting married."

"Charlie is different."

"You think you're the first woman to believe that?"

"You weren't always so cynical."

She shrugged. "I am French, and I married a man with multiple mistresses. Of course, I am cynical."

We needed a new topic. Immediately. "Tell me about the night Ghislain died."

"He was in high spirits and insisted we go to a place called The Magic Pan."

"You went to a crêperie?" Disbelief crept into my voice.

"You know Ghislain. He chose it so he could mock American attempts to mimic French food. But it was…good. He drank. We all drank. When Sophie asked him why he was in such a good mood, he told us you were engaged and would be desperate to finalize the divorce. Sophie pointed out that he should be desperate to finalize the divorce. He told her he was, but there was no reason he shouldn't make a few francs."

I clenched my hands beneath the table. "And then?"

"We returned to the hotel. I think it was around nine. Sophie and Pierre decided they wanted a nightcap. I went to my room."

"Ghislain?"

"He said he had business to attend to."

"Who do you think killed him?"

Her face tightened, and she glanced down at her hands. "A misadventure."

That was just silly. One didn't have a misadventure in Ellison's backyard. Actually, one did. It had happened at least once. Maybe twice. Possibly three times. It was hard to keep track. But I found it hard to believe that a stranger had killed Ghislain. There were three reasonable suspects. Pierre, Sophie, and the woman sitting across from me.

After lunch, we strolled the Plaza. She took in the stucco buildings, the red tiles on the roofs, the intricate iron work, and the lacy towers. "It is beautiful here."

"Thank you."

"I'm glad to see you again, Libba."

"I feel the same way."

We were admiring a Halston dress in the window at Woolf Brothers when I asked, "Did Sophie come back last night?"

Marie tilted her head as if trying to imagine herself wearing an Ultrasuede coat dress in burnt orange. "I don't know."

"You don't seem worried."

"Sophie always lands on her feet." She shook her head sharply. "I'd like to try that on."

We stepped inside Woolf, and I breathed deeply. There was something about perfumed air that eased the tension in my shoulders. Nothing bad happened in places that sold expensive scents. Woolf, Swanson's Harzfeld's—they were all stores that kept the real world and its problems at bay. It was no wonder Ellison and I loved them.

CHAPTER EIGHT

arie bought the Halston at Woolf Brothers. I found a silk blouse at Harzfeld's that would finally— finally—go with my Pucci pants. At Swanson's, we debated whether American designers had truly bested the French at the Battle of Versailles. They had. I graciously refrained from gloating.

We chatted about fashion, fine food, and the best shops in Paris. If a silence fell, one of us was quick to fill it. Better to talk of hemlines than of murder.

It was nearly five when Marie suggested a drink. "Let's go to the bar at the Alameda," she said. "I'm not ready to see our afternoon together end."

I felt the same. Despite everything—the murder, the suspicion, the years that separated us—spending the afternoon with Marie felt easy. Natural. As if no time had passed at all.

I left my bags in the car. Marie carried hers.

The bar was heavily influenced by Kansas City's relationship with its sister city, Seville. Wrought-iron chandeliers hung from dark wood beams. Octagonal terra-cotta tiles covered the floor, softened by brightly patterned rugs in deep reds, mustard yellow, and olive green. The walls were sepia—the perfect backdrop for paintings of conquistadors.

A woman sat alone at a table by the floor-to-ceiling windows, a glass of wine in front of her, untouched. She held herself rigid —marble statues had more give. She turned, and I immediately recognized her hooked nose and sharp cheekbones. The French had a term to describe women like her. Une belle laide. Not beautiful, but arresting; impossible to ignore. She was wearing something black and chic, and her figure looked infuriatingly youthful, as if the past two decades hadn't touched her.

Sophie.

Marie's breath caught, and her many shopping bags rustled in her hands. "She's back."

"I need to make a phone call." I didn't wait for a response. I turned on my heel, my heart pounding against my ribs.

The phone booths were across from the entrance to the Pam Pam Room. I fed a dime into the slot and dialed Ellison's number.

She answered on the third ring. "Jones' residence."

"It's Libba. Sophie is here. At the Alameda. In the bar."

Ellison inhaled sharply—the sound carried down the phone line. "Don't let her leave. I'll call Anarchy."

Don't let her leave? Her whole life, Sophie had done as she pleased, when she pleased. How exactly was I supposed to stop her? "I'll do my best."

I hung up, smoothed my dress, lifted my chin, and returned to the bar. Maybe, if I were lucky, Sophie would answer a few questions. If I were very lucky, she'd still be here when Anarchy arrived.

Marie had joined Sophie at the table. Two dark heads bent toward each other. Marie looked up as I approached, and a shadow flickered across her face.

Then Sophie glanced my way. "Libba." Sophie's voice was cool. Controlled. She didn't rise, didn't offer her cheek for a kiss.

A thousand sharp words danced on the tip of my tongue. I swallowed each of them and kept my expression smooth—even aloof. Sophie had always seemed so sophisticated. She still was. But I wasn't the same naïve girl she'd once known. "Sophie."

Her gaze flicked to the shopping bags piled at Marie's feet. "Marie usually shops on Boulevard Haussmann. I can't imagine what you convinced her to buy."

"Halston. Oscar de la Renta. Surely you've heard of them." Marie had gone a little crazy, as if each silk dress, each linen blouse, each pair of shoes could erase the memory of murder. I didn't envy her next credit card bill. I pulled out a chair and perched on its edge. "You've been missed."

"Have I?" One perfectly arched brow lifted. We both knew I hadn't missed her.

"Pierre has been worried." That was an assumption, but a safe one.

Sophie's lips curved into something that wasn't quite a smile. "Pierre worries too much."

A waiter appeared. I ordered a martini. I needed it.

"I hear you're engaged." Sophie's gaze swept over me. "How nice that you finally found another man willing to marry you."

I might have dated relentlessly, but I'd had fun. Sophie had wasted half her life waiting for a man who'd put her father's money above his feelings for her. A better woman might have pitied her.

I didn't.

"You look good." Her words were grudging. "Village life agrees with you." She waved her manicured hand at the Plaza, and I ground my teeth. Insulting me was one thing, insulting Kansas City was quite another.

I kept calm. "It does."

Her mouth formed a disappointed moue. I'd ignored her taunt.

The French loved diplomacy, dancing around a point for days

on end. I didn't have that kind of patience. "Where have you been? Marie's been worried." And the police were curious. I was, too.

Sophie lifted her wine glass and sipped. "Why would I tell you?"

"Sophie," Marie's voice was soft but firm. "Please."

Sophie glanced at Marie, and something passed between them. She sighed. "I needed time to think."

"About?" Marie asked.

"Ghislain." She set the glass down with a precise click. "I need to speak with him. Then Pierre." Her gaze drifted to the window, to the Plaza beyond. "I've been a fool for twenty years. Unable to see what was right in front of me."

Marie's jaw dropped.

Mine did too.

After spending half her life pining for Ghislain, Sophie had finally come to her senses? Also, she was acting as if she didn't know Ghislain was dead. And she seemed sincere. A flicker of doubt had me tightening my jaw. If she didn't know he was dead, she hadn't killed him.

Marie made a tiny, pained noise in the back of her throat and lifted her fingers to hide her gaping mouth.

Sophie looked between us. "What? What is it?"

The waiter appeared with my martini. I took a sip—I needed it—then crossed my fingers, hoping Marie would answer.

Marie shook her head, eyes wide and panicked.

I took a second, larger sip and scanned the bar for the waiter —I was going to need another martini. Sooner rather than later.

"What's wrong?" Sophie sounded more annoyed than worried.

"Sophie," I said slowly, "Ghislain is dead."

The wine glass slipped from Sophie's fingers. It didn't shatter—just tipped, sending a river of pale gold across the white tablecloth.

Sophie stared at it, unmoving. "Dead?" The word came out flat. Disbelieving. "That's not amusing, Libba."

On that, we agreed.

"He was murdered. The night before last."

Sophie's face drained of color. "But I saw him. I spoke with him. He was alive when I—" her voice faltered.

"When you what?"

Her hand rose to her throat. "Who killed him?"

"The police don't know yet," I said. "They've been looking for you."

"For me?" Her voice pitched higher. "They think I killed him?"

"No one thinks that," Marie said quickly.

I thought that. I could totally see Sophie as a cold-blooded killer. The surprise and horror she was displaying could easily be an act. What if her emotions were real? Was I letting my dislike cloud my judgment?

Sophie was quiet for a long moment. She lit a cigarette, the lighter shaking in her hand. "Ghislain told me you refused to sign the divorce papers. I was furious. I drove to your house to confront you."

"And?"

"Ghislain was there. Pacing the sidewalk in front of your house."

Her lip curled, and she blew a plume of smoke in my direction. "He told me to go back to the hotel. He had everything handled. I refused"—she shifted her gaze to the view—"there were too many things I wanted to say to you."

"What things?"

"He never loved you."

"I know."

She seemed surprised by my easy admission, her face falling as if my indifference disappointed her. She'd wanted to see my pain.

"What happened when you refused?"

"A light went on in the living room, and I told him to go get your signature. That's when he told me he was demanding money from your fiancé."

Poor Charlie. He'd been dragged into this mess because of me. When we finally got a moment alone, I would make it up to him.

"I stared at Ghislain, and it was as if I were seeing him for the first time. A con artist. A man not worthy of me."

"And then?"

"I left. I checked into another hotel. The Raphael." She picked up a napkin and began blotting the spilled wine, her movements precise and controlled. "I spent decades waiting. Twenty years of believing we would be together. And all along, he was..." She tapped her cigarette against the edge of the ashtray. "I needed time to think."

It was a weak explanation the first time she said it. It didn't get stronger with repetition.

"What time did you leave him?" I asked.

"I don't know. Ten? Ten-thirty?" Her eyes met mine. "He was alive, Libba. Pacing the sidewalk, alive."

I took another sip of my martini. Where was that waiter? Almost as important, where was Anarchy?

"The police will want to talk to you," I said.

"I didn't kill him." Sophie's voice was steady now, the initial shock fading into something harder. "I wanted to leave him, not bury him."

"Then you have nothing to worry about."

"Where did you go after you left him?" Marie asked.

"I came back here and grabbed a few things. I knocked on your door to tell you where I was going. You didn't answer."

Marie lifted one shoulder in an elegant shrug. "Jetlag. When I finally closed my eyes, I slept like the dead."

I was the same. Put me on another continent, and I needed sleep like I needed air.

I lifted my gaze from the last of my martini, and Sophie and I stared at each other across the wine-stained tablecloth.

She'd been at the scene. She'd argued with Ghislain. He died. And then she'd vanished. Everything pointed to her guilt.

But something didn't fit. Sophie was calculating. Controlled. If she'd killed Ghislain, it wouldn't be in a fit of pique. No, she'd poison him slowly.

Unless that was exactly what she wanted us to think. Maybe she'd had this planned long before they got on a plane to America.

The sound of footsteps made me turn. Anarchy strode into the bar, his expression grim.

He stopped at our table and looked down at me. "Libba. Ellison called."

"You're welcome."

The corner of his mouth twitched. "Thank you for the tip." Then he held out his hand. "Pleasure to meet you, Miss Marchand. I'm Detective Jones."

Sophie's head swiveled toward me. If looks could kill, I'd be six feet under.

Anarchy pulled out the fourth chair. "May I?" He sat before she answered. "Libba, I appreciate your help, but I can take it from here." His piercing gaze also encompassed Marie.

She didn't move. "Sophie, do you want me to stay?"

"Go," Sophie's voice was filled with ennui. She waggled her fingers at Anarchy. "This is a bêtise."

Marie hesitated, her gaze flickering between Sophie and Anarchy. "Not a bêtise, a murder." She crossed her arms over her chest. She wasn't going anywhere.

Oh, dear.

I stood, hoping she'd take the hint.

She didn't. She remained in her chair, ready to defend her friend.

Sophie offered her a small smile. "I'll be fine. Go hang up your American finery." She wrinkled her nose at the mere idea.

"You're sure?" Marie's doubt was obvious in her tone.

"I'll be fine," Sophie insisted. "I have nothing to hide."

Again, repetition did not make her more convincing.

Marie collected her bags and stood, staring at Sophie as if she might wordlessly convey the answers to Anarchy's questions. Then she turned to me, offering a smile that didn't reach her eyes. "Thank you for today."

"We should do it again before you leave."

She turned her back on me and stalked out of the bar.

I took that as a no and searched for a reason to linger.

Anarchy was already leaning toward Sophie, his voice low. I couldn't hear what he said, but Sophie's chin lifted in defiance.

I wished I could be a fly on the wall. How did Ellison make it through a day without knowing all the details? I glanced around the bar, found no way to discreetly eavesdrop, and sighed, digging in my purse for the valet ticket.

I still hadn't found it when I reached the lobby and ran smack dab into Pierre.

CHAPTER NINE

"Oomph." An apology rose to my lips and died when I recognized who I'd run into.

Pierre's eyes narrowed. "Libba." He made my name sound like something unpleasant he'd scraped off his shoe.

"Pierre." I clutched my handbag against my chest.

His gaze swept past me, toward the bar, as if he suspected I'd hidden Marie behind a barstool. "Where's my sister?"

Anarchy needed time with Sophie. I planted my feet and smiled brightly. "She went to her room. We had the most wonderful afternoon. Marie found the most divine Halston at Woolf Brothers. Burnt orange Ultrasuede—it's going to look stunning on her."

He stepped to the left as if he meant to go around me, as if he doubted my word.

I moved with him. "And a few things at Swanson's. Oscar de la Renta, I think. Your sister has excellent taste."

"She does." He shifted right.

I shifted with him. "Of course, Harzfeld's had some lovely pieces as well. I found a silk blouse that will finally go with my Pucci pants. You know how hard it is to find exactly the right—"

"Excuse me." His patience had evaporated. He tried to pass me.

How long had it been? Four minutes? Five? Anarchy needed more time. "Have the police spoken to you again? About Ghislain?"

Pierre flinched.

"Anarchy, the detective who's investigating, has an impressive clearance rate. He's married to my best friend. But you knew that. Ellison and I have been inseparable since we were girls." I lowered my voice. "She finds bodies. Often. That's why she wasn't traumatized over Ghislain." That sounded cold. "Not that she's heartless, it's just when one finds bodies like most people find pennies, one becomes inured to horror."

"Enough." He grabbed my arm and moved me aside as if I were a piece of furniture.

I stumbled but caught myself. Rude. Insufferably rude. But I'd bought Anarchy a few extra minutes.

Pierre strode into the bar, and I followed, my heels clicking against the terra-cotta tiles.

He saw her and stopped dead. "Sophie." His voice was raw.

Her head turned, and something flickered across her face—relief? Surprise? It vanished too quickly to read.

Pierre crossed the room, weaving between tables. For a man who cared about appearances, his rush to get to Sophie was jerky, uncoordinated, gauche.

I followed. Anarchy had told me to leave. But I wasn't missing this reunion. Not for anything.

Pierre pulled Sophie to her feet. He crushed her against his chest, one hand cradling the back of her neck, the other pressed flat against her spine. His eyes squeezed shut, and his lips moved against her hair—words too soft to hear.

Sophie stood stiff in his arms, her hands hovering at her sides. Then, slowly, her fingers curled into the fabric of his shirt.

I hadn't been able to read his lips, but I read Sophie's. "Je suis désolée."

What exactly was she sorry for?

Anarchy watched them, his expression unreadable.

Pierre pulled back just far enough to look at her. "Where have you been?"

"I needed time to think."

Again with the time to think. Ghislain had been an ass. Pierre still was. No extra thinking needed.

"About?" Pierre's voice was sharper than a knife's edge.

"The future." Sophie dropped her forehead to Pierre's chest and inhaled audibly, as if she were breathing in his cologne. Her arms circled his waist. If it were anyone but the two of them, I might have found the way they held each other romantic.

The hand at Sophie's back flexed. "And?"

She lifted her head, and her gaze flickered between Pierre and Anarchy. "This isn't the time."

"Don't." Pierre's voice broke. His hand at her back tightened to a fist. "Don't offer me hope if you don't mean it."

If he hadn't been such a complete ass, I might have felt sorry for him. He'd carried a torch forever, and finally—finally—the woman he wanted saw him. Wanted him. Looked at him with real emotion. Too bad she was probably a murderer.

The possible killer offered Pierre a small smile. "I mean it."

Two days ago, she was planning on marrying Ghislain. One would think she'd at least pretend grief. Instead, like a rat fleeing a sinking ship, she'd switched men. Not that I blamed her for dumping Ghislain. Although I might blame her if she'd killed him. Also, she hadn't exactly traded up.

"Please, don't ever leave like that again."

Her fingers grazed the rigid lines of his jaw. "I won't. I promise."

Pierre leaned into her touch. "I thought I'd lost you."

She opened her mouth as if an excuse was poised on the tip of her tongue.

If she said she needed time to think, I was going to punch her in the nose. I wasn't a violent woman, but Sophie was asking for it.

Fortunately, she remained silent.

"I've been so worried." Pierre tucked a strand of hair behind her ear. "Where did you go after we left the bar? It was late."

"How late?" Anarchy asked.

"Nearly eleven," Pierre replied.

Sophie's eyes widened, and she swallowed. Hard.

My gaze bounced between the two of them. Sophie, who hadn't seemed overly upset to learn the man she'd waited on for twenty years was dead, and Pierre, the man with an excellent motive for murder. One of them was lying. One of them had probably killed Ghislain. But which one?

Sophie's words came in a rush. "You're mistaken, chéri. We went upstairs just before ten."

Pierre tilted his head, studying the taut lines of Sophie's face. He raked a hand through his dark hair and nodded. "My mistake. It was ten o'clock."

"Interesting." The words slipped out before I could stop them. Not that I wanted to.

Anarchy quirked a brow and bit his lower lip as if he were hiding a smile. "Care to share, Libba?"

Yes. Yes, I did. "The way Pierre just changed the time is interesting. He said eleven, and he sounded certain. Not fifteen minutes ago, Sophie told me she saw Ghislain on my sidewalk around ten-thirty."

Sophie regarded me with eyes as dark and bitter as an open grave. "Pute."

I'd been called worse.

Anarchy ignored the slur, but his brown eyes glinted, and I

was glad his gaze wasn't fixed on me. "You were with Mr. de Fevre the night he died?"

"Briefly." Sophie's voice was icy. "I went to confront Libba about her refusal to sign the divorce papers. Ghislain was there, and I learned the problem wasn't her. It was him. We argued." The light pouring through the window illuminated one side of her face. The other was cast in shadow. It was nearly impossible to read her expression. "I left him in front of Libba's house. Alive."

The clench of her hands and the harsh set of her shoulders made me doubt her.

Anarchy rubbed his chin. "What time was this?"

"As Libba said, ten-thirty." She shot me another venomous look. "If I'd known you kept company with flics, I would have kept quiet."

"Fleeks?" Anarchy asked.

"'Cops' in French," I explained. I didn't add that it wasn't exactly complimentary. Nor did I grin at Sophie. But I really wanted to.

Anarchy gave his chin a second rub. "Miss Clemenceau, we should continue this discussion at the station."

"No!" Pierre barked. "I did it. I killed Ghislain."

I jerked my gaze toward him. His eyes were wide. His expression was tortured. The absolute certainty that he hadn't killed Ghislain settled on my shoulders, heavy as a wool coat on a summer's day. Pierre had admitted to murder. For Sophie.

A lie like that might send him to prison for the rest of his life.

Sophie wasn't worth a single night behind bars.

CHAPTER TEN

Ellison must have seen me arrive home, because ten minutes later she showed up with a pitcher of martinis. "Tell me everything."

I eyed the pitcher and forced a grateful smile. Ellison always used too much vermouth. But beggars couldn't be choosers, and I was positively parched.

We settled on the smaller patio, the one that didn't have a view of crime scene tape, and I took a moment to breathe. A light breeze carried the scent of grilling meat. Children laughed in a nearby yard. A handful of fluffy white clouds drifted across the deepening sky.

I stretched out my legs, rolled my shoulders until something popped, tasted the decidedly wet martini, and told Ellison about Sophie's reappearance. "Either she's an Oscar-quality actress, or she didn't know Ghislain was dead. That said, her reaction was…off. I saw shock, but not grief." Which gave me pause. "Surely if she'd killed him, she would have faked grief."

Ellison shrugged. "People do odd things."

I couldn't argue that. "She claims she finally realized that Ghislain was a waste of her time."

"Just like that?"

"She wasn't too happy that he'd lied to her."

"Then what?"

"Pierre arrived. They gazed into each other's eyes like lovesick teenagers." I took a tiny sip of my drink. "He lied for her. Heck, he confessed to murder for her."

"No!" Ellison's eyes were saucers. "How romantic."

"He might be the killer." It was my dislike talking. Not that I liked Sophie any better. In a perfect world, Anarchy would arrest them both, lock them in jail, and throw away the key. I sighed. "You should have seen his face when Anarchy said he was taking her to the station—the panic, the horror."

"He's protecting Sophie." She pressed a hand to her heart.

This wasn't a romance; it was a murder. I swirled my martini and wished for less vermouth and more gin. "He's loved her for twenty years. And now that Ghislain's conveniently dead, she's finally chosen him. He's not about to let her go to prison."

"Such a grand gesture."

I snorted. "Love makes people do stupid things." But was it love, or was it just wanting a woman he couldn't have? Now that she'd chosen him, would he continue to want her?

Ellison held up the martini pitcher in a silent offer.

I wondered if there was a way to add more gin without her noticing. Sadly, no.

"Did Anarchy say anything when you left?" she asked.

I lifted my left eyebrow. Anarchy hardly shared details about his cases with her. He wasn't about to tell me anything. "He took them both to the station. I imagine he's picking apart their stories as we speak."

A proud smile curled her lips. "He's good at that."

I sipped my drink. Had she used a whole bottle of vermouth? I could barely taste the gin.

"What if it were someone else?"

I frowned. "Who? I didn't kill him. Neither did Charlie."

"Marie?"

I shook my head. "She was kind to me in Paris. The only one who was."

"Kindness doesn't mean she's not a killer."

"What's her motive?"

"Love, money, sex?"

"She wasn't in love with him. She didn't benefit from his death. And Sophie would have killed her if she had sex with him."

Ellison frowned. "So we're back to Sophie and Pierre. Did Sophie know about the extortion?"

"She found out the night Ghislain died. She says that's the moment the scales fell from her eyes."

Ellison tucked her feet beneath her. "If it were me, I'd be furious. She'd waited all that time, and his greed made her wait even longer."

"You make a good point, but it's Pierre who confessed."

"To protect her."

"Or he did it." We were talking in circles. "He's loved Sophie for twenty years. With Ghislain dead, Pierre finally gets what he wants."

Ellison was quiet for a moment. A squirrel chittered in a nearby tree, and a woman's voice called the children inside. "So either Sophie killed Ghislain in a fit of rage, or Pierre killed him to have Sophie for himself."

"Either one is possible."

"Walk me through the timeline. From the beginning."

I took a sip of my martini. "Ghislain approached Charlie at the hospital around five. That night, they had dinner at The Magic Pan—Ghislain, Sophie, Pierre, and Marie. Marie says Ghislain was in high spirits. Now I know why." I couldn't keep the bitterness out of my voice. "They got back to the hotel around nine. Marie went to her room. Sophie and Pierre had a nightcap in the bar. Ghislain said he had business to attend to."

"The business was obviously extortion." Ellison tucked a strand of hair behind her ear. "What time did Charlie leave the hospital?"

"Ten." I swirled what was left in my glass. "He says he went for a walk. To think. He got home around midnight."

"Two hours is a long walk."

"I know." I sounded defensive.

"What about Sophie and Pierre?"

"Sophie says she and Pierre went upstairs just before ten. But Pierre said it was nearly eleven."

"One of them lied."

I nodded. "Sophie corrected Pierre, and he changed the time. Quickly." I set down my glass. "She claims she left Pierre and came to confront me about the divorce papers. She found Ghislain pacing the sidewalk in front of my house. They argued. She says she left him there—alive—around ten-thirty."

"And then?"

"She went back to the Alameda, gathered her things, and checked into the Raphael. She needed time to"—I raised my free hand and made air quotes—"think."

Ellison frowned. "So between ten and ten-thirty, Sophie was with Ghislain. But where was Pierre?"

"That's the question, isn't it? He claims they were together until eleven. She says they parted before ten."

"Someone is lying." Ellison tucked a strand of hair behind her ear.

"All we know for sure is that someone stabbed Ghislain in my backyard." I swallowed. "Maybe feet from where we're sitting. Then he dragged himself to your patio. And died."

"Why would Ghislain come to your house at all? Charlie told him to wait until morning."

"When I knew Ghislain, he was...calculating, but also impetuous. I wonder if he didn't come to our house to ask for more. Twenty thousand is worth a lot less now than when my father first paid him off."

Before Ellison could answer, a shrill voice cut through the evening air.

"Libba!"

I closed my eyes. Maybe if I ignored her, she'd go away.

"I can see you."

She wasn't going away.

Martha DuPuy pushed through the hedge that separated our houses. She was a tall woman. And boxy. Almost mannish. She wore her gray hair in a pageboy. A pageboy that had frizzed in the late-summer heat. Her eyes blazed in her squarish face, and she waved gardening shears at me as if they were a weapon. "Your dog," she spat, "has destroyed my borders. Again."

"Good evening, Martha." I kept my voice pleasant, pretending she didn't intimidate me. There was something impressive about a woman who regularly voiced her rage. Good for her. More women should voice their fury. Too bad she was directing her ire at me. "Lovely to see you."

"Don't you 'lovely' me. That beast ripped through my ornamental kale as if she were trying to make a salad."

Ellison snorted. She wasn't helping.

"I'm sorry to hear that. Charlie and I will pay to replace them."

"That's not good enough."

Ellison raised her glass to her lips, hiding what I suspected was a smile.

"I've had it." Martha was seething. "The stress caused by that dog has taken years off my life. I'm suing for emotional distress."

Emotional distress? If she wanted to talk about emotional

distress, I had her beat. My ex-husband, who wasn't my ex, had been murdered. And, as far as I knew, I was still on the suspect list. Just the thought had my stomach tightening into a painful knot. Also, I'd had to deal with two people who deeply disliked me. It didn't matter if the feeling was mutual; dealing with antipathy left me wrung out and…angry. Finally, Ellison made a lousy martini, and I longed for a good one. A touch of my own well-deserved rage gave me courage. "Fortunately, I already have a lawyer on retainer. I'll be sure and tell him about the emotional distress that comes from living next door to a woman who complains about absolutely everything."

Ellison choked on her martini.

Martha's face went purple. She stepped closer, shaking her shears in our faces. "You think this is funny?"

Compared to murder, Pansy destroying Martha's damn kale was funny. "A man was killed. I think your kale is a minor annoyance. If you had an ounce of empathy, you'd hand me a receipt and go home."

She sneered, leaning over me until the shears were mere inches from my nose. Their sharp tips glinted threateningly, and I drew a ragged breath, taking in the scents of metal and fresh-cut greenery.

My heart skipped a beat.

"Don't pretend you're grieving. You're just a boozehound who's using a murder as an excuse to drink."

I might have argued, but I didn't like the wild expression in her muddy brown eyes. She was furious. So furious she might lose control. I held up my hands. "Let's calm down. It's just ornamental cabbage."

"Martha, lower those shears." Ellison sounded like her husband. Calm, collected, in charge.

The shears inched closer, and my eyes crossed watching them.

"Martha!" Ellison barked. "Have you lost your mind?"

Martha lowered the shears and retreated a step.

I drew a deep breath.

"This isn't over." Martha waved her shears like a conductor's baton. "Next time that dog sets foot in my yard, I'm calling animal control." She spun on her heel and marched away.

"Martha," Ellison called.

Martha looked over her shoulder.

"You just threatened Libba with a potentially deadly weapon. She could have you arrested. I suggest you drop any idea of a lawsuit."

Martha's jaw clenched so hard I heard her teeth grind.

"You needed a new enemy?" I whispered.

Ellison shrugged.

"You'll replace the kale?"

"Of course." I let Martha have her win. "I'll even pay to have someone plant it."

"As if I'd let a stranger dig in my yard." She stalked across my lawn.

We watched her go.

"It would be wonderful," I said, "if Martha were the killer."

Ellison tilted her head. "Who's to say she's not?"

"Just imagine her with those shears, lurking in the bushes, ready to pounce on unsuspecting trespassers."

Ellison grinned. "Maybe she has a secret life as a vigilante, protecting her precious kale at all costs."

"Or perhaps," I suggested, warming to the idea, "she's part of an underground gardening mafia. Anyone who trespasses gets...pruned."

"Ghislain had to die because he cut across her lawn, trampling her hostas." She sounded almost empathetic.

"It's a lovely thought," I admitted wistfully. "A satisfying solution."

"Isn't it?"

Sadly, it was highly unlikely. I raised my glass. "To Martha. May she be guilty of something."

Ellison clinked her glass against mine. "To Martha."

"Hopefully a killer."

Ellison eyed me over the rim of her martini. "Be careful what you wish for."

CHAPTER ELEVEN

I woke to the smell of coffee and the sound of Pansy's toenails clicking against the hardwood floor.

Charlie stood in the doorway, a mug in each hand. "I thought you might need this."

I did. I'd drunk extra martinis last night, sure that the extra vermouth meant I was safe from a hangover. I'd been wrong. A dull ache pounded at my temples. I pushed myself up against the pillows and accepted the coffee. "Thank you."

"Aspirin?"

"Please."

Charlie disappeared into the bathroom, reappearing a moment later with the aspirin bottle. He shook two pills into my open palm and settled beside me on the bed.

I tossed the pills into my mouth, washing them down with coffee.

Pansy leaped up to join us.

I swore softly as the coffee sloshed in my cup. "Pansy!"

Unconcerned with spilled coffee, she circled twice before collapsing between us with a contented sigh.

We sipped in silence. The morning light filtering through the curtains looked almost golden. The man next to me smelled faintly of Z14, and stubble darkened his jawline—very sexy. Without the headache, the morning would be perfect.

Almost perfect.

I eyed Charlie over the rim of my mug. He leaned against a stack of pillows with his eyes shut. His right hand held his coffee mug. His left hand rubbed his temple. He looked tired.

Of me?

The girl who'd been humiliated in Paris anticipated the day that Charlie came to his senses and found a nice, conventional woman. One who greeted him at the door each night, made dinner (not reservations), and drank less. The girl winced at the sharp pain of losing him, even as she flexed her fingers, ready to tear into the imaginary woman who'd replaced her.

The woman I'd become sat straighter and faced her problems. "Charlie, we need to talk about the night Ghislain died."

He stiffened. "What about it?"

"You were missing for two hours..." My voice trailed away. I didn't want to be accusatory, but what had he been doing?

"I'm aware." He met my gaze. "I walked to Loose Park and sat on a bench by the duck pond. My fiancée had a husband she'd never mentioned."

The hurt in his voice made me wince. "I should have told you." In my defense, I'd believed my ex-husband was a girlish mistake best forgotten.

"Yes. You should have."

I had not brought up the missing hours to revisit my failings. "I'm truly sorry I never mentioned Ghislain."

"I was blindsided, Libba." He took a breath and stared into my eyes as if searching for the solution to a vexing puzzle. "What were you thinking, marrying a man like that?"

"I was young and naive." The coffee churned in my stomach. "He was handsome. Sophisticated. And he made me feel...desirable."

Charlie's eyes narrowed, and something flashed in their depths. Understanding? "He hurt you."

"Badly." My hand trembled, and I blinked back unwelcome tears. "Badly" was an understatement. Ghislain had ripped the heart clean out of my girlish chest. I'd rather talk about anything else—car engines, politics, murder—than revisit that pain. "Pierre confessed to Ghislain's murder."

Charlie exhaled sharply. "So it's over?"

I shook my head. "I don't think Anarchy believed him. You still need an alibi. Did anyone see you at the park?" A corroborating witness would be handy.

"Teenagers drinking beer. They ran off when they spotted an adult." He rubbed his palm across his chin. "I'm not helping myself, am I?"

"Anarchy knows you, knows you're not a killer. So do I." That didn't mean a prosecutor wouldn't press charges. "I'm sorry I got you mixed up in this." A nice, conventional woman would never implicate Charlie in a murder.

Charlie waved off my apology.

"I mean it."

"Libba." His voice was soft. "I love you. You know that, right?" Charlie wasn't one for voicing his feelings, and the moment felt...important. "There's nothing I wouldn't do for you."

A lump tightened my throat, and I leaned over Pansy, whose tail thumped excitedly against the mattress, and pressed a lingering kiss on his cheek. "I love you, too."

Silent seconds passed. It was the kind of silence that made me aware of every beat of my heart. Every beat of his heart. The silence was both heavy and hopeful. So hopeful that I indulged in a dream of a happy future. And then I remembered Martha.

"You should know, Pansy's been busy. We'll be getting a bill from the DuPuys."

"Of course, we will." He didn't sound remotely surprised.

"We may also be hearing from someone in Linus's firm."

His brow furrowed. "What did Pansy do?"

"Dug up Martha's ornamental kale. She was...displeased."

"That hardly seems actionable."

Pansy grinned up at us and wagged her tail harder.

"Martha was quite upset. She says Pansy has caused her undue stress. She threatened me with her garden shears."

Charlie, who'd been reclining against his pillows, jerked forward. "What!"

I patted his knee. "It's handled."

Charlie's gaze searched my face and body as if looking for damage. Finding none, his expression hardened. "She threatened you."

"I'm fine."

He huffed and shifted his attention to the garden-destroying problem stretched out between us. "It's a good thing the kids love you."

Charlie loved her, too. The man had a weakness for difficult females. Present company included.

I WAS A BACK-DOOR FRIEND, BUT I COULDN'T QUITE FACE walking across the patio where Ghislain had died. The pool of blood, the pallor of his skin, the knife—they were all too fresh. Instead, I went to the front door and rang the doorbell.

Aggie answered, resplendent in a bright blue muumuu with a red-cherry print. Dangling red cherries swung from her ears.

"You're back." I hadn't been expecting Ellison's house-keeper. "How's your sister?" Aggie's sister often needed her, and Aggie never said "no."

"Much better. Thank you for asking." Ellison's dogs danced around her legs.

"I'm sure Ellison is thrilled to have you home." I was, too.

Aggie was a phenomenal baker, and the sugar-laced scent in the air promised something delicious. I grunted as the Weimaraner, Max, thrust his nose into my crotch.

"Max! Shame on you! Don't you know Libba's a countess? Use your manners." Her blue eyes twinkled, and she bobbed a curtsy.

I rolled my eyes as I pushed the dog away. "Don't start, Aggie."

"It's very exciting." She stepped aside, allowing me full entry into the foyer. "It's not every day I chat with nobility."

"Stop."

There was mischief in her answering grin. "I just took the muffins out of the oven. Would you like one, Your Grace?"

"I'm a countess, not a duchess."

The grin widened.

I followed her into the kitchen, where she poured me a cup of coffee and placed two still-warm muffins on a plate.

"Thank you."

"The second one is for Mrs. Jones. She's in her studio."

I climbed the stairs to the third-floor ballroom that Ellison had claimed as her artist's studio. The large room smelled of linseed oil and coffee. Canvases leaned against the walls, and a vase filled with late-summer flowers sat on a table cluttered with brushes and paint tubes.

I sank into a cushy club chair, its upholstery faded by the light pouring through the north window, and pulled the paper wrapper off the muffin. "Any news?"

Ellison, who'd been studying a half-finished painting, looked over her shoulder at me. "Anarchy got home late, and he left early. We barely had a chance to talk." Her gaze caught on the muffin.

"Did he arrest Pierre? Sophie? Both of them?"

"No." She picked up a mug of coffee from a side table near her easel, then claimed her muffin. "But he took their passports."

"He wants more than a confession?" What more did he need? "Isn't that enough to hold Pierre?"

Her teeth sank into the still-warm muffin, and she chewed for a moment before replying, "He doesn't believe Pierre did it."

I sank deeper into the chair, bit into my muffin, and moaned. "It would make life easier."

Ellison raised an eyebrow. "Do you think Pierre did it?"

I brushed a crumb off my blouse. "He was awful when I knew him in Paris, and age hasn't changed him. If anything, he's worse." I allowed myself a small, catty smile. "I want him to be guilty. He'd look ghastly in prison orange, and he'd hate that."

"You've given this some thought. What about Sophie?"

"She'd look even worse in orange than Pierre." I indulged in a moment of picturing Sophie in a shapeless prison uniform, her hair in desperate need of a trim. "Too bad she seemed genuinely shocked when I told her Ghislain was dead."

"Well, it has to be one of them."

"Agreed." I took another bite of the muffin.

Ellison, with more self-control than I possessed, put down her half-eaten muffin. She picked up her paintbrush, a clear signal that our time together was over. Painting was something she did alone.

Still, I lingered, chewing slowly.

"What are you doing today?" As hints to leave went, it wasn't subtle.

"I thought I'd pay Marie a visit. She was rather put out that I called Anarchy." That call had ultimately led to the confiscation of her brother's passport; I didn't expect her to forgive me. Nor did I expect her to leave him now that he was in trouble. Marie was loyal. Did that loyalty extend to helping him get away with murder?

CHAPTER TWELVE

I found Aggie in the kitchen, where the delicious aroma of freshly baked muffins still lingered. She looked up from wiping the counters when I entered. "May I pack some muffins for you to take home, my lady?"

My lady? "You're not letting this go, are you?"

"Not a chance." She lifted her nose in the air and reached for a paper bag. "It's not every day that I rub elbows with the nobility."

"I wouldn't call this rubbing elbows."

Aggie stepped closer and rubbed her elbow across my arm.

I chuckled. "You're ridiculous."

She tucked a muffin into the bag with exaggerated care. "I'll tell my grandchildren about this."

"You don't have grandchildren."

"I'll get some." She added another muffin to the bag. "Are half a dozen enough for Dr. Ardmore?"

Aggie's muffins were nearly irresistible. The temptation to splurge would be dreadful. Charlie and I would have to exercise like fiends to burn the extra calories. "That's too many."

"He's a man who appreciates a muffin." She nodded as if

loving muffins were an admirable character trait. "I approve. Did your count like muffins?"

Ghislain had never been mine. Our whole relationship had been a lie. "Probably not."

She tsked. "I suppose nobody's perfect."

Especially not Ghislain.

The back stairs creaked, and Grace burst into the kitchen with Beau and the dogs trailing behind her.

"Grace, don't." Beau's voice was tight with worry. "You'll make things worse."

"You're wrong."

Beau's nose twitched. His gaze landed on the muffins cooling on the counter, and for a moment, their current drama took second place to gluttony. "May I have one, please?"

Aggie smiled and handed him a muffin. "Of course, sweetheart."

He took an enormous bite, his cheeks puffing out like a chipmunk's. The dogs settled at his feet, their eyes locked on the muffin, their stubby tails sweeping the floor.

"Grace, would you like a muffin?"

"No, thank you. I have to go."

"Ish nah whir it." It's not worth it—at least that's what I thought Beau said. Hard to be certain when his mouth was full of muffin.

"It is." Grace's jaw was set. When pushed, Grace revealed her grandmother's steely determination. Something had pushed her. "You're my brother."

Beau stilled as if Grace's casual claim had shocked him. Beau was a new addition to Ellison's family. He was still finding his way. Right now, he looked at Grace as if she'd hung the moon.

"What's going on?" I asked.

Grace turned to me. "Stewart Hawkins has been bullying Beau."

"Grace." Barely a whisper, a quiet but desperate plea to keep his secret.

I understood that plea for privacy in a way that Grace, who was beautiful and strong and unscarred, didn't. A memory flashed through my mind—I was at a café near Place Maubert, penning a letter to Ellison. I remembered the smell of exhaust and cigarette smoke, the rude waiter, melting a sugar cube into my cup. I'd taken a sip of my café au lait and decided not to tell Ellison about how serious things were with Ghislain. She'd ask questions I wasn't prepared to answer, and I was too embarrassed to be honest, even with myself. Lordy, I'd been a fool. I pulled out a stool and perched at the kitchen island. "Beau, may I tell you a story?"

He nodded and crammed more muffin into his mouth.

"When I was just a few years older than Grace, I went to Paris to study, and I met a man."

He wrinkled his nose. "Is this a romantic story?"

"Not really. I did fall in love, and the man asked me to marry him."

"He was a count," Aggie stage-whispered. "French nobility."

I shot her a look. "Not important."

"You were married?" Grace's eyes were as big as saucers. "You're a countess?"

"For a week. Turns out the man didn't really love me. He wanted my father's money. And I was humiliated. So humiliated that I never told anyone about him. All the hurt I felt—I carried that with me. All by myself." I focused my gaze on Beau. "I should have told your mom, let her help me."

Beau's eyes narrowed. "You're saying I should let Grace help me?"

"Along with your mom and Anarchy."

He glanced down, scuffing the toe of his sneaker against the floor. "It's embarrassing." He tore off two pieces of muffin, tossing one to Max and the other to Finn. "I look weak."

I resisted the urge to smooth his blond hair. "It's not weak to tell your family when you need them. There's nothing they won't do to make sure you're happy. Trust them."

Grace rested her hand on Beau's shoulder. "She's right. Come on. Let's talk to Mom."

Reluctance warred with resignation on his face before he let her steer him toward the stairway.

"You don't have to say anything," Grace said, her voice softer now. "I'll handle it."

When the sound of their footsteps faded, Aggie shook her head. "That girl."

"She's protective." A terrifying combination of Frances's will and Ellison's loyalty.

"Those two would do anything for each other." Aggie ran a hand through her corkscrew curls and smiled. "It's a blessing, having someone like that in your corner."

"You and your sister?" Seeing the look on her face, I wished (for a brief instant) that I wasn't an only child. But I didn't need a sister; I had Ellison. And she had me.

"I'd help her bury a body." She glanced at the window to the patio and winced. "Not that she'd ever kill anyone."

I thought about that as I walked home, the bag of muffins warm against my hip. Family loyalty. The fierce, unquestioning kind. The kind that made a sixteen-year-old girl ready to declare war on a bully.

Marie was loyal to Pierre. Had she lied for him? Covered for him?

Did her loyalty extend to helping him get away with murder?

I intended to find out.

CHAPTER THIRTEEN

"Muffins." I set the bag on the kitchen counter.

Pansy stared at me with pleading eyes and wagged her tail so hard her butt shook.

"Nope," I told her.

She shifted her gaze to Charlie, who opened the bag and peered inside. "Aggie's back?"

"She is." I kissed him on the cheek. "I'm heading to the Alameda."

"For?"

"To see Marie." I grabbed my handbag and keys. "I thought I'd smooth things over."

Charlie claimed three muffins and arranged them in a neat line on the counter. "You should take her the rest."

"You're sure?" Charlie loved Aggie's muffins.

"If they're here, I'll eat them."

I reclaimed the bag and headed toward the door.

"Libba, be careful."

I glanced over my shoulder. "I'm always careful."

He raised an eyebrow, but wisely said nothing.

I drove past Marie on the Alameda's sidewalk. She wore a

sage green wrap dress and had her dark hair pulled into a French twist. She walked with purpose, a woman on a mission.

I left the car with the valet and hurried after her. "Marie!"

She turned, her expression shifting from surprise to wariness to something carefully neutral. "Libba."

I caught up with her and held out the bag. "These are for you."

She accepted my offering and looked inside. "You bake?"

"Not exactly. Where are you headed?"

"Harzfeld's. That camel wrap dress I tried on when we were shopping, I can't stop thinking about it." A clear sign she was meant to buy it.

"Mind if I tag along?"

Her pause was almost imperceptible. "If you like."

We crossed the bridge over Brush Creek.

"So much concrete," she murmured.

"It's been this way since the '30s. There was a boss in Kansas City who owned a concrete company. Some people say his enemies are buried beneath all that concrete." I was a believer, and I'd often wondered how many secrets lurked beneath the cement's weight.

Marie shuddered. "A graveyard." She clutched the bag tightly enough to rustle the paper. "Where will you bury Ghislain?"

I tripped over my own feet. "Me?" I had no intention of burying Ghislain.

"You were his wife."

And wasn't that a bitter pill? "Pierre was his best friend. Pierre should plan the funeral."

"At present, my brother cannot return to France." She scowled as if she'd just remembered my role in Sophie and Ghislain being taken in for questioning.

The morning sun was warm on my shoulders, but I shivered.

"The only good thing to come of this trip is that Sophie has finally come to her senses."

"You know, I always had the feeling that you didn't like her."

"I don't. But my brother loves her, and his happiness matters to me."

The Plaza buzzed with shoppers. My mind buzzed with random thoughts. Aggie telling me she'd help her sister bury a body. Grace ready to do battle with a bully. Frances staring down a police officer to get to her daughter. The pieces fell into place.

Not Pierre.

Not Sophie.

Marie.

I closed my eyes against the sun's brightness and searched for a different answer.

There wasn't one.

"You killed Ghislain." The certainty in my voice surprised me. This was Ellison's job—unmasking killers. I was around for comic relief.

Marie's step faltered. For a single heartbeat, she froze. Then she kept walking, her pace unchanged. "Tu es folle."

But I wasn't crazy. Sophie had knocked on Marie's door, and Marie hadn't answered. Not because she was asleep, but because she wasn't there.

We reached the first of Harzfeld's windows, and I asked, "Why?"

Marie took in the display. Mannequins wearing floaty dresses and suede boots. So different from her French style.

"Why?" I repeated.

"He was a terrible man."

"He's been terrible his whole life. Why kill him now?"

"I did you a favor." Her voice was ice cold.

Same as my blood. Marie had killed Ghislain and was trying to pass it off as a public service. "You didn't do it for me."

A cold sting jabbed through my shirt, pressing directly against my skin. I gasped at the sudden pain, and my gaze fell to my torso. Marie held a knife, small but wickedly sharp, and half-hidden by her handbag.

She grabbed my arm, holding me close. "Let's walk." Her voice was pleasant, conversational, terrifying.

Shock rendered me stupid, because I did as she demanded.

We rounded the corner, and I wondered if I could shake her off.

As if she'd read my thoughts, the knife's tip dug deeper. "What's that?" She jerked her chin at a short flight of stairs that led to a gray metal door.

"It leads to the parking garage. Marie—"

The knife pressed harder. "Keep walking. Don't make a scene, Libba. I'd hate for anyone to get hurt."

I walked.

The stairwell led up to the second floor. Despite the Plaza's best efforts to keep it clean, the stairway always smelled faintly of urine and overwhelmingly of ammonia. I wrinkled my nose and tried to formulate an escape plan. I refused to die with the combined odors in my nose.

"Marie—"

"Keep going."

We stepped into the garage, and Marie guided me between a powder-blue Lincoln Continental and a black Cadillac Eldorado. Two yachts masquerading as cars, they blocked us from view.

"You're not a killer. It had to have been an accident." I was grasping at straws. Especially when the opposite was true. She'd stabbed Ghislain in the ribs and left him for dead. She was going to do the same to me.

Acrid fear coated my tongue, but I lifted my chin and met her gaze.

Marie studied me for a moment. Then she shrugged, as if I hardly mattered. "I followed Ghislain that night. What business could he have in Kansas City? We'd come for a signature. Nothing more. Ghislain engaged in dalliances over the years, so I assumed he was meeting a woman. If I proved to Sophie that he was cheating on her again, maybe she'd finally give him up. He left the hotel on foot, climbed that blasted hill, and cut through the park. I thought he'd noticed me, so I hid behind a tree. When I came out, I'd lost him."

"And then?"

"I wandered through your neighborhood until I heard voices. By the time I found him, he was alone. Smoking. Staring up at an enormous English Tudor. Smirking."

"What did he say?"

"Nothing. He didn't see me. He slipped into the backyard, and I followed him. He stretched out on a chaise longue and lit another cigarette as if he owned the place. I confronted him, demanding to know what he was doing. He told me he was making sure he got his money. When I asked what he meant, he told me he'd asked for twenty thousand dollars to give you a divorce."

My gaze flickered over the Cadillac's glossy black surface, and I caught the reflection of Marie's blade and my own pale face. I just needed to keep her talking. It was a busy parking garage; surely someone would happen by. "He asked my fiancé for the money."

"Quel connard."

I didn't disagree.

"I threatened to tell Sophie about his delaying their marriage so he could get more money out of you, and he laughed. He said Sophie wouldn't care. He could murder Pierre, and Sophie wouldn't care."

"Quel connard," I repeated her words back to her.

She nodded. "He called my brother pathetic for caring about a woman who was in love with another man."

"So you stabbed him."

"I had a knife with me. For protection." A chilly smile curled her lips. "Paris can be dangerous."

She'd left that knife sticking out of Ghislain's ribs. Another knife poked my ribs. Just how many knives did she have?

Now didn't seem the time to ask.

She offered up a Gallic shrug. "In the end, everything worked out. Sophie came to her senses, and she and Pierre are finally together."

"You killed a man."

"Don't pretend you care."

"I care that you murdered someone."

She met my eyes. "I'm sorry about this, Libba. I always liked you." The knife's tip sliced through my flesh, and a sudden rush of blood stained my shirt and the waistband of my pants.

Before she could drive the knife home, I twisted away, stumbling backward.

My heel caught on something—a crack in the pavement or a stray pebble—and I went down hard, my palms scraping against the concrete.

Marie stood over me with the knife raised.

This was how I died? Absolutely not! I had things to do—things to accomplish. Charlie and I had living to do—a wedding to plan, a honeymoon (any place but France), years of sipping coffee together as we read the morning paper, passionate kisses, and quiet hugs. She couldn't take that from me. Clutching my side, I inched away from her.

Marie smiled, as if my attempt to get away was amusing.

Something—a kelly-green blur—crashed into her head.

She crumpled sideways, the knife clattering across the concrete, the paper bag slipping from her fingers, spilling muffins around me.

Ellison stood behind her, breathing hard, clutching her Hermès handbag like a weapon.

"Haven't I warned you about parking garages?" she demanded.

I let out a shaky laugh. "It's not like I chose to be here."

She dug in her handbag, withdrawing a small, pearl-handled gun, which she pointed at Marie. "Libba might like you. I don't. Make a move, and I will shoot you."

Marie's eyes widened, and she pressed her open palms against the Caddy's shiny paint. "I understand."

"Are you hurt?" Ellison's gaze landed on my bloody white blouse. "You're bleeding."

"I'll be fine. How did you know where to find me?"

"Aggie asked me to bring over more muffins. Charlie said you'd gone to meet Marie. I got this terrible feeling in my stomach and drove to the Alameda. The valet told me that you and Marie had walked to the Plaza. You're lucky I couldn't find any street parking." Ellison avoided parking garages like the plague. "You're even luckier I heard your voice."

"Thank you." The words felt inadequate.

"You can thank me by never confronting a murderer alone again." She extended a hand, pulling me off the pavement. "I mean it, Libba. My heart can't take it."

"Neither can mine."

She pulled me into a hug, even as she kept her gun trained on Marie. "Are you well enough to find a phone? We need to call Anarchy. As soon as the police arrive, we'll get you to the hospital."

I glanced at Marie, who slumped against the Cadillac. Her hair had come loose from its pins, and she looked older somehow. Smaller. Diminished.

"I really did like you, Libba," she said quietly. "For what it's worth."

"Not much."

With my best friend holding her at gunpoint, I went into Harzfeld's and asked to use the phone. A bloodied woman, attacked in their parking lot, got immediate service.

CHAPTER FOURTEEN

Hospital emergency rooms all smelled the same, like antiseptic and anxiety. They all looked the same, too—oatmeal-colored, windowless walls, and bad lighting.

I perched on a narrow exam table while a nurse cleaned the wound in my side.

Charlie sat next to me, holding my hand so tightly that my fingers had gone numb. He'd sent the ER doctor away. Not good enough. Instead, we waited for the head of the plastic surgery department.

What seemed like an hour later (but was probably ten minutes—time moved differently in hospitals), the doctor arrived.

"Adam, thanks for coming."

"Sure, Charlie. Just remember, I'm pulling you off the course if I ever have a heart attack." The doctor glanced at my chart. "Knife wound?"

"Libba confronted a murderer." Charlie didn't say, "She's lucky to be alive," but the unspoken words hung in the air.

"Will it scar?" A vain question, but it mattered.

The doctor shifted the pale blue gown and examined the wound. "Minimal. Let's give you a shot for the pain, then we'll get you sewn up."

Latex gloves. Thread. A needle. The room tilted, and sweat beaded on my hairline.

Charlie squeezed my hand. "Don't watch."

"I wasn't planning on it." I focused on his face instead. He was wan beneath his tan, and a muscle jumped in his jaw.

"Sharp prick," said Adam. "That's the painkiller."

Charlie paled. For a cardiologist who dealt with life-and-death situations daily, he was not handling this well.

"You okay?" I asked.

"That's my question."

"Answer mine first."

"I'm furious."

I winced. And not from the needle currently sewing my skin shut. "At me?"

"At the woman who stabbed you." His voice was rough.

The needle bit, and I sucked in a breath.

Charlie's grip on my hand tightened.

"I'm fine, Charlie."

"You are not fine. You have a gash in your side."

"A small gash." I attempted a wry smile. "Minimal scarring."

"I don't care how small it is." His thumb traced circles on the back of my hand. "When that police officer called and said you'd been stabbed—" He stopped, swallowed, and glanced at Adam before looking into my eyes. "I never want to be that frightened again."

The rawness in his voice had my eyes filling with tears. "You're not going to lose me."

"You confronted a murderer. Alone. In a parking garage."

"Technically, we were on the sidewalk when I confronted her. She moved us to the parking garage."

"That's not the defense you think it is."

Adam tied off the last stitch. "Six stitches. Keep them dry for forty-eight hours. Come back in ten days to have them removed." He peeled off his gloves and tossed them into the trash can. "No more knife fights."

"I'll do my best."

Charlie stood and held out his hand. "Thank you, Adam."

"You'd do the same for me. Although the most trouble my wife gets into is spending too much at Swanson's."

"Libba does that, too."

"Hey, now," I objected.

Adam offered me a tired smile. "Forget Swanson's. Go to the drugstore and buy yourself some calendula salve. Start applying it as soon as the wound begins healing. Now, if you'll excuse me." The curtain swayed in his wake, and the sounds of the ER —beeping monitors, murmured conversations, the squeak of rubber soles on linoleum—filled the silence.

Still holding my right hand, Charlie got down on one knee. "Marry me."

"You've already asked. I said yes." I waved my engagement ring in front of his face.

"I mean now. This week. I don't want to wait."

"Charlie." I studied him closely. His eyes were bright, almost feverish, and his set jaw ticked as he waited for my answer. He was…afraid. He'd nearly lost me.

"Libba," he replied.

"The invitations take eight weeks." My voice wobbled because I didn't want to wait either. Life was short. Today proved that.

"I don't care about invitations."

"Frances will care about invitations."

"Frances isn't getting married." He lifted my fingers to his lips and kissed the back of my hand. "Besides, you don't need a divorce anymore."

He was right. I was a widow. Had been since Ghislain's death. The Comtesse de Fevre. "No," I said softly. "I don't suppose I do."

"So?"

I looked at this man—this good, decent, handsome man who vacuumed when he was anxious and loved a dog who destroyed everything in her path. "Your children?" They lived in Texas with his ex-wife.

"They can hop on a plane."

"Then, yes. Just family."

His smile could have powered the hospital for a month. He stood, pulling me into his arms, but careful to avoid pressing against my stitches. "Will I be a count when we're married?"

I laughed, and the stitches pulled. "Ow. No. It doesn't work that way."

"Pity. Count Ardmore has a nice ring to it."

"It absolutely does not." I rested my forehead against his chest. "As much fun as it would be to swan around the country club as a countess, I'm going to renounce the title."

"Are you sure?"

"Positive. Let the next heir deal with the moldering château." I had no use for a crumbling estate in a country that had broken my heart. My life was here—with Charlie, with Pansy, with Ellison next door, and a club full of people whom I'd known since kindergarten. I didn't need a title.

"You're sure you won't regret it?"

"Charlie."

"What?"

"Ask me one more time, and I'll change my mind about marrying you."

He grinned. "Understood."

The curtain flew open.

Ellison stood there, her kelly-green Hermès bag—the one

that had felled a murderer—hooked over her elbow. Her eyes were red-rimmed, and her chin trembled. "Don't you dare get married without me."

"How long have you been listening?" I asked.

"Long enough." She swiped at her eyes with her free hand.

My throat tightened, and I blinked hard. I was not a woman who cried. Except I'd been stabbed, and stitched, and proposed to (again), and my best friend, who had saved my life with a handbag and a pearl-handled pistol, was crying. The tears came. I couldn't stop them.

"Stop it," Ellison whispered, her own voice thick. "If you cry, I'll cry."

"You're already crying. You started this."

"Liar." She swiped beneath her eyes again. "You're getting married next weekend?"

"That's the plan."

"Mother is going to kill you."

"She'll get over it. Frances warned me about dilly-dallying just the other day."

"Mother said 'dilly-dally'?"

"I think her exact words were, 'Don't waste time. There are plenty of women interested—Charlie Ardmore is a catch.'"

Charlie grinned. "A catch?"

I swatted his chest. "As if you didn't know."

"Family only?"

"You and Anarchy are my family. I couldn't get married without you."

"Okay then. I'll host a small party afterward."

"Ellison."

"For the people who attend the wedding. And Mother and Daddy. Mother would kill us both if we didn't invite her. You're practically her third daughter. And we have to include Jinx and Daisy."

"Ellison." I didn't have the energy to argue, but I had a feeling her small party would be a soiree for two hundred.

"Libba," said Charlie, "you look tired."

I was tired. I leaned into him, grateful for his steadiness. "We need to nip this in the bud."

"Ellison, we're grateful for the offer. Family only. Family includes your parents, but not your bridge group."

She pouted.

"I mean it, Ellison."

"Fine," she conceded. Then she leaned forward and kissed my cheek. "I'll stop by in the morning. Aggie's baking a Bundt."

It usually took dying to get a Bundt cake from Aggie.

My side throbbed, a persistent reminder of my terrible day. Still, it was a manageable pain. Easily ignored with the promise of Bundt cake. Or gin.

PANSY GREETED US WITH HER CUSTOMARY ENTHUSIASM—spinning in circles, barking, launching herself at Charlie's chest. She licked his face with the desperate devotion of a dog who'd been abandoned for days.

"Down, you beast." His voice was fond.

I changed into loose pants and one of Charlie's button-downs—clothing that wouldn't rub against my stitches—and settled on the living room sofa. Pansy leaped up and arranged herself at my feet, her muzzle resting on my ankle.

Charlie sat next to me, and I settled my head against his shoulder. "There's so much to plan."

"There isn't. I'll call and make an appointment with a judge tomorrow."

"A dress."

"Go to Swanson's and buy the most expensive thing they have."

How could I argue that?

We sat like that, the three of us, grateful to be together. I never wanted the moment to end. As soon as I had the thought, a knock at the door shattered our peace.

Pansy erupted from the couch, barking as if invaders had breached the gates. Her claws scrabbled against the hardwood as she raced to the door.

Charlie sighed. "I'll get it."

He returned with Anarchy, who settled into the wingback chair and declined a drink.

"How are you feeling?" he asked me.

"Six stitches and a ruined blouse. I'll survive."

The corner of his mouth twitched. "Ellison told me that she whacked Marie with the bag she bought in Paris."

"Ironic, n'est-ce pas?" Then I saw the opportunity. "Who knew Hermès bags could be weapons? See, Charlie. I need a new one."

He winced before turning his attention to Anarchy. "What's happening with Marie?"

"She's been charged with Ghislain's murder and Libba's attempted murder. She's cooperating." He rubbed his palm against the back of his neck. "This confession is real."

"Pierre?" I asked.

"Both his and Sophie's passports have been released. He's free to leave the US."

"Idiot." It was the nicest thing I could think of to call him.

"He only confessed because he thought Sophie was guilty."

The doorbell rang again. And Pansy, who'd finally calmed down, launched herself off the couch with a bark that could shatter eardrums.

Charlie groaned and went to the door.

He returned with Linus DuPuy.

Linus did not acknowledge me, which was just as well. I wasn't in the mood.

"What do you want, Linus?" Charlie didn't offer him a seat.

Linus thrust an envelope at him. "This is the itemized receipt for Martha's plantings. I trust you'll handle this promptly."

Charlie accepted the envelope but didn't open it.

"Of course, that bill doesn't include her time. Kale doesn't plant itself."

Charlie crossed his arms over his chest.

"Additionally," Linus continued, tugging at his collar, "there's the ongoing stress caused by your dog. Martha has suffered—"

"Linus, stop right there." I shifted on the couch, unable to get comfortable without Charlie and Pansy. "Your wife threatened me. With wickedly sharp garden shears. She brandished them inches from my face."

The blood drained from his face.

"Ellison witnessed the whole thing. If you and Martha pursue a claim against us for emotional distress caused by a golden retriever, I will press charges for assault with a deadly weapon."

Linus opened his mouth. Closed it. Opened it again. Clearly, Martha hadn't told him the whole story.

"We'll pay for the kale." Pansy had almost certainly destroyed the blasted cabbage. "But the lawsuit talk stops here."

He nodded. "I'll speak with Martha."

I narrowed my eyes. "You do that."

Charlie saw him out, returning with Pierre and Sophie.

Pansy went into a fresh tizzy.

I leaned my head against the back of the couch. I didn't have the energy for Pierre's disdain or Sophie's derision.

Anarchy, who'd been heading for the door himself, took one look at the two of them, muttered something about it being his cue to leave, and hurried past them.

Pierre jammed his hands into his pockets and shifted his weight from foot to foot. He looked up. He looked down. He looked at the painting above the mantle (Ellison's work). He didn't look at me.

Sophie stood beside him with her hand tucked around his arm. She wore black—chic, understated, and entirely appropriate for a woman whose fiancé had been murdered two days ago.

I braced myself for a cutting remark.

It didn't come. Instead, he swallowed. Hard. "I owe you an apology. I was unkind to you in Paris."

Of all the things I'd expected him to say, that wasn't one of them. I waited, because a smart woman never rushed a man who was eating crow.

Pierre finally looked at me. "My sister tried to kill you—"

Pansy chose that moment to stick her nose into Pierre's crotch.

He squeaked.

Sophie's lips twitched.

Mine did, too.

"I accept your apology." I was gracious because I wanted them gone. "Are you staying in Kansas City? For Marie?"

His expression fractured. "She is my sister. I will see that she has the best legal representation."

"Of course you will." Because that's what family did. They showed up. Even when—especially when—it was hard.

Thankfully, they didn't stay long. Pierre shook Charlie's hand. Sophie inclined her head with regal grace. And they left, the door closing behind them with a quiet click.

When I heard that click, I exhaled.

Charlie reappeared in the entrance to the living room. "That was unexpected."

"And how."

He crossed the room and sat beside me. Pansy wriggled between us, her tail a metronome of contentment. "What can I get you?"

"A decent martini."

Charlie laughed. "There's my girl." Then he kissed the tip of my nose, eased himself off the couch, and headed for the bar cart.

The martini would probably have too much vermouth.

I'd drink it anyway.

HAVE YOU MET FREDDIE?

Inspired by Lois Long, one of the first real-life columnists at The New Yorker, Freddie pens a column about the glamorous 1920s New York scene.

I stumbled across a column by Lois and wished we could be friends. Time machines being hard to come by, I did the next best thing and used her as a muse for Freddie Archer instead.

MURDER IN MANHATTAN

CHAPTER ONE

Taken from A Touch of Rouge— June 20, 1925, issue of Gotham magazine

When I tell you the weather is hot, I'm hardly reporting news. Nor is it news when I say our fair city bears a striking resemblance to the place where my last young-man-about-town's dear mother said I would be going when I toddle off this mortal coil.

When my invitation to the North Shore for last weekend fell through, I had no choice but to embrace the rising mercury.

Embrace I did—the weight of over-heated air, the cloying scent of wilting flowers pinned to pretty girls' shoulders, the sheen of sweat on orchestral brows, and butter-and-egg men thick on the ground. Imagine my surprise when Zelda and Scott Fitzgerald floated into the evening's boîte on a cloud of gin and Tabac Blond. Scott, who claimed a meeting with his publisher kept him in this sweat box masquerading as a city, suggested a change of venue and nothing would do but piling into a taxi and motoring to the

Biltmore Cascades. Who was I to argue? What could be cooler than a rooftop garden? Besides, sometimes a girl needs caviar.

Roses and out-of-town visitors bloomed in profusion. Nestled in the bower, the latest favorite guest of every hostess on the Upper East Side charmed members of the fairer sex. One wonders how the much-in-demand Jake Haskell found time to dine al fresco.

Afterward, a visit to Tex Guinan's club of the moment. Tex, in her usual good humor, was unfazed by the showgirls who deemed the mercury too high for their costumes. The men, in particular, enjoyed the floor show. One man with the look of a dyspeptic county judge was so taken by a flamboyant redhead with obvious assets, he failed to notice his necktie marinating in his drink. As far as this correspondent knows, he may yet be there. Drooling still... A

A Touch of Rouge

FREDDIE ARCHER ADJUSTED THE COOL CLOTH DRAPED ACROSS her forehead and eyes—not that the cloth was terribly cool. Nothing stayed cool in this heat. It was hardly morning—barely 9:00 if the sounds outside her office were any indication—and already the day was stifling.

"Freddie? Are you decent?"

The gentle utterance of her name was accompanied by the sound of the door opening. Such were the dangers of sleeping on the divan in her office—someone was bound to disturb her. In this case, someone was her secretary, Annie.

"I am dying." Given the knitting needle lodged in her brain, the declaration wasn't remotely dramatic.

"Sorry to hear that." The unseasonable heat had curdled whatever milk of human kindness Annie had once possessed. The lack of genuine sympathy was positively galling.

Why hadn't she held out for a secretary with a nurturing soul?

"I brought you a bottle of aspirin and a glass of water."

Maybe Annie wasn't completely lacking in compassion.

Freddie lifted onto her elbows. That accomplished, she pushed herself to sitting and lifted the cloth hiding her eyes. The office was brighter than the gleam in a chorus girl's eyes when a rich man came calling. Why must the sun shine with such verve in the morning? She closed her eyelids, but the light burned a red halo in the darkness.

"Here." Annie pressed a glass into her left hand. "Two or three?"

"Four." Freddie held out her empty right palm.

Annie shook the tablets from the bottle, then her footsteps crossed to the window. The sound of blinds being closed was lovelier than a symphony. "You have messages."

"Do I?" Freddie tossed the pills into her mouth and washed them down with a swig of water.

"The writer of A Touch of Rouge has messages," Annie amended. "There's a reader who takes umbrage with your description of The Fox and Hound as a club best reserved for those chasing the dragon."

"There's an opium den in the back room."

"Also, the police are here to see you."

"The police?" Freddie opened her eyes and surveyed her now dim office. Her shoes were abandoned near the door. A single silk stocking draped over the back of a chair facing her desk. The other stocking circled her ankle. Last night's frock was a pool of crumpled silk next to the divan. An open beaded clutch rested atop the dress. "Whatever they want, I didn't do it." She spoke with assurance she did not possess.

"Do what?"

"Anything. Drink in a speakeasy. Dance on top of a patrol

car. Go for a late-night dip in the fountain outside the Plaza Hotel." She'd done that and more. Many times.

"He's a detective."

"A detective?"

"I thought you'd want to see him before Gus arrives."

Freddie rested her throbbing head against the back of the divan. While the stories of her antics earned her an enormous readership, the antics themselves shocked her boss to the bottom of his born-in-Iowa soul. Gus would frown upon a morning visit from the constabulary. "I supposed I'd better see him." She raked her fingers through her bobbed hair and kicked the stocking from her ankle. "How bad do I look?"

"Like something the cat spit up." Annie bent and picked up the stocking.

If Freddie bent like that, her brains would leak out of her ears.

"A detective, you say?" What could a detective want? Freddie scrubbed her face with the damp cloth. The white linen came away smudged with the remnants of last evening's mascara, rouge, and powder. Her lipstick had long since decamped—she'd wager it was on a young man's collar. "Do I have anything to wear?"

Annie opened the narrow wardrobe in the corner of the office, pulled out a deceptively simple crêpe de chine dress, and held its hanger aloft. "This?"

"Perfect." Freddie glanced down at her bare legs. "I don't think I can manage stockings." The mere thought of reaching for her toes made her stomach flip like a Ringling Brothers' trapeze act. But no stockings meant she wouldn't be able to leave the cover of her desk. So be it. "Do you have a comb?"

"Of course."

"A lipstick?"

"Of course."

"What's his name?" Freddie stood. Just stood. She could do

no more—her stomach and head needed time to adjust to their new fully-upright positions.

Annie chose not to answer her question. "Finish your water, and I'll get you some more."

Freddie drained the glass. "I need coffee."

"You need to write your column then go home for a long nap."

"The new column is written." She pointed at her desk, an oasis of calm in the disorderly room. Pad of paper. Pencils in a cup. Typewriter. A stack of letters from readers who either loved A Touch of Rouge for her breezy writing style or hated her for glamorizing night clubs. And neatly-stacked pages waiting for Annie to take them to an editor. "As for a nap, that sounds positively luxurious. Too bad there's a detective here."

"His name is Mike. Mike Sullivan." Was that a touch of pink on Annie's austere cheeks?

"Mike, you say?" Freddie ventured a step—a small one. Somewhat surprisingly, the floor did not open and swallow her whole. She took a second step. A third shuffle forward carried her to the mirror hanging on the back of the office door. There, she gasped. Even in the blessedly dim light, the woman in the mirror looked positively haggard. "I'll need some powder, too."

"What did you do last night?" Annie held out a comb.

"Nothing nearly as exciting as last week. I didn't encounter the Fitzgeralds. I didn't hop in a fountain. Nope. Last night was nothing special. Dinner at the Colony, a show in Harlem, dancing at Corona de Oro." Freddie ran the comb's teeth through her tangled hair. "It's all there in my new column."

Annie, who was a huge fan of Scott's short stories, harumphed. Freddie suspected Annie was also a secret fan of Scott and Zelda's escapades, not that she would ever admit it.

"Nick Peters was there. Apparently, he's in the city working on his new show." She tried—tried—to keep her tone casual as she tugged at a snarl.

Annie wasn't fooled. "You spoke to him?"

"We were very civilized." Had being civilized hurt him as much as it hurt her? "He was there with his leading lady." Why were all leading ladies impossibly beautiful? Last night's had been a honey blonde with rounded cheeks and bowed lips painted a brilliant cherry red. Freddie had hated her on sight. On good days, Freddie could best be described as pretty—such an anemic, little word. She didn't need a second glance in the mirror to know today was not a good day.

Annie reclaimed the comb and put the frock in Freddie's hands.

The dress whispered over her shoulders. She smoothed the fabric over her slip and patted a stray hair into place. "I believe I'll take you up on that second glass of water." She kept her voice light and airy as if spotting Nick dancing with another woman hadn't left her breathless. And thirsty. For copious amounts of Champagne. She wasn't carrying a torch for him. She absolutely was not. But it was galling how quickly he'd moved on.

"Of course." Bless Annie for pretending not to see the cracks in the façade.

The price for all that Champagne was this—a painful morning. "And coffee."

Annie collected the stocking hanging from the chair. "Of course."

"Are there any shoes in that wardrobe?" Last night's black satin pumps and today's crepe de chine dress would be ridiculous together.

"No."

"I'll go barefoot."

Annie's brows rose.

"I'm not stepping out from behind my desk. Your Detective Sullivan will never know."

"He's not my detective." Annie's voice was a shade too sharp.

"Yet."

Annie flushed a deep pink.

"Give me a minute or two to fix the wreckage—" Freddie circled her hand in front of her face "—then bring him in."

Five minutes later, a ginger-haired man the size of a rhinoceros settled into the chair across from her.

The chair groaned.

Freddie forced a smile. "How may I help you, detective?"

"I read your last column, Miss Archer." Detective Sullivan, with his size, open features, and maleness, did not resemble her usual reader.

"Oh?"

He held out last Saturday's magazine, carefully folded to her column. "You were at the Biltmore Cascades with the Fitzgeralds."

"Are they in trouble again?" What had they done now? Freddie rested her arms against the desk. "They mean well. They do!" Zelda had a tendency to get caught up in wild moments and forget she was an adult. And Scott egged her on. Either too drunk, too enamored, or too desperate for material for a short story to care that Zelda had flashed a wide-eyed beat cop walking Fifth Avenue.

"They're not in trouble."

Well, that was a relief. She leaned back and considered Detective Sullivan's bright blue eyes. "Who is?"

"Who is what?"

"In trouble. Someone must be, or you wouldn't be here."

"How do you know Jake Haskell?"

Jake Haskell. "Tall. Blond hair. Midwestern accent. Divot in his chin. And—" she tapped a finger on the center of her own divot-less chin "—terrible taste in neckties."

"How do you know him?" Detective Sullivan fixed his gaze on her.

The intensity of that gaze made her feel like a butterfly pinned to a board. Freddie shifted in her chair. "I don't know him. Not really. I met him at a party."

"But you put him in your column?"

"Say what you will about New York, with this heat, the city is most attractive to those who can leave. While I don't begrudge anyone a single breath of ocean-cooled breeze, half the city has gone missing. That means finding warm bodies for the column is a challenge." A bead of sweat formed between her breasts and trickled down her torso. Freddie ignored the tickle of perspiration and waved a languid hand at the closed blinds. "By the end of August, I expect I'll be writing about shoeshine boys."

"Who introduced you?"

So many questions. Freddie snuck past the ice pick lodged in her brain and searched her memories. The night blessedly cool. The stars impossibly bright. She'd danced on a veranda overlooking the ocean. "John. John Burcham introduced us."

Detective Sullivan pulled a small notepad from his jacket and made a note. "Who is John Burcham?"

"A reporter. A friend of my brother's."

"Was your brother there that night?"

"No." That was all he was getting. She didn't talk about Gray. Ever.

"When did you meet Mr. Haskell?"

"I think we met in May." The breeze had made her shiver. What she wouldn't give for a shiver now. "Definitely May. Early in the month."

"And you didn't see him again till the other night at The Cascades?"

"I might have." Haskell was a bootlegger—a bootlegger who brought bottles of scotch as hostess gifts to cocktail parties. Real scotch. From Scotland. Not the brown-tinted bathtub swill some speakeasies passed off. As such, Haskell was a sought-after guest —it was that popularity that had earned him a mention in last week's column. But Freddie wasn't about to tell a police detective about Jake Haskell's bottles of scotch. The admission would land too many friends in the soup.

"You're aware of Haskell's profession?"

When, oh when, would the aspirin kick in? "His profession?"

"You're aware Haskell was a bootlegger?"

"I might have heard something to that effect." A nice, safe response. "Did he retire?"

"Retire?"

"You said he was a bootlegger. Was."

"He didn't retire. He died."

The gasp that escaped her said almost everything—what a pity, and how awful, and he was much too young. "How?"

"He was murdered."

The air in her office stilled, and her lips struggled to form a simple word. "Murdered?" Maybe the fault was not on her lips but in her throat. The one word emerged as a strangled plea.

Detective Sullivan's eyes searched her face. Thoroughly. What was he looking for? Surely he couldn't suspect her? "He was shot."

"Shot?" Yet another strangled word. "Who shot him?"

"We're hoping you could help us with that."

"Me?" She crossed her hands over her chest and winced as the ice pick in her brain bored another inch toward the center of her gray matter. "I barely knew the man. How could I help?"

"Who was at the Cascades the night you dined with the Fitzgeralds?"

"No one."

"No one? You mean it was empty?"

"Of course not. But there was no one there to write about—a crowd of out-of-towners—"

"You can tell someone is from out of town just by looking?"

"Can't you? There you are." The last she directed to Annie who stood in the doorway with a tray.

"I brought coffee." She'd also taken time to comb her hair and powder her nose.

"Bless you."

"And Danish."

"You're an angel." The Danish was for Detective Sullivan. Annie never brought pastry when Freddie was alone. "Isn't she an angel, detective?"

Sullivan flushed and pulled at his collar.

Annie stepped into the office and put the tray on the desk. "Do you take cream or sugar, detective?"

"Sugar, please."

"One lump or two?"

"One." The detective returned his notepad to his jacket and watched Annie use tiny silver tongs (where on earth had she found those?) to plunk a sugar cube into his coffee.

"Here you are." She held out the cup.

Their fingers brushed, and the cup rattled against its saucer. The two made calves' eyes at each other for a long second.

Detective Sullivan finally accepted the coffee. In his enormous hand, the cup looked as if it belonged to a child's tea service.

Annie, whose cheeks were flushed a becoming shade of rose, abruptly turned to Freddie. "Black?"

"Please." She always drank her coffee black. If one was going to drink calories, there'd better be liquor involved.

Annie poured a cup and handed it to her.

Freddie took a grateful sip. "Where were we, detective?"

"You were telling me who was at the Cascades."

"That's right." Freddie closed her eyes and pictured the rooftop dining room—tables covered with crisp white linen, tuxedoed waiters, the pleasant hum of genteel conversations, the less pleasant sounds of the streets rising up to them. She went often enough that one night melted into another. "Haskell was there at a table for two."

"Who was he with?"

"A woman."

"What did she look like?"

"Silk dress—sky blue with crystal beadwork—quite stylish. Ropes and ropes of pearls. Light brown hair—bobbed. Pretty in a kittenish way." Freddie opened her eyes in time to see Detective Sullivan lean toward her, an avid expression on his freckled face.

"Kittenish?" he asked. "Do you know her?"

"Never set eyes on her before."

He slumped. "Would you recognize her if you saw her again?"

She was good with faces. And names. Skills that came in handy when writing a weekly feature on the places to see and be seen in New York. "I'd definitely recognize the dress and the pearls. Why all these questions?"

"The woman might know something that can help us catch Haskell's killer."

Freddie stared at the giant across from her. He still held the cup and saucer, and they still looked like a little girl's toys in his meaty hands.

He stared back at her. "I need your help."

"My help?"

"She'd be happy to help." Annie, who'd forgotten to leave after serving the coffee, wore the slightly stunned expression of a woman who'd met the man of her dreams.

Freddie lifted her brow and stared at her secretary. "I would?"

The detective rubbed his chin. "I've talked to everyone we can find who was at the Cascades that night. You're the first person who could give me a decent description of the woman Haskell was there with."

"What could I possibly do?"

"Let me know if you see her again."

Freddie put her cup down on the corner of her desk. "You mean search her out at clubs?"

"No!" Detective Sullivan held up his hands and shook his massive head. "Absolutely not. If you see her, you let me know. Nothing more."

Freddie stared at her lap and pressed two fingers against each of her temples. God save her from this headache and from men who wanted women to be nothing more than pretty—in this case, talking—accessories. "If I spot her, it will likely be in the middle of the night." She raised her gaze. "Are you in your office then?"

A cloud passed over Detective Sullivan's face. She'd presented him with an unforeseen wrinkle. "I'd still like to know where you see her. Like I said, she might know something about the murder."

"This sounds too dangerous." Annie's voice fluttered like a chiffon hemline.

A second cloud passed over the detective's visage, this one darker than the first. His face cleared, and he spoke to Annie. "Miss Archer will be perfectly safe as long as she doesn't approach the woman."

Annie's forehead wrinkled. "You're sure?"

"This mystery woman is just a witness. If a female decides to kill, she doesn't do it with a gun."

The detective was dead wrong. If she ever decided to kill someone—say, someone like Nick—she'd use a gun. She even knew exactly where she'd shoot him.

"If you see her, you'll call me?" Detective Sullivan held out his card.

"Call you—" she glanced at the number on the card "—and do nothing else."

"I would never ask a lady such as yourself to do anything remotely dangerous."

Annie sighed as if she actually saw the gauntlet Detective

Sullivan had thrown on Freddie's desk. "She'll call you if she sees her. She won't approach her. She won't follow her. She won't speak to her." Annie might be directing her words at the detective but she was speaking to Freddie. "I'll see you out, detective."

Freddie stood and extended her hand.

Detective Sullivan hauled himself from his chair and shook her hand. "Thank you for your assistance, Miss Archer. Remember, if you see the woman, call me. Do not interact with her."

Freddie ignored Annie's worried gaze. "I'll remember."

Annie closed the office door on the detective's broad back and whirled around. "Don't."

"Don't what?"

She held up a restraining finger and jabbed at the air. "I know you. You'd run into a burning building if a man told you not to. Please, don't go looking for that woman. Do not."

"This is New York. The chances of seeing her again are slim." Not exactly true. Despite more than five million people in the city, she still ran into Nick with disturbing regularity.

"If by some miracle, you do see her, call the detective. Nothing more."

"What else would I do?"

They both knew the answer to that question.

ALSO BY JULIE MULHERN

The Country Club Murders

The Deep End

Guaranteed to Bleed

Clouds in My Coffee

Send in the Clowns

Watching the Detectives

Cold as Ice

Shadow Dancing

Back Stabbers

Telephone Line

Stayin' Alive

Killer Queen

Night Moves

Lyin' Eyes

Big Shot

Fire and Rain

Killing Me Softly

Back in Black

Tight Rope

Bad Blood

Rich Girl

Evil Ways

Freddie Archer Series

Murder by Moonlight (a free prequel novella)

Murder in Manhattan

The Poppy Fields Adventures

Fields' Guide to Abduction

Fields' Guide to Assassins

Fields' Guide to Voodoo

Fields' Guide to Fog

Fields' Guide to Pharaohs

Fields' Guide to Dirty Money

Fields' Guide to Smuggling

Fields' Guide to Secrets